CONTENTS

Streetlight

A Novel By **Ernest Brawley**

New York at its 1970s Nadir

For information regarding permission, please write to:
info@barringerpublishing.com
Barringer Publishing, Naples, Florida
www.barringerpublishing.com

Design and layout by Linda S. Duider
Cape Coral, Florida

ISBN: 978-1-954396-14-2
Library of Congress Cataloging-in-Publication Data
Streetlight / Brawley

Printed in U.S.A.

CHAPTER ONE

The Things You Do for Love

Following a trail of stolen travelers' checks and credit card receipts, relying on tips from bribed hotel receptionists, airline clerks, service station attendants, and the proprietor of a holiday house rental agency, Ray and his partner traced a pair of runaway lovers to a villa on the outskirts of a little, whitewashed, fishing village on the east coast of Ibiza. Fortin was the name of the place, sitting on a cone-shaped hill beneath a crumbling Moorish castle, hemmed in by cane fields, olive groves, bare jagged mountains, and a tiny, crescent-shaped beach.

This all went down in the spring of '75, a spring so hot it might as well have been summer, so hot it's been written up in all the record books.

Tired, dirty, and overheated after ten days on the road, they arrived on the afternoon bus from Ibiza Town. Ironically, since they'd left the States with two suitcases full of cash and five thousand dollars in pocket money, they were short of funds, the contents of the suitcases having disappeared into their boss' numbered Swiss bank account, and much of the pocket money into the kit bag of an intrepid second story man who had burglarized their Barcelona hotel room.

So, they checked into the Casa Campello, a long, low, tile-roofed establishment run by an expatriate Australian and his fat, little, Spanish wife. The facilities were crude: cold saltwater showers, communal bathrooms and kitchens, hard-wooden pallets and straw mattresses for beds. And it was a kilometer into town and the beach. But the price was right, no deposit was required, and the guests—seedy, backpacking hitchhikers from all over Europe—were not the nosy type.

First thing they did was shower. One by one. Ray's partner, Monika—a gorgeous, six-foot Swede with the body of a pole dancer—was the boss' current squeeze, so even when she came prancing out of the bathroom in a towel and hung her dripping bra and bikini panties on the window bars to dry, even when she rolled on her bed and did her siesta in the raw, Ray kept his mind strictly on business.

The wind was so hot, so hard—a *Sirocco* blowing off the North African desert—that her things were dry in an hour. She crawled off the bed, strode to the window like she was the only one in the room, wriggled into her panties, pulled a purple tie-dyed mini dress over her head, slipped on her sandals, and capered around the room. Tan, blond and long-legged, she modeled it for him.

"How do I look, Pard?"

"How do you think?"

"Like a fucking fox!"

"Then why ask?" he said, thinking: *It's a dog's life.*

"See you!"

"Hey, wait up! What am I gonna do for food?"

"Here, take this!" She tossed her wallet at him. Inside, there were a hundred dollars American.

"This is all we got left?"

"Till the 'boss man' wires us some more."

"For that we gotta wait."

"For what?"

"A nice, quiet, out-of-the-way place. All it needs is a phone and a telegraph office."

"Where's that?"

"You're the traveler, babe. I never been outta the States."

"We'll think of someplace."

"Meanwhile, we better hold onto this," he said, slipping the C-note under the sweaty waistband of his jockey shorts. "You never know how these things are gonna work out."

She split and he sat up in bed for hours, sleepless with hunger, reading a dog-eared Penguin mystery that he found in a drawer in the bedstand, pausing from time to time to reflect on the ironies of life and love.

These lovers they'd tracked across Europe, who'd given up everything for each other, once had other lovers. Ray knew this for a fact. He was a witness. Yet, how long had those loves lasted? And how long would this love last, given a chance? So where was the percentage? This he would never understand.

At noon the next day, Monika showed up, all smiles, and

smelling so good you could live in her hair.

"I've just had a freshwater shower! Wow, you should see their place."

She'd brought a plastic bag full of white, Spanish rolls and hard salami. Ray wolfed it down, stopping only to ask, "They got the money?"

"Lost it in Monte Carlo, they said."

"Gee, that's too bad."

"Maybe I should talk with them some more?"

"What for?" he said, with his maw full of bread and salami.

"You never know."

"They surprised to see you?"

"Nah, they figured something like this might happen. I don't think they've quite grasped the meaning of what they've done. They're treating it all like some kind of lark."

"A lark? I mean, Jesus, they not only . . ."

"They threatened."

"You can't threaten the boss."

"I know that."

"Okay, whaddya say? Twenty-four hours?"

"Sounds pretty reasonable to me."

"Listen, I . . . I didn't break the C-note."

"That was the wiser thing to do."

"Yeah," he said, finishing the sandwich, licking the crumbs from the wrapper. "But . . ."

"Hey, you eat too much, buster," she said, laughing, punching him softly on his hard, furry paunch. "You ought to watch your weight."

"You oughta watch your mouth."

"I'll raid their fridge again," she said, heading out the door, "and bring you something at siesta time."

At siesta time, there was still no sign of Monika, so Ray went native for a couple of hours.

As night fell, hunger, boredom, and the relentless sawing of cicadas drove him into the narrow, winding streets of the town again, though the boss had warned him a dozen times if he'd warned him once: "Keep a low profile."

It was the hour of the *paseo*. Slender, young Spaniards, dressed in gay colors and separated by sex, circled each other on the seaside promenade, flashing their dark eyes at each other, singing sketches of Flamenco.

The foreigners were all out on the beach below the seawall. And they were the focus of great curiosity and attention from the natives as they squatted around their bonfires drinking beer, flaunting their baked, half-naked bodies, bellowing at each other in guttural North European dialects.

Stepping down to the beach, Ray hit on a trio of skinny, pimpled, London girls with Cockney accents. Not for what they thought. But only to slurp foam from the bottom of the beer bottles they left behind when his hulking, hang-dog presence turned them off and they moved to the other end of the cove.

He padded along home in the moonlight, through the cane fields and olive groves, his bare toes squeezing dust, his sunburn hurting. The cicadas still going like mad.

It occurred to him that he was getting tired of this shit, and soon it would have to end.

First thing in the morning, the Australian proprietor showed up at the door, long and lean in his khaki pants and bush jacket, demanding immediate payment in full.

"Seen you on the beach last night, mate, suckin' on empty bottles. This ain't a charity establishment, you know."

"Wait till my girlfriend comes back. She's got all the money."

"Righto. I'll give you till eight tonight, but I'll have your baggage as security."

Ray waited, and he waited, but Monika never showed. He began to suspect her of harboring charitable feelings toward the lovers. Not that he hadn't doubts of his own.

The boss drove them to this. Ray even defended them, tried to make him see reason. At first, he listened. Then, just to show who was running things, he changed his tune. Which was typical. And he was the kind of guy, that when he made a wrong turn, he took others along with him. Dragged Ray along with him one time when they were kids, on some stupid dope heist up in Spanish Harlem; they spent the next two years in Warwick Reformatory together, regretting it. And yet, to this day, the whole issue and challenge of Ray's life was tied up with the boss man: the way he took you and touched you and turned you around; the way, when you tried to change him, you got changed yourself.

So, this thing with the lovers, it was more than a question of right and wrong. It was about relationships.

After siesta, Ray put on the same soiled, white, tailored shorts he'd been wearing for days, a lightweight canvas shoulder holster, with a 9-millimeter Czech military pistol inside, a grungy Hawaiian shirt, white perforated loafers and hoofed it up a red dirt road toward the villa on the hill.

Halfway there, he heard a car coming and slunk behind an

olive tree. Cicadas were sounding off all around him. Flies and bees buzzing. Vipers and scorpions rattling in the grass and the cactus plants.

A big, blue Jaguar, a Mark IV, rumbled by, trailing a cloud of red dust.

Inside was Monika, throwing her head back, laughing, sitting between a pretty, sunburned, little redhead with long curly hair, and a thin, spiffy-looking, spade cat with a beard and a modified 'fro—the lovers. Penny O'Riley and Bobby O. One the boss man's wife, the other his former associate. Hadn't been long since Ray called them both amigos.

When the dust settled, Ray stole up the hill to the villa, belly low to the ground. He climbed the garden wall, scratching a paw on the purple wisteria, and entered the house through the open patio door. Expecting some cook or maid to start screeching any minute, he sniffed the place out and came up with three hundred dollars in New York Citibank travelers' checks, a couple of twenty-pound notes, assorted *pesetas*, a quarter key of cocaine, and a pair of open-date plane tickets to Paris, France. He whoofed a gram of the coke, pocketed one of the twenties, and left everything else just as he found it.

Enveloped in a bright, fissionable cloud of power and self-confidence, he dogtrotted into town through the olive groves and exchanged the twenty for two thousand seven hundred *pesetas* from a little man in a barber shop. For a thousand *pesetas* he bought a steak dinner and a bottle of Rioja at an outside restaurant on the plaza. For twelve hundred more, he paid the Aussie what he owed him and redeemed his bags.

Next evening, Monika still hadn't shown, and Ray's

radioactive glow was long gone, so he humped it up the hill again. The *Sirocco* had died down at last and the air was amazingly soft. Not a breath of wind. Not the faintest tinge of heat or cold. Though the cicadas had not ceased their rending of the peace (and wouldn't till October, he'd been told), the mosquitoes at least had not made their appearance yet. The white-walled, red-roofed, little town, spilling down the terraced hillside to the cove, glowed pink, as did the clouds, the mountains, the line of surf, and the fishing boats setting out beyond the point. From down the hill came the sound of small waves splashing, the chatter of home-bound farm workers in *Ibicenco* dialect, the cries of children, the barking of dogs. A donkey brayed in the distance. On the highway outside of town, a truck blew its air horn and brakes squealed.

In the villa's backyard, under the grape arbor, he removed the Czech military pistol from its holster and screwed a silencer onto the barrel, while all around him half-wild bantam chickens were clucking, with baby ones peeping and pecking in the red dust.

The three old friends, clad only in their bikini bottoms, were seated on the open terrace, gathered round a blue, metal table, under a blue and white striped Calvados umbrella. Ignoring a neat little white mound of powder-like substance on the table, they were facing the precipice and the sea below, sipping at tall, green iced drinks, while a procession of small, fluffy clouds, clouds like the tails of lambs, moved slowly across the horizon.

The lovers had their chairs pulled up close, and were leaning against each other, arms and fingers entwined. The young man's long, shapely, black head was thrown back and his eyes were half-closed, his pose indicating that he'd just said something that he found immensely funny. His mouth was wide open, and his large, even white teeth, framed by his wooly beard, glinted in the light. The fair, sunburnt, young woman—a woman Ray had once considered his protegee, who'd worked for him at his topless joint and came to him and confessed when she had a drug problem, a woman he'd gladly helped and would again—was leaning forward, and her curly, red hair had fallen over one eye. Her lips were parted only slightly, demurely, yet her thin delicate shoulders and small childish breasts were shaking, as if she, too, was tickled by what her mate had just said.

And the injustice of it all struck Ray again. For these lovers seemed to him so young, so alive, and he'd once loved them—still loved them both so dearly—that the very skies ought to have cried out in protest at his intentions.

"Hi, there, kids!" he called, bobbing up from under the wall, propping the weapon—long and black and evil, distinctly out-of-place among the purple wisteria—upon the bare, hairy crook of his arm. "How ya doin'?"

Their eyes popped, mouths hung open, chests heaved in terror at his sudden appearance.

Ray smiled at them, shook his head, and clicked his tongue, almost apologetic.

"Sorry, guys. But you know the drill, right? Blood in, blood out."

And bap-bap, bap-bap. No chit-chat. Just like that. Two for each of the lovers.

Monika leapt to her feet, holding her hands over her ears.

"Goddamnit!" she shrieked, "Why'd you do that, Ray?

Why'd you fucking do it?"

"I was afraid," Ray said, stepping over the wall and up to the table, nosing into the mound of cocaine.

"Afraid of what, for God's sake?"

"Afraid!" he said, coming up for air, licking shit off his snout, feeling the burn in the crook of his arm start to hurt, right through the buzz of the coke, as he'd known it would hurt. "Afraid you was gettin' a little too chummy here."

"You dirty dog!" she yelled, charging around the table, beating him on the back with her fists. "You stupid sonofabitch! They were just about to tell me where they've got it."

"They ain't got shit," he said, shaking her off like a fly, stepping over to give the lovers each a quick *coup de grace* behind the ear, bap-bap, and then winding up, flinging the weapon far out to sea. "They blew it. Now come on, help me roll 'em over the side. We got a plane to catch."

CHAPTER TWO

Welcome to Fear City

1975 was called "the year of the terrorist." All over the world, innocent tourists and business travelers cowered in air terminals, fearing instant annihilation at the hands of The Red Army Faction, The Popular Front for the Liberation of Palestine, or some previously unknown organization sprung into life overnight.

Shelley Friedman was terrified of the very notion of air travel. If it hadn't come to divorce, she'd have abided on the island of Ibiza forever until she was as brown and gnarled as the olive trees. If Tobias Jr. had not been with her, she'd have floated across to the mainland on an inner tube.

Finally, though, out of desperation, she took the plane.

Predictably, the trip was a disaster.

Halfway to Madrid and the friendly young Moroccan student who'd just been sitting beside her, playing with two-year-old Toby, making him howl with laughter at his clever hand tricks, suddenly leapt up, rushed to the front of the plane, whirled, spread his feet, placed his hands on his hips and scowled ferociously, as if awaiting some momentary command. At the rear of the cabin another young Arab hastened to take up a similar position.

Stewardesses abandoned their smiles and stood transfixed in the aisles.

Passengers stopped breathing.

Even the plane seemed to pause in flight.

Shelley, her heart frozen in mid-beat, grabbed her little, part-Jewish son and nearly smothered him in her lap.

The tension lasted perhaps a minute. A lifetime. Then the Arabs smiled—cruelly, mockingly, it seemed—and returned to their seats.

A single great sigh of collective wonder and relief resounded throughout the aircraft.

A few minutes later, with a double Scotch in her hand, and the Moroccan sitting calmly beside her again, sharing a Diet Pepsi with Toby, Shelley began to doubt her own senses. Did what she think happened really happen?

Another double, and her curiosity got the better of her. Swallowing her fear and embarrassment, she turned to the young man and said, *"Excusez-moi, monsieur, mais pourquoi est-ce-que vous avez fait ça?"*

"Pardon, madame?" he asked politely. But he had such a self-satisfied grin plastered across his blunt, snub-nosed, Berber face that it was clear he'd caught her drift.

"Why'd you do that?" she repeated in English. "What you did a few minutes ago."

"Oh, that!" he laughed. "Well, answer me this, madame. Why do black people in your country sometimes follow white people in the night?"

"I don't know. Why don't you tell me?"

"There is no law against it if no threat is made. But they want you to keep it always in mind."

"Keep what in mind?"

"The power of fear," he said, smiling.

The Arabs got off in Madrid. Shelley and Toby stayed aboard for Paris, where they would make their connection to New York.

The plane took off and flew over the Pyrenees.

Toby laid his head in his mommy's lap and started talking slowly, softly to himself, "dis and dat, dis and dat, *esto y aquello, esto y aquello.*"

Shelley switched her console to classical music, stuck the rubber plugs in her ears, and leaned back against the headrest.

"Now relax," she told herself. "And think of it this way: You've still got your baby. You've still got your looks. You've still got your talent. And it's day one of your brand-new life."

Just then she happened to glance up and found herself looking at a huge, jowly, Italian-looking dude, sitting eight or ten rows ahead beside a tall, spectacular, blond Swede. Shelley recalled standing in line behind them in the Ibiza terminal but had paid them no mind at that time.

Now, with his New York Mets ball cap pushed back on his head, the guy was scrutinizing Shelley quizzically, as if trying to establish where they might have met in the past.

For an instant they regarded each other frankly.

Then a light of recognition flashed, and they turned away, as if by mutual consent, and ignored each other for the rest of the flight.

His name, she recalled, was Ray Pagano. They had met in September of 1966, when he and his friend, Al Rakozi, answered an ad she'd placed in the *San Francisco Chronicle:* "Riders wanted to share driving expenses to NYC."

Ray and Al were recovered drug addicts and had been doing an internship at a New Age drug rehab center called Synanon. Shelley had done a year's journalism internship at the *Oakland Tribune.*

And they had all started out, she recalled now, with great excitement. Excited not only about heading back to New York and starting new lives, but about each other as well.

Shelley found both Al and Ray attractive, in different ways—Ray for his large, dark, muscular body, Al for his golden tongue—and they felt the same way about her.

There was also the fact that they were low-class ex-druggies and small-time criminals from Brooklyn, and she was an Upper Eastside Jewish girl with a Princeton degree. It was the 1960s, after all. The cross-cultural baggage only added to the attraction on both sides.

Then one night in Cheyenne, Wyoming, they were all lying around stoned and half-naked on their motel bed after a hot, dusty day's ride, and Shelley cried out, "Oh, God, I just can't choose between you guys!"

"Then why should you?" Al replied, puffing at the Mexican torpedo he'd just rolled (pot, he maintained, was not a drug but a "medicament"), passing it to Ray, who passed it on to Shelley.

"Hey, you're right," she murmured, feeling the cannabis

invade her. "Why should I?"

And so, a night ensued the likes of which Shelley had never known before and never would again. A windstorm came up in the middle of it, and then the moon came out; and whenever she recalled the scene now, it was with alkali dust settling on the skin of the three lovers like white ash, like *Hiroshima Mon Amour.*

There were another couple of nights on the road. Then they reached their destination and went off to pursue their dreams.

Shelley wanted to snag a job at the *New York Star.*

Al wanted to start his own drug outreach program, called "Streetlight," based on his experience at Synanon.

Ray wanted to open a topless bar and make a lot of money so he could do what he really wanted to do: raise pit bulls.

And each of them would succeed, in certain ways. Yet each of them would fail as well, in ways they couldn't have imagined.

Shelley knew how she had failed at life. And she wondered now in precisely which way Ray had failed, for it to show so clearly and indelibly on his countenance.

Hours later, to the sound of '70's Punk Rock, Shelley rode a battered, old Checker Cab through the squalid streets of New York City at its 20th century nadir. And while Toby napped in her lap, she snapped photos with her Kodak Astro Zoom . . .

A gigantic, hooded skeleton with "WELCOME TO FEAR CITY" painted on the side of an abandoned factory . . .

A wrecked car lying in brick rubble, surrounded by fire-gutted apartment buildings . . .

A gang of junkies nodding off on the stoop of a boarded-up brownstone . . .

A bunch of "gangstas" and their "ho's" lolling on an ill-lit corner, warming their hands over a fiery garbage can . . .

A beautiful, broken, young girl nodding off against a brick wall . . .

A pair of long-haired, long-side-burned white cops laying back, smoking cigarettes, and chatting in their battered, old squad car, uninterested in the chaos around them . . .

The taxi pulled up at a shabby hotel. Shelley dragged her suitcase, stroller, and baby inside with no help from the sullen driver.

A newsstand by the door displayed a copy of the *New York Daily News* with a photo of President Ford and the headline:

"FORD TO CITY: DROP DEAD."

CHAPTER THREE

Making for the Light

Midnight. A sometime, merchant seaman named Jim Range descended the ladder of a container ship with a sea bag flung over his shoulder, and a narrow musical instrument case in hand. Tall, long-haired, robust, he strode across the pier, exited at the front gate, waved at the security man, crossed 2nd Avenue and turned into ill-lit 36th Street.

Crossing the dark alleyway between two abandoned warehouses, he jumped when a pair of skinny, jittery boys with amphetamine eyes rose out of the darkness. The black boy wielded a gun, the pimpled Puerto Rican kid a long knife.

"Just got paid off, sailor man?" the black boy wanted to know.

The Puerto Rican kid laughed and danced around him, chanting, "Give it up, give it up, give it up, sailorman!"

Jim dropped his sea bag and raised his hands.

"Okay, listen; I give you what I got," he said, then waved his musical instrument case at them. "But I keep my ax."

Slipping the case between his legs, Jim took out his wallet, extracted some cash, and handed it over.

The black kid stuffed it in his pants, grabbed the sea bag, and dragged it off around the corner.

Jim took his instrument case by the handle, turned, and started to walk away. But the Puerto Rican kid followed him, laughing and dancing again, waving his long knife.

"Give it up, sailorman, give it up, give it up!"

Jim whipped around to face his attacker.

"I'm warning you, man. Stay back!"

"What you got in there?"

"I told you."

"Why you keep it so . . ."

He imitated the gesture of a mother holding a baby.

"You wouldn't understand."

"Try me. Try me."

"It's the one thing I value most."

"I dig what you say, sailorman, the kid said, smiling. Then he snarled and came at Jim with his knife, faking it to the left and right, switching it from hand to hand. "And that's just why I want it."

Jim slammed the instrument case down on the boy's wrist, breaking it with an audible snap. He screamed, dropped the knife, and stared down at his wrist, which now hung at an odd angle, limp.

In a swift, smooth, practiced move, Jim felled the kid with a karate chop to the neck. Supine in the gutter, mouth open, he seemed incapable of doing anything but blink up at his assailant.

Jim scooped the knife off the pavement, pulled the boy's head back by the hair, and pressed the blade to his throat, drawing blood. About to slice it through, he shook his head, took a deep breath, rose to his feet, and knocked the kid out with a kick to the head.

Sticking the knife in his pants, he opened his instrument case on the pavement, inspected his flute, and smiled to himself when he found no damage. He shut the case, picked it up, and strode off down the dark street, making for the light.

CHAPTER FOUR

The Boss Man

Hair bound up in a towel, Shelley stepped out of her bathroom in a robe, flicked on a battered TV and sat on the bed to listen to a TV news announcer.

"Run by a former gang member and drug addict named Al Rakozi, Streetlight is currently the most successful drug rehabilitation facility in New York."

A photo of Al's distinctive Hungarian American face appeared on the screen, and Shelley's eyes went wide in fear at the sight of him. "Charismatic and well-connected, Rakozi, known to his followers as 'the boss' or 'the boss man,' has supporters in law, banking, industry and government. At a time when New York is drug infested, crime-ridden, and bankrupt, Streetlight is one of its few bright lights."

The news program cut to a clip of Rakozi, about to address a loud, raucous, young crowd in Washington Square Park. Dressed like a Rock star, he leapt across the stage and reached for the microphone to thunderous applause.

Shelley jumped to her feet at the sight, shook her head in fury, and switched off the TV.

"No! No fucking way!"

CHAPTER FIVE

Female Commiseration

The street was narrow and cobbled, with tall shade trees, buckling sidewalks, and fancy grillwork on the fire escapes and stoops. In the pale light of morning, it seemed to Jim charming, almost picturesque. The place he was looking for had been described to him as a basement apartment in an old, five story, red brick building, and he found it easily. It was at 76 Charles Street. As it turned out, the only red brick building on the block, just across from a row of elegant brownstones, with tall narrow windows and beautiful carved wooden doors.

Plucking a white rose from the bush beside the stoop, he went down a flight of mossy, crumbling brick stairs, swung his rucksack off his shoulder, leaned it against the wall, punched the buzzer, and waited, praying his old friend would be home. Hoped for maybe a touch as well. A meal. A night's lodging. Yet he was not particularly surprised when no one answered. The address was months old, and Monika had never been one to let grass grow under her feet. He even had a flash that she might be dead.

Heaving the rucksack on his shoulder again, turning to go, he glanced at the front window, noticed that there was a crack in the straw curtain, and couldn't resist stopping a moment to peek inside. Adjusting his eyes to the light, he could see that the apartment was long and narrow—a three-room, railroad flat that ran all the way through to the other end of the building. Bookshelves and posters crowded the exposed brick walls. Futons and large, fluffy pillows lay about the straw-matted floor. Indian bedspreads adorned the ceiling, the beds and what remained of wall space. Big potted coleus plants dangled in the windows.

Peering in at that leafy, little wonderland of bohemian domesticity, yearning to be let in, Jim let his mind wander to the farthest, furriest edges of possibility . . .

The last he'd seen of Monika was when they'd run into each other outside Karachi. They were headed for the same place, it turned out. Frank's place. Frank was this enormously fat, incredibly black, old Pakistani who ran a teahouse in Victoria Road as a front for his other, nefarious activities. A pimp, a smuggler, a bootlegger, and black marketeer, a dope dealer and fence for stolen goods, a usurer and counterfeiter and gunrunner, and probably worse, Frank was at the same time a devoted husband and father, a faithful friend, a generous employer, a devout Christian who attended High Church services regularly and an incorrigible Anglophile who wore a blue, woolen blazer, a cricket club tie and white flannels in even the steamiest sub-continental weather, and spoke English with an impeccably pukka accent. In short, Frank was the man to see in Karachi. And they had things to sell, fruits of the Great Grass Road: Gold coins from Andorra. Timex watches from Istanbul. Black market rupees from Teheran. Opium from Kandahar.

Concluding the deal, Frank suggested that they all retire to his back garden for a little shot of "Country," the potent local moonshine, and a blow at the gun. The gun was a sort of Oriental waterpipe that you sucked on very hard with nothing coming out and your face going all red and then suddenly, BOOM! The thing would go off and you'd get this powerful and instantaneous blast of opium that went right down to your socks. Five hits off the gun and they were out of their gourds. When they finally came to, they were sitting with Frank on the deck of a leaky, old, Indian Christian, pilgrim ship, bound for the World Anglican Congress in Bombay.

Jim would never forget that voyage, nor the boats with sails like swallowtails that ran out from the Rann of Kutch, delivering a troupe of fancifully attired Gujerati musicians and players who sang and danced wildly, wonderfully, then quite suddenly got seasick all at once, fell to the deck, and went to sleep piled up on their own vomit. And later, the squall that came up out of nowhere to cleanse the deck and drive the wogs below, leaving Jim and Monika alone on the aft cargo hatch when the moon came up yellow and dripping from the Arabian Sea. And then tearing crazily at each other, rolling off the hatch and onto the slippery wooden deck while the creaking old steamer heaved and lunged and fell away beneath them and the ghost of another Jim—Conrad's *Lord Jim*—rose pale and dripping out of the brine.

Afterwards, lying entwined with Monika on the wooden deck, drenched in sweat, sea water, and sexual secretions, Jim grew suddenly, urgently tumescent again. Yet, as soon as she perceived the direction of his thoughts, she leapt up—statuesque in the moonlight, a halo of salt spray round her wild, blond hair—and said, in her Abba accent. "Sorry, but that's all she wrote, Jim."

"What?" he gasped.

"After that," she said, mock serious, pointing to the place where they'd lain together on the deck, "there can be no second act."

"Aw," he whined, clutching her arm like a child. "Come on, Monika, please."

"No," she said, flinging him off, moving away, around the bulkhead, down the promenade deck stairway, laughing tauntingly. "Never take a good thing too far, boy. Always leave yourself wanting a little more . . ."

Monika stayed aboard for the leg to Goa.

Jim disembarked with Frank in Bombay, and he'd never run into her again, barely even heard from her except for a card now and then, via American Express, from some exotic locale. Her last note had come from this same address. She'd finally cleaned up her act, she said, got into drug rehab and settled in . . .

"What're you looking at?" a female voice demanded from behind the door.

"Uh, looking for Monika," he said, jumping in fright. "She in?"

"Who's asking?"

"Jim," he said. "A friend."

"Jim? Jim? Is it really you?" she said, opening the door.

And there she was, bigger than life.

Immensely tall, even in her bare feet, she wore a red, silk, Chinese, dressing gown, with a green and blue peacock design, long hooped jade earrings, an African trade bead necklace and jangling silver bracelets. Her full-lipped, sharply chiseled Scandinavian face was deeply tanned, as if she'd just returned from a month in Guadeloupe.

"Monika," he said, gaping at her. "I, uh, just got in from Oslo this morning."

"Still out there kicking up dust, huh?"

"Actually, I'm thinking of packing it in."

"It happens."

"Yeah. A few years on the road and a house, a car, a spouse, a kid or two—that's the exotic thing. Right?"

"Don't make me laugh," she said. And then, throwing her head back, rolling her eyes at the sky, showing her tongue, her strong white teeth, she proceeded to do just that.

"It was only a thought," he said, grinning helplessly.

"Why, you poor thing, you don't know your own mind, do you? Well, come on in, dear. The least I can do is offer you a cup of coffee."

Seating him on a large, yellow, Indian pillow, she lit some incense, put Phoebe Snow on the stereo, brought out a plate full of Danish and a couple of hand-turned ceramic mugs full of steaming café-au-lait, and set them down on her low, cable spool coffee table.

"Wow," he said, lounging back on a pile of pillows. "This can't be real."

"You're right. Gotta go to work in a couple of minutes."

"Mind if I stick around?"

"Be my guest. Use the bath if you feel like it. There's a *djellaba* in the closet. Fits all sizes. I'll be back at six."

Jim took her advice. Then he curled up on one of the futons and didn't know a thing till she came in the door that evening.

"Now, where were we?" she asked, going behind the closet door, stepping out of her work clothes and into her kimono again, slipping Earth, Wind & Fire into her tape deck.

"I was about to catch you up on my most recent adventures."

"Nothing I'd like better." Folding her long, long legs, she sat down beside him on the futon, produced a vial of cocaine, a twenty-dollar bill, and poured out a couple of lines on the coffee table.

"Hey, wait a minute, Monika. Last I heard, you were in rehab. Place called 'Streetlight,' you said."

She rolled the bill, covered one nostril, and snorted coke with the other.

"Dunno." She dipped down for a snort up the other nostril and handed Jim the bill. "Must've had some kind of relapse, I guess."

He grinned, snorted, and pointed at a big red hickey on her neck. "Boyfriend?"

"Boss man." She shrugged. "What you're you gonna do, huh?

"Uh-huh. Well, lemme see. Where to start?" he said, snorting deep and long, feeling his heart take off like a quail. "A month ago, I found myself in Tokyo. I had a five-tatami room in a colorful neighborhood called Shinjuku, a pretty roommate named Yasuko, and a job as an extra in the movies and on TV. Every time a white man was called for, I was it. But the winter had been long, and the Japanese, for my taste, were too cloying and inquisitive. Even the viewing of the cherry blossoms in Shinjuku Park left me cold. That's the trouble with Japan. Everything leaves you cold. Even the good things. Besides, I had this yen for round-eyed ladies again, a nostalgia for my own culture."

So, one dull morning in May, he said, he caught a local train to the Yokohama docks. He'd told no one he was leaving. Not even Yasuko. And he was taking the long way around. In his pocket, he carried a ticket on a Russian passenger ship to Nahodka, Soviet Far East, and another on the Trans-Siberian Express.

Two weeks later he fetched up in Helsinki without a kopek, sold his winter coat in the flea market on the quay and started hitchhiking around the Gulf of Bothnia in a light, woolen sweater and a hooded rainslicker. But auto stop in Northern Europe was chancy at best, the weather in May, more wintery than spring-like. The Nords themselves were not notable for their solicitude toward shaggy and itinerant young strangers and there were several times when it was touch and go.

In Turku, he broke into a university dormitory and passed the night in a tubful of hot water. Near Haparanda, he got caught in a snowstorm and spent the night running up and down the empty highway, waving his arms, beating his chest, and shouting into the forest. In Stockholm, he kipped in a pederast-infested city park. In Karlstad, he had to go to the police and ask them to lock him up for a night in jail. The whole way he ate nothing but handouts and amphetamine tabs, and by the time he hit the Norwegian frontier he was seeing things: giant white marmots in the roadway, white bats swirling about the car, white mice running up and down his sleeves.

Then in Oslo he got lucky. Steered by a Panamanian seaman he met in a waterfront bar, he signed on the *Balboa Trader* as an unpaid "workway" hand an hour before she was to sail for New York. After eleven stormy days at sea, he landed in New York this morning nearly penniless, a fugitive from justice, and still three thousand miles from home. But the prospect did nothing to discourage him, he said. On the contrary, it left him feeling breathless with excitement and nervous anticipation. And he wished he could go on living this way forever. Every time he found himself in another great city with his pockets empty, his stomach growling, it was like being born all over again.

"Oh Jim," Monika said, when he was done recounting his adventures. And there was an expression of warmth and affection on her beautiful, strong-jawed face that was unfamiliar to him. "What a wonderful liar you are!"

"It's God's truth, I swear."

"Bull pucky! You cannot flimflam this daughter of the road, man," she said, exaggerating her Swedish accent. "I've been there, too. You know?"

He grinned. "Well, I do have a little insurance."

"Uh-huh."

"Got another berth. If I really want it. Container ship. Sails out of Brooklyn in a month."

"Where to this time?"

"Cape Town, South Africa. Then on to Christchurch, New

Zealand."

"About as far as you can get, huh?"

"Just the way I like it."

"MPs still after your AWOL ass?"

"Anyone come asking for me?"

She laughed and shook her head.

"Hey. A few months ago? I had to jump ship in Panama."

"What?"

"No shit. Right on the fuckin' Canal. US Navy came aboard. Caught me with my pants down. I bailed. Hit the water buck-naked, not a penny to my name."

"How'd you get away, then?"

"Long story."

"Right," she scoffed.

"Thank God I had a friend in Panama City who owed me. Gave me some clothes. Printed me up a new passport."

"Well, come here then, Mister Swaggerific," she said, sniffing and shaking her head in sympathy. "After all you've been through, whether real or imagined, you deserve a little female commiseration."

She wouldn't let him do anything. Pushed him down on the purple coverlet. Ran a hand up under the *djellaba* and worked at him till he grew big in her palm. Then flung a leg across and settled with a sigh, her kimono hiked up over her broad, tan-lined hips.

Later, she made him pull out the old, Gemeinhardt flute that he'd packed around the world and play her favorite piece, Debussy's *"Pavane for a Dead Princess."* Then she put on an Abba tape, laid out another line or two, stripped him to the skin, and anointed him with olive oil. Smelling of tossed salad, slippery as eels, they rocked and rolled on her tatami mat till they looked like straw dummies.

Later still, Jim sat on the futon, playing his flute in a beautiful rendition of Ravel's *"Pavane for a Dead Princess,"* while Monika, spectacular in her nakedness, lay with her head on his lap, eyes closed.

Toward morning, they made love again, to the tune of Bob Marley's "No Woman, No cry" on her record player. When the song ended, Jim shook his head in sadness, and a tear ran down his cheek, which seemed to annoy Monika.

"Now, what in God's name are you crying about? After all the fun we just had."

"I ... I don't know. For ... For all the wrong turns I've taken. All the missed opportunities. All the shit I ..."

Monika went stiff beside him.

"I'm sorry, Jim," she said, "but I just can't deal with that kind of ... *need* right now. Way, way too much on my plate as it is. You can kip here till you get your act together, but ..."

CHAPTER SIX

The Fish Tank

A vast, brick, fortress-like facility at 103rd Street and West End Avenue appeared to have once been a National Guard arsenal. 'STREETLIGHT' said a huge sign, aimed at air traffic, on its flat roof.

Down in its basement, an alarm clock rang in a tacky, little bedroom. Ray Pagano, puffy from a hangover, rolled out of bed naked, pulled on his pants and a t-shirt with 'Blood Bros' written on it and did a line of cocaine.

He shuffled out the door, threaded his way through the labyrinthine corridors of the building, walked up some coiling stairs and into a luxuriously furnished room in one of the arsenal's old brick turrets. There, he found Al sprawled across an enormous circular bed. A pretty, bruised, young, Latina girl with a shaved head lay conked out by his side, a puffy red love bite on her neck. "Hey, Boss!"

"Wha? Wha?"

"Come on, Al. You got an inspection tour at nine, and a Board meeting at eleven."

A few minutes later, Ray accompanied him through the corridors of Streetlight. Soon, a pair of bodyguards joined them: an enormous, black man named Jazeel, and a huge, tattooed Mohawk named Tall Boy, both shaved bald and wearing Blood Bros t-shirts like Ray's. Monika fell in line behind them, dressed like a secretary now in a neat skirt and blouse, a large pad and pencil in hand. Inspirational slogans plastered the walls of the facility. The same slogans—in the rhythmic, rapping voice of Al Rakozi—sounded out over the omnipresent intercom system.

"You think you got a drug problem? Wrong! You got a thinkin' problem. Thinkin' is what got you in here. Stop your stinkin' thinkin'! Utilize, don't analyze!"

The boss swept into a dining room full of white, black, and Latino junkies of both sexes, ages eighteen to fifty, all with shaven heads. Joyful, worshipful, the whole crowd of them turned from their breakfast trays to greet the guru-in-chief—"The boss, the boss, the boss man!"—while behind him Monika took notes on the proceedings.

"That's what I like to hear, Streetlighters," Al shouted back at them. "Energy. Spirit. Motivation!"

Next stop was the reception room. Tall Boy and Jazeel pushed a heavy, steel door open and stepped inside. Al, Ray, and Monika followed them in.

Seated on a long-wooden bench, nine ragged, dejected-looking junkies waited as Al bounced across the room at them, grinning.

"Hi guys. I'm Al Rakozi, this is my secretary, Monika, my

blood bros, Ray, Tall Boy, and Jazeel, and we're here to welcome you to Streetlight!" A moment later, he led his draggedy-ass newcomers into a large, fluorescent-lit, gym-like room with an enormous sign on the wall: "FISHTANK." Several other signs hung on the walls. One of them said: UNDERSTAND RATHER THAN BE UNDERSTOOD. Another said: LOVE, RATHER THAN BE LOVED.

In one corner, there was a table full of medical accoutrements including a phlebotomy chair, a medical lab fridge, a table with a neat array of needles, syringes, blood collection tubes, antiseptics, bandages, long razors, and hair clippers. A plump, smiling, old, Filipino nurse stood before the table at attention.

The boss motioned the newcomers inside while Tall Boy and Jazeel stood guard by the door and Monika headed for the nurse's table. He and Ray led the newbies to the center of the room and motioned for them to sit around them cross-legged.

"Welcome to the 'Fishtank', gang!" the boss said, exuding enthusiasm. "This is where you're gonna spend your first week. We call it 'Hell Week.' And it's gonna be tough. You know? But if you pull together, Fish, you'll make it. You understand what I'm sayin'?"

No one said a word in reply until a middle-age white woman spoke up.

"Uh, yeah," she sighed, with a total lack of enthusiasm. "I guess."

Ray growled and pointed a finger in her face, making her jump.

"Hey, listen up, Fish!" he hollered. "When the boss man asks a question? You answer him in a loud and clear voice. Together. Awright?

Now, lemme ask you again. Do you understand what I'm sayin'?"

"Yes!" the group replied in unison.

"Can't hear you!"

"Yes! Yes! Yes!"

"'Yes, boss!'" Ray yelled at them.

"Yes boss, yes boss, yes boss man!"

"A little better," Al said, shaking his head. "Now lemme tell you what I'm doin' here, Fish. Just passin' on what I learned from my own hard-ass experience. Awright? And what I learned is this. The road to wellness?" He paused and pointed a finger at them. "It does not begin with the ego, with 'Me, Myself, and I.' No way! It starts here . . . Here in our Streetlight family." Al spread his arms, as if to embrace the group as a whole and smiled, beatific. "And how do we reach our goal? We give ourselves up. Abandon all that ego shit that got us in here and yield to the will of the clan. Awright?"

"Yes boss, yes boss, yes boss man!"

Al motioned toward Monika and the nurse in the corner.

"We start with the drawing of your blood. This is for medical reasons, so we can assess your health needs, but it's also symbolic. In fact, over the years, it has become an almost religious rite for us, an act of contrition, the draining of the bad blood that got us in here. Next, we shave you bald, both men and women, so you can start fresh, clean, and new. Awright?"

"Yes boss, yes boss, yes boss man!"

CHAPTER SEVEN

A Shocking Discovery

Long hair tamed, all business now in a dark, Biba, business suit, Shelley high-heeled it through a busy newsroom and stopped outside a glassed-in office with a sign above the door: 'Benjamin Hirschberg, Managing Editor.'

Peering in at a slight, balding, thin-lipped, middle-aged man bent over a printout on his desk, she rapped at the window.

Annoyed, he raised his eyes from behind his reading glasses, started in surprise, and leapt to his feet.

Shelley stepped through the door, a belabored smile on her face.

Benjamin, or "Ben," shook his head and grinned back at her.

"Well, I'll be good goddamned. How y'all doin', honey-bunch?"

A Jew from South Carolina, Ben seemed to take the utmost pleasure in drawling it out for all it was worth.

Shelley tried a laugh and gave him a hug.

"You in town for long, hon?"

"Let's put it this way, Ben. I'm looking for an apartment, and I'm out on the job market again.

Ben glanced at his watch.

"Hey, you know what, Shell?" He grabbed his coat, took her by the arm, and headed for the door. "Let's do lunch."

They walked out of the newspaper, around the corner, and into an old café full of loud, gesticulating reporters who all seemed to know Ben.

He smiled, waved, and shook hands all the way to the back where a smiling waiter awaited them. "Hey there, Nicasio. Listen here. Can you gimme one of them Fettucini Alfredos? And a Wild Turkey on the rocks? Thanks, buddy."

Shelley ordered Perrier and *Salade Niçoise and* picked at it.

"I just quit smoking," she said, "and already I'm starting to worry about my weight."

"Oh, I wouldn't fret about that none, hon. You look like Sunday mornin."

"You don't look so bad yourself," she said.

But the truth was he looked awful. Though they were only seven years apart in age and had started out together at the *Star* at the same time, Ben stayed on and made it to the masthead a couple of years back. As managing editor, he was responsible for running the paper on a day-to-day basis. But he still had to answer to Corvo, the chief editor—a journalism "legend" who spent less than a third of his time in the newsroom and the rest chasing after friends' wives—and to its playboy publisher, David St. Godens, as well. They were both delighted to give Ben a free hand, but the instant he screwed up they were all over him.

And the strain showed. His huge, yellowish eyes were starting to bulge behind his thick bi-focals. He'd lost most of his hair. His mouth was pinched and nervous, his chin beginning to sag, his flowered tie was years out of style, and the cowboy boots he wore to increase his height looked ridiculous with his rumpled seersucker suit.

"So, what's up, Shell?"

"Tobias and I have decided to part ways."

"Hate to say I told you so."

"Don't rub it in."

"Classic fuckin' case," Ben said, shaking his head, smiling in triumph. "Your old man's a writer, an expat, and a Jew, and he dies—idealized—when you're very young. So, what do you do? Run off and marry the first old . . ."

"I have my memories. Tobias' boys have grown up now, but they still write me, they still call me 'Momma.'"

"What about the baby? What you gonna do with him?"

"Toby's with me, of course. And you should see him, Ben. He's two now, and utterly unflappable. A bit of a piggy though. Haven't been able to wean him from his bottle yet. But he's a hit with the ladies. He's romancing our Mexican chambermaid at the moment."

"So, what's the plan, hon? No openings at the *Star* right now. Nowhere else I know of. Even for someone as talented as the world-renowned photojournalist, Shelley Friedman. We just start comin' out of that damn recession and the city goes bankrupt. Right now, our advertising revenues are zilch. We're firin' people, not hirin' 'em, Shell. Just want to say that up front, so's you don't get your hopes up."

"I didn't think it was going to be easy," she said.

And for an instant, she was tempted to use her sex appeal on him. But then she read his face and observed all the conflicting emotions there . . . Sympathy, affection, nostalgia, cruelty . . .

Though Ben honestly wanted to help her now, he very much enjoyed his new power over her, like the power she had once held over him: the power to deny. He had once pursued Shelley, plied her with Southern charm and Southern Comfort and came near to carrying her away. Meanwhile, her friend and fellow reporter, Wendy Smith, pursued him just as relentlessly. When Shelley turned Ben down, Wendy got him on the rebound. And neither Ben nor Wendy had ever really forgiven her for it.

"Sorry to come asking favors, after all this time," she told him as they were about to leave. "But it seems all my other New York friends have scattered."

"Tell me about it," he said, and proceeded to mark off their fellow cub reporters on his fingers, as if they were soldiers fallen in battle. "Bonnie in Rome with Reuters. Don, *Times* bureau chief in Hong Kong. Greg in D.C., runnin' the congressional press gallery. Wendy, locked in with the kids and the dogs and the station wagon out there in Long Island . . ."

"Yes, but you do have Wendy. Think of that. And you've had the chance to make new friends. I've been out of touch."

"Hey, your only real friends are the ones you start out with."

"Which is precisely my point," she said, but he didn't seem to like being reminded of it very much.

Two days later, two days of fruitless job and apartment

hunting, Shelley wheeled Toby down to the mail room at American Express and found a large manila envelope from Tobias. Inside, along with a scribbled note, and a check for Toby, there was a copy of the *Ibiza Mercury*, their local English language newspaper. The *Mercury* wasn't much. Only came out every couple of weeks. Mostly full of local expatriate gossip. But this time Shelley found the headline—"DOUBLE MURDER IN FORTIN!"—so captivating that she decided to swallow her pride, park Toby outside a phone booth, and call Ben at the *Star*.

"Ever hear of a guy named Ray Pagano?" she asked, after his secretary had kept her on hold for five minutes.

"No, ain't, Shelley, and I'm real busy right now."

"How about Al Rakozi? That ring a bell?"

"Yeah. Runs a drug rehab outfit named 'Streetlight.' The darlin' of the media, for the moment."

"What else you know about him?"

"Man's got a lot of charm, apparently. Got backers in law, banking, real estate, city government. Got this whole self-supporting communal society of addicts and former addicts with chapters in every borough except Staten Island. He's in with the Libs, blacks, Hispanics, gay liberation. Right now, he's got about four thousand members. At election time, he has 'em out canvassing door to door, registering unregistered voters, bussing people to the polls, handing out literature. Nearly every politician in New York owes him something."

"Anything on the downside?"

"Got an eye for the ladies, they say. Got this tight, little coterie of rich society bitches that help him raise money. But there's only been one hint of anything weird or fucked up, far as

I know."

"What's that?"

"People come out of his outfit accusin' him of mind games, manipulation, intimidation, megalomania. Say he runs the place like a cult. Now don't get me wrong. Most of his people swear by him. And no one disputes the fact that he's done great things for his drug addicts."

"What would you say if I told you that I used to know Al Rakozi, and his pal, Ray Pagano, and I've discovered something grisly, shocking, horrific about them, something that will be very, very big news?"

"Why don't you come down to the office, hon, and we'll talk about it."

"That's what I thought you'd say," she laughed. "Let me find a babysitter for Toby and I'll be right over."

Yet, crossing the crowded, clamorous newsroom of the *Star* two hours later, making for Ben's glassed-in office at the far end, she was acutely aware of the fact that she didn't know one face, and the majority of them were years younger than her own.

"Okay. I'll bite," said Ben, as she walked into his office. "But I'm warnin' you, girl. Do not fuckin' waste my time."

She reached into her bag, pulled out the *Mercury*, and slapped it down on the desk in front of him.

"The hell is this?"

"My ex sent it." She pointed to the front page: "BODIES WASH UP IN RINCON COVE."

He grabbed the paper, scanned the story twice, then waved the paper at her.

"So, what we got here?"

"Okay, the female victim, Penny O'Riley? Guess who she is." He shrugged and raised his hands.

"Al Rakozi's wife."

"No way."

"Look at this."

She handed him a photocopy of an old edition of the *New York Star*. The headline read "STREETLIGHT WEDDING," and in a black & white photo below it, Al and Penny stood before a grey-bearded Indian guru on the roof of Streetlight.

"So, Al's wife, she got herself killed in Ibiza," Ben said, sniffing, raising his hands, still playing hard-to-get. "So fuckin' what?"

"You ready for this?"

He rolled a hand at her, as if to say, 'Get on with it!'

"Ray Pagano, Al's best and oldest friend, was on the plane with me from Ibiza. On the night of the murder."

"No fuckin' way!"

She nodded, slowly, smiling.

"He was with a beautiful, six-foot, blond woman. And guess what?"

"What?"

"A neighbor in the village saw the suspects leave the crime scene, and they fit the descriptions."

"No way!"

"Way!"

"Any news service picked up on it?"

For the first time, he sounded interested, excited.

"Penny goes by her maiden name. O'Riley. No one's made the connection yet."

"So, tell me this," Ben said. "What's the famous Al Rakozi's wife doin' over there in Ibiza with some black dude, a gram of cocaine in her veins?"

"And more importantly, why is she dead?"

"So, tell me this, Shelley. How do you know this . . . Al? And his pal, Ray."

"Okay. We're talking about . . . years ago. I'd just finished my internship at the OAKLAND TRIBUNE. So, I took out an ad. 'Share driving and expenses to New York City.' And they answered it."

"What were they doin' out there?"

"Working in drug rehab at Synanon."

"Ain't that some kind of cult, too?"

"Some people say so."

Ben took in his breath. Seemed to be getting more excited.

"Now, out there on the road? Guess you got to know them boys pretty good, huh?"

Ignoring his sardonic, insinuating tone, Shelley attempted to convey, without much success, a sincere, straightforward manner.

"Yes, I did, Ben . . . And the more I learned, the less I liked. They grew up as druggies and petty criminals in Brooklyn. And they hadn't risen very far, from what I . . ."

"Reason I asked?"

He dipped his head and waggled a finger at her.

"Ben, it was a four-day road trip, years ago."

A guilty look crossed her face, and she took a deep breath.

"Come on now, Shell. 'Fess up. Cain't be takin' any chances of conflict of interest here."

"No. Really," she insisted. "I'd ... I'd forgotten their existence till I saw Ray on that plane."

"Well, if you say ..."

Shelley zoned out, and Ben's voice faded into the distance.

In hazy black and white, an image appeared before her
eyes: beautiful, naked, young Shelley and squat, hairy Al having
rough sex on a wet, dirty bathroom floor.

Al slaps her hips, the back of her head, hard, rides her butt
like a bucking, fucking mare.

Covered with bruises, Shelley writhes beneath him,
shrieking in pleasure and pain.

Al hollers like a cowpoke when he comes. "Eeeeehaw!"
Then he leans forward, kisses her long white neck, bites into it,
and begins to suck. Just as she begins to moan in orgasm, Ben's
annoyed voice recalled her to the present.

"You listenin' to me, Shell?"

"Uh ... yeah."

"Any photos of you with them?"

"They don't have any. I had some, but I destroyed them."

"Witnesses?"

"Gas station attendants. Motel clerks. The ninety-year-
old lady across the hall from Al's old apartment in the East
Village ..."

"Thought you said you were with him only on the ... ?"

"No one who would remember," she said, avoiding his eyes.

Ben aimed a doubtful look her way, shook his head, and
gave her obvious subterfuge a pass.

"Then we're good to go, Shell. Anyone raise a fuss? It's just,
'He said, she said.' Right? And ... I'm startin' to sniff a really big

one here . . ."

"You offering me a job, Ben? You sound pretty excited."

"No, I ain't offerin' you no damn job. You're lucky I don't just steal the fuckin' story and hand it over to one of my own reporters. That's what Corvo'd do. Hell, think of the disadvantages you're operating under here. You been out of the country for years. You lost all your local sources. And a reporter . . ."

"I know, Ben. You told me a hundred times: 'A reporter is his sources.'"

"Still just as true as it ever was."

"So, what *are* you offering me?"

"A challenge."

"How much?"

"Completely on spec. I can't even give you expenses."

"Now why would I want to do that?"

"You pull this one in for me, honey, I swear, I'll go right over that Wop bastard Corvo's head. I'll go upstairs and talk to the publisher, David St. Godens, in person. I'll find a place for you on the *Star* or break my ass tryin'."

"Look, I can't do it on spec."

"Why not?"

"I . . . I'm nearly broke. I didn't ask my husband for alimony, I've got Toby, and . . ."

"Well, hell, why didn't you say so, hon? I'll take it out of my own expense account if I have to. Never use the damn thing, anyway.

"Now here's what we're goin' do," he went on, after they'd solemnly shaken hands across his desk. "Come around the back door at the sonbitch. Lull his ass into complacency. The cocksucker will sue at the drop of a hat. Got all these bleedin'-heart lawyers workin' for him free of charge, some of the craftiest in New York.

"He's slippery as a pig in shit, and he's got this captive press corps. Knee-jerk Liberal columnists he's bamboozled over the years. Won't hear a word against him. Including some of the shitheads that work for me.

"So, I don't want you comin' out with anything negative till we got him surrounded with irrefutable facts. Your first piece is gonna be straight bio. 'Early Life of Drug Rehab Guru Al Rakozi.' Then we nail the sonbitch when he ain't lookin'. When he's hot."

"When will he be 'hot?'"

"In a couple of weeks, the mayor's gonna give him a special award 'for service to the City of New York.' And you, dear? You gonna hit 'em with your killer piece in that mornin's paper."

Shelley leapt to her feet, hooting, and clapping.

"Yes!"

Ben jumped up as well, and they bumped fists.

"And oh, my, but the shit will fly!"

CHAPTER EIGHT

Hunger

Monika asked nothing of Jim after their spat, made no demands. She even cut his hair, shaved his beard, gave him some clean clothes to wear—a tee shirt, sweatshirt, Levis and sneakers that had belonged to some previous lover—and let him sleep on the futon across the room from her. Yet she kept the refrigerator bare, and most of the time, he was left entirely to his own devices.

After she went out to work each morning, he would stay on in the apartment for hours, practicing his flute or recorder, watering the herbs and plants that hung from her windows and filled her kitchen, feeding the tropical fish in her aquariums.

Later, he would patter barefoot out to her tiny, overgrown back garden and recline on a rusty, mildewed, lounge chair to read her old *HIGH TIMES* magazines, her books on astrology, on the occult, on obscure Eastern religions, listening to the IRT subway trains rumble by under Seventh Avenue, smoking stale cigarettes he found in odd crannies around the apartment and drinking gallons of water from her garden hose to stave off the hunger pangs. Sometimes the phone would ring, and he'd listen to the answering machine, cryptic calls from someone called Ray, someone called Al. Not that he was interested, but just to break the monotony. Finally, hunger would drive him into the streets. He didn't have a key, so once he was out, he had to stay out till Monika got home. Most nights she returned late. Sometimes she wouldn't get back till three or four o'clock in the morning. Weekends she didn't come home at all.

He could've sneaked on the subway and ridden up to the George Washington Bridge. Could've walked across to the Jersey side and stuck out his thumb. Might've gotten a ride with a traveling salesman, or a long-haul truck, all the way out to the Coast. But Monika had somehow milked him of his will.

He could've called his dad, a prison guard in Folsom, California, asking for enough to get him home, and there were times he was tempted. But when he thought of their harsh parting words, when he confessed that he'd gone AWOL and the MP's were after his ass, he figured it wasn't worth the effort.

It was the height of spring. The air was full of pollen, buzzing insects, the smell of flowers, sunshine. And it was all wasted on Jim. For days and nights on end he wandered the Village, ransacking garbage bins for refundable bottles, hawking stolen newspapers, playing his flute for nickels and dimes in the subway, sleeping in parked cars, on the sparse grass of Washington Square Park, dreaming of a warm bed, a cozy, yellow lamp, a decent novel to read, patiently awaiting his benefactress' return.

One night, plopping down Jane Street in the rain, he saw a short, muscular Hispanic boy in white tennis shoes leap to the trailing end of a fire escape ladder, catch it, swing up like a trapeze artist, climb the steps and disappear into an unlit window on the second floor. It was such an amazing performance, and it happened so fast—in a blink or two of the eye—that Jim barely realized what happened. And it occurred to him that he might do something of the same. In high school, he'd been on the gymnastics team. In college, he'd done some rock climbing. He was still nimble and light on his feet. It'd be a cinch. He'd crawl up Monika's fire escape to the roof, run across to the rear, slide down the rain drainpipe and break into her place through the back window. But when it actually came down to it, he couldn't. She might get pissed, he thought, and throw him out on his ass.

Locked out again on another long, rainy, weekend night, he found a battered Volkswagen bus on Hudson Street with its rear door unlocked. Checking to make sure no one was looking, he heaved it open, crawled in, and closed it behind him. Inside, it was chill and musty, smelling of sex. He rolled up in an old rug blanket that he found, and in no time his cold, wet clothes were warm and sweaty. The windows of the bus steamed up, cutting the street and traffic light. The atmosphere turned humid and close. His shivering stopped. And toward morning, despite the persistent itch of the woolen blanket against the exposed portions of his skin, he was able to get some sleep.

Four days later, sitting at the end of an abandoned pier at the foot of Little West Twelfth Street, singing Otis Redding's "Sittin' On a Dock of the Bay" to himself, he felt himself start to itch again. All up and down his crotch and ass and under his arms his skin was on fire. He swung down under the pier, stood on the black scummy rocks, and had a piss in the green waters of the Hudson. Peeling his trousers down, examining himself in the harsh sunlight, he found a myriad of tiny, white, crab eggs clustered at the roots of his pubic hair. From years of experience in India—he'd once acquired such a virulent strain that it followed him around for months, spontaneously generating again and again at the most inopportune moments— he knew the exact prescription: Wash and dry all clothes and bedclothes at high temperature, shave pubic hair, generously apply Pyrinate 200 lotion to roots. Trouble was the laundromat and the treatment were going to cost a lot more than he could make hawking stolen newspapers or playing his flute in the subway. Yet, he had to do something, because he and Monika had shared her *djellaba* in the last couple of days, and there was a chance that she'd become infected as well. Racking his brains, trying to come up with some quick money-making scheme, he finally settled on a second-story job.

That night he watched and waited on Charles Street, lurking in doorways, clutching a short, sharp, metal rod he'd found on the pier. When the street was dark and quiet, he thrust the rod into his belt, went up the stoop to the first floor of Monika's place, stood on the handrail, leaned out, reached for the ledge, pulled himself up, grasped the bars of the first floor window, hoisted himself onto the next ledge, and continued crawling up the wall like an ant, gripping it with his ragged fingernails and the rubber tread of his sneaker soles, until he reached the fire escape on the second floor. Breathing hard, he paused, listening for some sign of discovery. But all was tranquil on Charles Street. After that there was nothing to it. Ascending swiftly and silently to the roof, he slipped across to the roof next door, and the next, and kept going until he was four or five doors up the street. There, he crept down a rear fire escape past open windows and blaring television sets until he found an unlit, unbarred window on the fourth floor. Waiting, breathing hard again, he listened until he was sure that no one was home. Then he pulled the sharpened rod from his belt, rose up and punched it through the window just above the latch, making a small, jagged, hand-size hole. The glass fell onto the ledge with a light tinkling sound, drowned out by tinny TV laughter from the floor below. Listening again for any sign of discovery, he slipped the latch, levered the window slowly, silently upward a few inches, and squeezed through.

Inside, he threw a doily over a table lamp, switched it on low, latched the door chain to prevent surprise, and found himself in a small, crowded apartment with musty wall-to-wall carpeting, faded overstuffed furniture, yellowing photographs, stained brown wallpaper, green plastic light fixtures and a low ceiling. Though the place was neat, and the beds were made, it smelled of old people, and dust lay thick on all the furniture. Breathing easier, imagining its elderly residents in some shabby condo on the West Coast of Florida, he proceeded methodically to search the place for money and valuables. He went through the bedroom, the bathroom, the living room, the guest bedroom, the kitchen. He went through the closets, the bed clothing, and drawers. He searched under the furniture and above the shelves. But he found nothing. Not a penny. Not a strand of pearls. On the point of giving up, he thought of the refrigerator. And there, in an old green Mason jar, he found a crisp, cold, twenty-dollar bill.

"Awwwright!" he shouted, shadowboxing around on the kitchen linoleum. "Awwwright!"

Replacing the twenty with an IOU, he stuffed his crabby clothes in a plastic, supermarket bag, slipped out the window in a double-breasted white linen suit that looked like it hadn't been worn since 1944, climbed up the fire escape, and scampered across the dark roofs to 76 Charles Street.

Monday evening, when Monika came home from work, he was waiting on her stoop.

"What's with all the laundry?"

"Listen, I hate to tell you this . . ."

"You're kidding me, Jim. Not that."

"I'm sorry," he said, fishing in his bag for the big green bottle of Pyrinate 200. "But I got the cure."

"You better have, boy," she said, though she didn't appear to be much put out. In fact, she was already starting to laugh.

Like Jim, she'd been through it all before.

But then inside the apartment, when they wanted to get into the shower and give each other the treatment, they discovered that the water had been shut off. Phoning upstairs to the neighbors, Monika found that emergency repairs were being done, and wouldn't be completed until tomorrow.

"Jim, if you don't do something about this . . ."

"Not to worry, love, I got just the place . . ."

Later that night they climbed the stairs to the fifth floor, went through the trapdoor and out onto the rooftops. A few minutes later, inside the old folks' place, everything seemed exactly as Jim had left it. Stealthily, by the light of the doily-covered table lamp, they crept to the bathroom, turned on the shower, shed their things, and hopped in together. Giggling in the half-light, shaving their crotches and up under their arms, lathering the Pyrinate 200 over all smooth and slippery parts, they began to grow aroused. "Here, rub me here, get those nasty things off me..." And ended up on the floor in a pile of arms and legs, in a puddle of water, soapsuds and spent crabs.

Sated at last, and shaved, rinsed, dried, parasite-free, fitted out in their freshly laundered togs, they crept back through the apartment and tossed their dirty things into the courtyard below.

"*This* is the way I like you, Jimmy," Monika said fiercely, as they clambered over the roofs in the darkness, with the lights of the metropolis in their eyes, a hot humid wind in their hair. "This is the way you were meant to be. Like me, man. Follow it out, wherever it goes."

CHAPTER NINE

The Taste of Blood

It was a neighborhood of five-story, brick tenements, narrow, treeless streets, Italian bakeries, coffee houses, salumerias, storefront social clubs, and Mom and Pop grocery stores, with pasta boxes, cans of olive oil and plum tomatoes stacked up behind the plate glass.

Poor and old, it was yet meticulously kept, with swept sidewalks, gleaming cobblestones, a profusion of potted flowers and plants and groups of elderly Sicilians lounging on the stoops watching and commenting upon each passerby.

"Know anything about a guy named Al Rakozi who grew up in this neighborhood?" Shelley kept asking. "How about the name Ray Pagano? That ring a bell?"

"Never heard of them," they solemnly intoned, in their Brooklyn accents—"Nevah hoyd of 'em"—shaking their heads.

The code of *omertà* prevailed even at the Ristorante Pagano, at MacDougal and Spring, and out front of the Rakozi Candy

Store, on Thompson Street, where Shelley succumbed to temptation and bought her first pack of cigarettes in two weeks.

Father Brian, the thin, studious-looking, old, parish priest at St. Anthony's, on Sullivan Street at Houston, was more forthcoming, though he delivered his lines into her tape recorder as if he'd spoken them to dozens of reporters over the years.

"Baptized them both, I did," he said, in a thick, Irish accent. "But I remember Al Rakozi much better than Ray Pagano. Al was the only Romanian lad in this Italian neighborhood."

"I thought Al was Hungarian."

"Well, that depends on how you look at it. His family is Hungarian, but from Romania."

When Shelley looked puzzled, he aimed a sardonic grin at her.

"There are millions of Hungarians in Romania. They've even got their own province."

"Really? What's it called?"

Father Brian bared his teeth, all drama. "Tran-syl-vania," he warbled, trilling his "R'" in a fake Romanian accent.

Shelley gaped in astonishment.

"Anyhow," the priest said, with a sardonic grin. "Al went to our parish school. And he was one of my . . ." He shook his shoulders, pursed his lips, and now his grey, long-lashed eyes seemed wily, furtive . . . "my altar boys for several years. There was even talk of him going into the seminary. But there was trouble in his family. His father was a great, bloody, brute of a man. Had a taste for drink, and an abusive streak. Beat his mum black and blue. Bit her like a rabid dog. The police hauled him in on it several times. But it came to naught. Several times after his elder siblings left home, little Al felt obliged to protect his mother. And he complained to me about how bloody awful he felt, how helpless and frustrated, being so small in comparison to his father.

"Up into his mid-teens, Al was active in parish charitable work, but he was cursed with what we call 'an over-scrupulous conscience.' Talked about this tremendous calling he had to do good works, to devote himself to others less fortunate than himself. Yet every time he did something good, he got this tremendous desire to extract some symbolic payment for it. And then he felt he had to go right out and do some more good works to salve his conscience. I told him that his affliction was not as uncommon as he thought. Told him that I myself had been tormented by it, as had every other priest I knew, and he ought to just try and forget about it."

The priest paused. Shelley smiled and nodded, encouraging him to continue.

"Poor lad. His mum cut her wrists in the bath when Al was only seventeen. And the poor, young feller, he was so distraught, they say, he dipped a cup in the tub and drank of her blood."

Shelley gasped in horror.

"Amazing what the lad has managed to achieve, though, isn't it? After such a start in life. Can't tell you how proud we are of him."

Shelley rose to her feet, struggling to regain control of herself. "Thanks so much, Father. Mind if I . . . ?

She whipped her camera out before he could reply and snapped a photo that captured Father Brian in all his sleazy faux charm.

Later, back at the *Star*, Shelley laid it all out to Ben.

"So, old Father Brian, with all that blood talk, he gave me an idea ... I went to the medical school at NYU and did some research. And like, everybody thinks it's all kind of Bela Lugosi, right? But what I found, all the myths about vampires are based on a real medical condition."

Ben raised his hands and stared at the heavens, scoffing at her.

"I know. You're gonna laugh. But it's called 'Clinical Vampirism Disorder.'"

"You are *shuckin'* me!"

"What I found," she went on, shaking her head. "It's a male thing."

"Now, why ain't I surprised by that?"

Shelley tried to grin back at him, but it came out as more of a grimace.

"Starts when a certain type of boy swallows blood for the first time and finds it exciting. Then, they start getting a sexual thrill out of sucking on their own scratched arm or hand. When they become adults, they look perfectly normal ... They don't have long fangs. They can see their reflection in the mirror. They sleep eight hours every night in a real bed, not a coffin. But they get off on a feeling of power and control. So, they start sucking blood from other people, either by force or consent.

"Consent?" Ben laughed. "What kinda crazy sonbitch would ever consent to that?"

"That's a whole other issue, Ben, but some people, believe it or not ..." She paused to draw in a deep breath. "They actually get off from having their blood sucked."

"No fuckin' way!"

She nodded at him very slowly, eyes shut.

Later that same day, Shelley flashed her new press tags at One Police Plaza and took the elevator up to see an old friend from her days as a court reporter, Detective Manny Rivera.

A tall, light-skinned Puerto Rican, with a fringe of black hair around his crown, a perpetual, five o'clock shadow, a pencil-thin mustache and the look of a man afflicted with constant acid indigestion, Manny was seated in his cubicle in the Narcotics Division, hunched over his computer terminal, puffing at a cheroot.

"Well, goddamn, look who the cat drug in!" he chortled when she leaned over his partition and gave him a fist bump.

Shelley gestured at the big, empty room.

"Where is everyone?"

"Out to lunch . . . What you doin' back in the World, girl?"

"Out on the beat again, Manny."

"Last I heard, you married a famous writer and moved to the hippest island in the world."

"Yeah, well you know how it goes."

"Tell me about it. I'm divorced twice, workin' on a third right now."

"Listen, can you do me a favor? The name Ray Pagano mean anything to you?"

"It might."

"Used to own a topless joint in the financial district. He was also into pit bulls. Raised them in his backyard and fought them out in Jersey somewhere. Word was, he financed his dogs with a wholesale drug operation sanctioned by the Gambino Family."

"Hmmm, lemme see," he muttered, and punched the name into his computer. "Yeah, he was busted about a year ago on a drug trafficking charge. Sold a couple of keys of coke to a guy I know in the First Precinct. Second offense. High bail. But he made it. He was indicted, tried, and convicted. He appealed, it was denied, and when he came up for sentencing, he jumped bail."

"When was that?"

"His court date was April 21, 1974."

"That fits."

"What's up?" Manny asked, peering up at her from beneath bristling black eyebrows.

"Okay, Ray Pagano is Al Rakozi's best and oldest friend.

The famous Al Rakozi? The guy who runs Streetlight?

"And Al's wife got murdered in Ibiza, along with her black boyfriend, just when Ray happened to be in town . . ."

"Hold it." Manny raised a hand at her. "Hold it right there."

"What? You don't believe me? I saw him there. On the very day . . ."

Manny shook his head and put a finger to his mouth.

"Ain't sayin' that, Shell," he whispered. "All I'm sayin'? This Rakozi dude? He's wired right up to the . . ."

He pointed upstairs.

"That's what everyone keeps telling me," Shelley said, shaking her head. "Okay. So why don't we just prove it, one way or the other?"

"How we gonna do that?"

"Hey, I have to do your job for you? It's simple."

"Lemme tell you. I think you're gonna find ... nothin's gonna be simple in this case."

"Just call the police in Ibiza, okay? You speak Spanish. Ask 'em to send any prints they got on the killers of Penny O'Riley and her boyfriend, Robert 'Bobby O' Osborne."

Manny seemed about to protest, but Shelley silenced him with a waving finger.

"And when you get the prints? Compare them with the prints you got on Ray Pagano and any you find on Monika Thorssen and call me a liar."

CHAPTER TEN

The Queen Bee

"THE ZOO," said a sign over the door of a huge room full of bald, cheerful, ex-junkies in shorts and BLOOD BROS tank-tops, all busy or playing volleyball, jogging around the perimeter, doing punk rock aerobic routines to The Ramones.

Several of them, male and female, sported love bites on their necks.

A bandstand extended from the bleachers, and when the boss man clambered up to the microphone all activity came to a halt, the music stopped, and his audience gazed up at him in awe.

He pointed up at the messages that hung from the walls, started chanting them out loud, and they all shouted back the refrains.

"In losing yourself!" "You find yourself!" "Don't agitate!" "Cooperate!"

When the chants came to an end, everyone, including Ray,

clapped, and yelled, "The boss, the boss, the boss man!"

Later, there was a Board meeting on the agenda. So, Ray had to climb all the way up the fire stairs to the Board Room with the Boss because the elevator wasn't working. Then he had to sit there with him for hours listening to piped-in Musak, facing these dreary, boring, rich people and professionals in dark business suits who pretended to advise and consult when in fact the whole show was just the boss man.

And worst of all, Ray had nothing to do with the proceedings. His only function was just to sit there beside him looking ferocious and twiddling his thumbs, even though had absolutely no need of an in-house bodyguard. Why? Because number one he already had these two big-ass dudes, Jazeel and Tall Boy, who followed him on his rounds of the boroughs like faithful hounds. And, number two, all of Streetlight worshiped him like a god; even the Board stood in awe of him.

But he kept Ray trotting after him anyway, at all hours of the day and night, opening and closing doors for him, fetching him this and that, obeying his commands like a fucking sheepdog.

"Hey, it's not for me personally, man," he claimed. "It's to maintain the dignity of the office."

Sure, boss, uh-huh. Ray had known him since he was shitting his pants, so he took it all with a grain of salt. Whatever kick he was on, whether it be trading baseball cards, boosting cars, group groping, or creating his own utopia, it was always "The Gospel According to Al."

The Streetlight armory used to belong to the National Guard, and it was built like a medieval fortress, with red brick walls five feet thick and turrets with gun slats cut in their sides.

The Board Room was way up at the top, in the tallest turret, so high that even after they'd sweated it up to the boss' office floor they had to climb another thirty feet on this tight little clanging spiral stairway.

Inside, the place was a perfect circle, twenty feet in diameter, and it might have seemed claustrophobic if it hadn't been for its domed skylight, its high-tech spotlights and smiling color photos of recovering drug addicts.

A great, round, oak table sat out in the middle of the room, surrounded by tall-wooden chairs. In front of each chair, there was a place setting and a stack of papers. On a side table nearby stood a two-gallon coffeemaker and a platter full of croissants.

The Board itself was made up of twelve members, including the boss, excluding Ray, and Monika his executive assistant. One of the board members, Chief Inspector Ron Nelson NYPD, according to his name tag, had a Band Aid on his neck, as if from a shaving accident.

A few members were missing today, but there was a quorum. And everyone was seated, waiting expectantly, when the Top Dog, trailed by his faithful companion, swaggered into the room.

Short and squat in his nondescript bush jacket, jeans, and desert boots, with a huge, battered face and head, a long droopy mustache, and a mop of sandy hair hanging down over his collar, the boss man was someone you wouldn't notice in a crowd. But get him one-to-one, or facing an audience, and a light came shining out of his dark, slitty, little eyes, a light that no one could face without blinking or bowing.

"Alright, let's cut the crap!" he shouted, though no one had said a word. And he stood there scanning their faces, taking great pleasure in their uncertainty and anxiety, while Ray fetched his coffee and croissants.

"What's he up to?" they all seemed to be wondering, as he fiddled with the gavel, raising it up like he was about to bang the meeting to order, then letting it fall into his open palm. "What's he up to now?"

The rudeness of his language offered them no clue because it was S.O.P. He habitually addressed them not as a respectable executive body, but like peers from his days in the drug trade. They didn't seem to mind. For the moneybags among them, it was even a drawing card because it gave them an illicit little thrill. They even joined in sometimes. Gave them a chance to let their hair down.

None of them had a clue as to what really went on in Streetlight. And none of them cared if he kept producing results and getting media attention. But sometimes he let them attend a sanitized, VIP version of one of his attack therapy sessions. Silk Stocking liberals from the Upper East Side, they were all guilt-ridden masochists at heart, and they loved nothing better than getting ripped apart by a bunch of dark, toothless, pop-veined members of the underclass.

"What's he up to?" everyone was still wondering. "What's he up to?"

And the reason they didn't know was because ... the boss himself didn't know. "Always Keep 'em Guessing," was his motto, and it referred even to himself.

With his junkies, though, he was even worse. He'd tell them to do something, explain it all in detail, and then turn around and tell them they were doing it wrong; they had to do it another way. He'd lay down a law, with a penalty of summary expulsion, and reverse it the next day without telling anyone. He'd feast the clan like royalty for a week, then, without warning, put them on a diet of bread and water, punishing all complainers.

His object was to instill fear and paranoia, he said, to have them wake up every morning scared to death that they might be told to get out and never come back.

Without fear, he believed, a junky valued nothing.

Without fear, there was no control.

Fear was what held Streetlight together.

"What's he up to? What's he up to?"

You could see it on their faces—well-groomed, middle-aged faces, do-gooder faces, willfully credulous faces—as they flitted nervous glances at each other around the table, trying to read his mood, trying to find out how they should feel.

To the Boss, Streetlight was like an extension of himself. When he thought of it, he said, he didn't think of it as a collection of separate individuals. He thought of it as an organism, with the communal property as the body, himself as the brain, and the members and residents as the body's many busy cells, going about their business in thoughtless, productive bliss.

"I'm the Queen Bee," he declaimed, without a flicker of irony. "Without me, the hive will die."

And there must have been something to it, because whenever he was in a good mood, the place rocked with laughter. If he got sick, it crept along at half-steam. When he got pissed off, everybody hid, and then let out their aggression on each other. If he quit smoking or drinking, or went on a diet, everyone else followed suit.

It was to the point now where he didn't even have to get the members to follow his lead; they did it automatically, out of love. Sometimes, they tried to anticipate his moves. But it wasn't easy; he couldn't even do that himself. And if he caught them out on any kind of philosophical limb, he was liable to cut it off. Not that they would resent him for it. They regarded his mood swings and petty cruelties affectionately, like those of an adored and eccentric uncle, or an unpredictable household god. Life in an institution tended to get boring, and the boss man could always be counted on to add spice.

Lately though, he'd been in a poisonous mood, and everyone inside had suffered for it. Suddenly one morning—not long after Ray got back from Europe with Monika and sought refuge again at Streetlight under the alias "Johnny Di Dio"—he decided to put everyone on a guilt trip. Over the in-house radio station, he went on tirades for hours on end, excoriating their sins of thought and deed.

"What kind of bug has he got up his ass now?" everybody wondered, and prayed he'd work it out soon.

Not that it was any mystery to Ray. Once a Catholic, always a Catholic. Penny had been his Madonna. One he'd created himself—his redheaded, Irish, Mary Magdalene. His *schtup* of *schtups*. Which is to say, he raised her up so high, he couldn't *schtup* her no more. That's the ultimate *schtup*. And then she broke his heart.

Not to say that Ray hadn't felt a pang or two of guilt himself for Penny's passing, from time to time. And if he had to do over again . . .

"Alright, let's bring this meeting to order," the Boss barked at last, having decided, for no apparent reason, to relieve the Board's suspense, to put an end to its fear and confusion. "There's something I'd like to run by you today. I mean, what do you think? Isn't it about time I started getting a salary for all the fucking work I do here? Other charitable foundations pay their directors. Why not this one?"

"Excuse me, Al, I'm sorry, but I don't think that's a very good idea," said old Dorothy Dayton Lewis, one of his moneybags. "To be perfectly frank, I'd say it's right down there with that notion we considered a year or two back to try and get Streetlight declared a religion. And I'll tell you why. The whole source of our power, and our funding, and our esteem in the community, comes from this: The founder and director and guiding light of the Streetlight Foundation lives with his patients. He's an ex-addict and an ex-convict just like they are. He shares their hardships. He shares their sorrows and their joys. And he takes nothing for it. Not a penny. No one in Streetlight does. Everything is plowed back into the organization. Everything is dedicated to one purpose, and one purpose only—the saving of bodies and souls. It's like a holy covenant. It's like a vow of poverty. And it can't be broken."

"It's easy for you to talk about poverty, Dorothy!" Al bellowed. "You live on Park Avenue. You got a country home in the Hamptons. When it gets cold, you fly down to the Bahamas. But I'd like to see you locked in here for a few days with these dope fiends. I'd like to see you 'commiserate' while they piss and wail and moan and blame everyone else but themselves for their problems. You'd be climbing the walls. And I've got to do it year in and year out.

"So why don't you just get with the program, dear," he said in a softer, yet somehow even more threatening tone, "or find some other way to while away your empty hours?"

For a long time after that, the Board members found it expedient to scrutinize their coffee cups, their half-eaten croissants, the papers on the table before them. The only sound to be heard was the scratching of Monika's pen as she summarized and censored the proceedings according to the Boss' longtime instructions.

Then doughty, old Dorothy cleared her throat and faced the boss man again.

"I hereby move that we take under study the suggestion from the floor that we offer some form of remuneration to our chief executive officer. Any seconds?"

The motion carried unanimously.

CHAPTER ELEVEN

The Messianic Calling

Heading into the subway at Church Street and Park Place, across City Hall Park from One Police Plaza, waiting for an uptown A Train, regarding the moldy tile wall on the other side of the tracks, the water dripping from the peeling mortar ceiling, the scraps of paper, orange peels and yoghurt cartons lying in pools of fetid water between the ties, the sleek gray rats running up and down the rails, the black splotches of gum, candy wrappers and cigarette butts on the concrete beneath her feet, Shelley lost all the self-assurance she had mustered for Manny and her other interviews, and was invaded by fears and doubts and paranoid fantasies.

She kept expecting to meet her mother—the demented, British, War Bride mother who'd plagued her youth and ran off to places unknown when Shelley was a senior in college—pushing a shopping cart full of plastic bags, begging alms on the subway platform.

The vision seemed so real, so vivid in all its details, that Shelley knew it was true. Somewhere out there, Phyllida roamed the subway—white-haired, wild-eyed, rifling garbage cans, talking posh to herself.

In the subway car, it was unbearably hot, crowded, and smelly, with squalid signs advertising foot balms, anal creams, and cut-rate abortions at eye-level, so there was no way to avoid them except by closing your eyes. But you couldn't close your eyes because the instant you did you got rubbed up against from behind by creepy, little, tattooed men in rolled-up tee shirts.

Later, coming out of the subway at Forty-First Street and Broadway, she felt that everything had become appallingly sleazy, slimy, and evil in some way she couldn't put into words. The streets were littered with filth of every description, even human excrement. Nasty, little, middle-aged, white, and Hispanic men made obscene gestures and remarks to her. Cunning, light-footed, young, black men followed her, menacing her with their eyes. She could almost feel hands reaching up her skirt, tearing her skin. Mugging, rape, murder, and mayhem awaited her, seemingly, around every corner.

Hurrying around Bryant Park to the front entrance of the monolithic New York City Public Library, she ran past the stone lions and up the marble staircase to the Newspaper and Periodicals Section.

Delighting in the order and silence, the waxy, pine-oil odor of the high-domed, wood-paneled, Victorian chamber, the murmured instructions of the young, bespectacled, female librarian, Shelley took a deep breath and made her way to the index file where she began to slowly work through the R's and

S's. As subjects, she found, Al Rakozi and Streetlight filled nearly thirty cards.

Hours later, Shelley marveled that in all the miles of news and feature stories she had scanned on the microfilm viewer, not one was less than favorable, that Streetlight was universally acclaimed as an unqualified success, that Al Rakozi came across as utterly charming and captivating, a blend of Peck's Bad Boy and Mahatma Gandhi.

The press' fascination with Al seemed to lie in his contradictory character. How, they wondered, had this little, foul-mouthed braggart, with a criminal record, a Napoleonic complex, and nearly total power over the lives and purses of thousands of people, managed to rehabilitate so many drug addicts? No one doubted that Al was capable of underhanded methods. Indeed, he frankly admitted to bending zoning laws, tax laws, building code and even civil rights laws. Yet, all his interviewers were prepared to wink at his transgressions, accepting without question his implied dictum that "the end justifies the means."

Just as she was about to leave the library, Shelley thought to look up "messianic cults," and spent another hour investigating that category, taking copious notes, summarizing her findings as follows:

"The precipitating factor in the messianic calling is virtually without exception a major early life crisis or failure. Overcoming this crisis, the future cult leader gains strength, develops charisma. Typically, he starts out as a sincere do-gooder. His success in helping others attracts followers and true believers. As a means of coping with his feelings of inadequacy, he starts believing in his own superiority, his invincibility, his exclusion from the rules that bind ordinary mortals. But he can never forget his early failure and feels vulnerable to its effects for the rest of his life. His vulnerability breeds fear. Fear breeds panic. This, coupled with great power over people's lives, is often a potent, if not tragic, mixture."

Later, descending the marble stairs to the library's main lobby, glancing at the Chagall painting—a pale, delicate young girl in a filmy pastel dress, a ramshackle village—that hung in an alcove there, she was reminded of Penny again. It occurred to her that not one of the many writers she'd read had thought to ask Al about his wife. She recalled from a news story she did on the Rakozi wedding in 1968 that Penny's maiden name was O'Riley, and she had been raised in Stuyvesant Town, a red-brick, high-rise, middle-income housing development at Fourteenth Street and First Avenue.

Down in the lobby, she consulted the Manhattan phone book, where eighteen O'Rileys were listed. Only one of them—Brenda O'Riley—lived in Stuyvesant Town.

Operating on instinct, Shelley decided to forgo a preparatory phone call and simply show up at her apartment.

"Hi, I'm an old friend of Penny's," she called into Mrs. O'Riley's speaker a half hour later, "and I just heard about her death."

She was buzzed in immediately.

A small, haggard woman, with stringy, faded red hair, a sagging face and huge dark circles under her eyes, Mrs. O'Riley appeared nervous and ill-at-ease when she opened the door, and kept looking around behind her, as if afraid that someone might be listening.

"Mrs. O'Riley, could I talk to you for a moment about Penny?"

"What's there to say?"

"Well, I don't know anything about how she died. Last thing I knew, she got married to Al, then this."

"Why you bringin' him into it?"

"I just wondered."

"Uh . . . you wanna come in?" Mrs. O'Riley asked, looking around behind her again.

Her living room was small and perfectly square, with a low ceiling, tiny windows, magazine pictures of no apparent pattern tacked to the wall and tattered overstuffed furniture.

"Can I get you somethin'?" Mrs. O'Riley said and motioned her onto the soiled red sofa in front of the TV set. The Merv Griffin Show was on, and she didn't bother to turn it down. "I got wine or beer."

"A glass of wine would be great, thanks."

"What'd you say your name was, Miss?" Mrs. O'Riley asked, carrying in a can of beer and a tumbler of red wine from the kitchen.

"Shelley Friedman."

"Jewish name?" she inquired with raised eyebrows, as she set the drinks down on the glass coffee table.

"Uh-huh."

"Don't remember her tellin' me about no Jewish girls," Mrs. O'Riley went on, as she sat down beside her.

"I was more like a friend of a friend."

Cracking her beer, taking a hefty swig, Mrs. O'Riley lit a

cigarette.

Shelley lit up one of her own, then sipped decorously but thirstily at her wine. "That 'friend of a friend,'" asked Mrs. O'Riley, suspiciously, "was it Tina Bowran?"

"Yes, Tina Bowran," Shelley replied, nodding firmly, committing the name to memory. "And I . . . I was at Penny's wedding. What a wedding, huh? In Tompkins Square Park, in November, under the changing leaves. A rock band. Everyone in costume. I mean, it would've been so easy to poke fun at, with all those street people and upper-class do-gooders rubbing elbows. But I remember it as beautiful and moving and almost . . . triumphant. Penny was so lovely. Al was so imposing. And then . . ."

"Yeah?" Mrs. O'Riley raised her thin, arched brows again. "If you don't mind me askin', Miss, what line of work you in?"

"I'm a journalist."

"Oh!" she exclaimed, shaking her head. "We're not supposed to say nothin' to any reporters."

"Who's 'we'?"

"Why, Penny's family," she said, in a loud stagy voice, as if to some invisible audience. "Her husband. Her brother. Myself. Penny got herself in a mess, over there in Spain, but she's gone now, and we want her to rest in peace."

Just then a young man in his late teens or early twenties lurched out from one of the bedrooms, wiping his eyes, shaking his head, as if fresh from many hours of deep, blameless sleep. Slight, smooth-faced, and fine-boned, he was not so much handsome as beautiful, in the same haunting way Penny was.

"You're Penny's brother, aren't you?" Shelley asked and found herself suddenly and perversely attracted to this young man . . . and his air of innocence and frailty that might be deceptive . . . his huge, spacey, blue eyes and pale brown hair and pale white skin.

"Yeah, I'm Mike," he replied, smiling disarmingly, flinging himself down on an armchair across the room.

"Mike just got out . . . he was over at Streetlight," his mother put in. "After Penny . . . Al thought I needed someone to look after me."

"Now I'm lookin' for my own place," said Mike, grinning.

"Where?"

"Anywhere," he replied, winking at her. "Got any ideas?"

And she wondered whether his suggestive attitude was because of her appearance or something deeper in her aspect that he perceived.

In appearance, Shelley was well-groomed, well-dressed, even glamorous, or at least that's the effect she had strived to convey in her new role as career girl. If her air of success was what attracted him, then maybe all he was looking for was someone to tide him over till he got his feet back on the ground. Whatever the case, there was nothing in it for her except sex . . . and certain intangibles. And she was not in the market for intangibles. Not at this point in her life.

"I'll let you know if I hear of anything," she murmured, setting the empty tumbler down on the coffee table in front of her, stubbing out her cigarette. And then, turning abruptly toward him: "What do you know about Penny's death?"

"I didn't even find out about it till a week after it happened."

"When did Al find out?"

"Al? Well, he . . . uh . . . he found out right after me. I mean, first Ma got a call from the State Department. I guess Penny listed her as 'next of kin.' Ma phoned me at Streetlight. Usually, they don't like you to talk with the outside. It's bad for therapy, they say. But they let Ma's call through 'cause she told them it was a death in the family. I told the boss."

"The boss?"

"That's what we call Al Rakozi. At Streetlight everyone calls him that."

"Why did Penny and Al break up, do you know?"

"Hey, that's pretty obvious," Mike sniffed. "She ran off with one of his best friends. Not to mention, they cleaned out one of Streetlight's safe deposit boxes."

"But you know, I'm her mother," Mrs. O'Riley put in, "and I keep thinkin', 'Why? Why? Why?' I mean, that girl had her life turned around."

"Now that's enough, Ma," Mike warned, raising a hand at her.

"Well, thank you so much," Shelley said, rising to her feet, heading for the door. "I thought so much of Penny, and I just wanted to set things straight in my mind . . ."

CHAPTER TWELVE

A Fateful Affliction

The boss led Ray into his big, circular office, located in another of Streetlight's turrets, featuring an enormous circular desk, a medical lab refrigerator, and bookshelves cluttered with photos of him with celebs and politicians. As soon as he was in the door, he stepped over to the fridge, pulled out a blood collection tube, opened it, and gulped it down. He tossed it in a trash bin, wiped his lips with the back of his hand, took a deep breath, and winked at Ray.

"Come in!" he hollered, a moment later, when there was a knock at his door. And his mood turned sour as soon as Monika walked in "What's up, boss man?" she asked, nervously, sussing his mood. "Another Cayman run?"

"Hear you got some dude crashin' your crib."

"Huh?" she said, big-eyed with fear.

"My crib. The one I pay for."

"Who . . . who said that?"

"I got ears," he growled. "All over town."

"He's just an old friend. A sailor. Needed a place to stay till his ship sails."

Al scowled.

Monika sniffed in terror.

"And this fucker, he could be anyone. You know? A cop, reporter, paid informer . . ."

"Now, hold on, boss. He . . ."

"He could threaten your ass. You know? Get you to turn state's evidence."

Monika seemed about to protest, but Al stopped her with a raised hand and a snarl.

"Now get the fuck outta here!"

After she left, he stood at the window, looking out over Central Park. Then he whipped around with a stricken look on his face and started scratching his balls and ass, really working them over.

"You know, man, I talk these junkies down. Call 'em this, call 'em that. They'd try the patience of a saint. But the bottom line is—this place, my work here, it's my life blood. Anybody fucks with it, jeopardizes it, I go for the jugular. Right?"

"Right," Ray answered, reflexively, although he hadn't a clue what he was driving at.

"Now lemme tell you something, something you are not going to believe. That fucking cunt, she gave me the crabs."

"Say what, boss?"

"All of a sudden she shaves her crotch, see? And she don't wanna ball no more. I couldn't figure it out. Now I got 'em in all my clothes, all over my bed."

"Wait a minute, what . . . ?"

"And she got that fucking sailorman staying at her place. The Super told me. My place, that I bought and paid for, that Penny used to have. Can you top that? And this guy? He could be anyone. You know what I'm saying?"

Ray finally got the picture.

"Jesus, boss, I don't know."

"The fuck you mean you don't know?" Al snarled, coming up and grabbing him by the chops, pinning him with his eyes. "Have I ever let you down, Ray?"

"Never," he said, though he could think of a time or two. "But it ain't easy, you know? I mean, Monika and me, we're like partners. She started out dancin' at my club. Like Penny. Like Tina . . ."

"Is that a yes, or a no?"

"Jesus Christ! A body like that?" Ray sighed. "It's a fuckin' crime, boss."

"Don't look so hang-dog, man, you look like one of your own mutts," Al laughed. Then he grabbed him by the ponytail and twisted, twisted. "Sure, it's a shame, a fox like that. But you and me, we're a team. We go back. We're even more than that, right?"

"Right," Ray admitted reluctantly, and the boss bit into his neck and sucked.

CHAPTER THIRTEEN

The Strongest Suspicions

The day after Ben offered her a job, Shelley signed a two-year sub-let on a furnished, two-bedroom apartment on West Eleventh Street in the Village. The place was a find because the tenant had fixed it up almost exactly according to her own taste, which ran toward blues and whites, with flowered mock-Victorian wallpaper, exposed brick, sanded plank floors, stripped pine furniture, hanging patchwork quilts, and lots of green plants.

There was even a cat thrown in. Shelley loved cats, and she had a horror of New York rats and cockroaches. Teresa—a delicate, glossy, black tabby with irresistible green eyes, a sweet disposition and a raptor's eye for vermin—was like a dream come true.

Exhausted from her long day of interviews, she paid off today's temp babysitter and saw her out. She put Toby to bed with his bottle and his favorite song, "Why is a Fire Engine Red?"

"I wub you, Mommy," he whispered when she tucked him in.

"I love you, too, Sweetheart," she replied, smiling to herself, noticing that his Spanish was rapidly disappearing.

After a kiss goodnight, and the ritual *"Buenas noches, te amo, duermes bien,"* left over from their life in Ibiza, she dimmed his light, and stepped out of the room.

Then she sat down in the living room, with Teresa curled up in her lap, and tried to read this afternoon's edition of the *Star*. But she couldn't read. Her mind kept wandering back and forth from Al Rakozi to Father Brian to Michael and Brenda O'Riley.

Throwing the paper down, she walked into her bedroom and lay down on the bed.

And there it came to her, as if by mental telepathy.

"Mrs. O'Riley," she said a moment later, her voice booming out over the speaker on her answering machine's recording mechanism. "I have a feeling you might've been holding something back from me about Al Rakozi, possibly because your son was in the room."

"Uh-huh," she replied, in a tone that indicated that she was still not alone.

"Just answer me yes or no. Do you have any misgivings about Al Rakozi?"

"Yes."

"Any strong suspicions?"

"Yeah."

"You think he might be involved in Penny's death?"

"Yes, I do. Well, thanks for callin', Fiona. I gotta go now."

"One second, Mrs. O'Riley. Is there someone I could talk to, maybe some friend of Penny's, who could tell me more about this?"

"Sure thing."

"Okay, I'm going to call this person 'the seamstress.' Can you please give me her number now?"

"The seamstress? Oh, yeah. There's actually two of 'em."

"Is one of them Tina Bowran?"

"Yes, it is. . . ."

Hanging up, Beth immediately dialed the numbers that Mrs. Enright had given her. There was no response at the first number, though she let it ring and ring, but an answering machine picked up at the second number, and a woman with a deep, breathy, Marlene Dietrich voice came on:

"This is Monika Thorssen . . ."

Beth left a message for Monika to phone her at the earliest opportunity. Then she made herself another drink, returned to her room, sat down at her desk, and pulled out her diary for 1966. Puffing at a cigarette, glancing distractedly at the family photographs arrayed before her . . . Toby as a three-month-old in his father's arms, the twins at eleven in their Spanish school uniforms . . . she remembered the kid that Al had been in '66. A jokester, a punster, a non-stop talker. Full of bullshit, maybe. Too puffed up with himself to be very likeable but a million laughs. She remembered his raspy voice, the voice of a man twenty years his senior, and the way he'd strut into a room full of people, high on himself, and boom out, "I'm beautiful, man. Have you ever seen anybody so fucking beautiful in your life?" And despite everything, you believed him.

Then she thought of what this same young man had

achieved, against all the odds. She considered the good he'd done in the world, the lives he'd saved, the non-profit empire he created. Not for himself, but for the benefit of others. And she wondered how this person could possibly do anything like what she suspected. Could anyone change so much?

She thought of herself. How had she changed? She wouldn't take the kind of risks she took back then. Wouldn't dream of traveling across the country with two strange men. But she was still capable of accepting risks, providing the rewards were great enough. And she wondered what kinds of risks might Al be prepared to accept, to attain his changing goals?

And she recalled their transcontinental journey. Driving for nearly five days with nothing to do but talk and sing along with pop songs on the radio ("*Walk on By*," by Dionne Warwick, was number one on the hit parade, and it became their theme song). You could learn a great deal about your fellow travelers. Especially, if the two men were old friends who'd grown up together and spent a lot of time reminiscing and poking good-natured fun at each other. Add to this the fact that they had still been young, obscure, with nothing to hide, and you could come up with a lot of data. And this data—filed away at the back of your mind for years but not forgotten—might have been of little value. Yet, now, taken in light of future events in their lives, it suddenly became vastly more interesting.

"...It started with them kissing my breasts," she read in her diary, "then Ray worked his way up and Al worked his way down..."

Blushing at the casual sexual explicitness of her twenty-three-year-old self—had she really said such things, done such things with men like these?—she turned to some later, more straightforward entries in which Al and Ray spoke of their past. Meanwhile, she was jotting it all down on a note pad, relying on her memories and research to fill in the gaps.

Just as Shelley finished writing up her notes, the phone rang. It was Manny.

"Hey," she said, "you're working late."

"Yeah, the old lady's gonna kick my ass."

"What's up?"

"Listen to this, Shell. They got two sets of prints, and they both fit."

CHAPTER FOURTEEN

A Gift from the Grave

After the episode with the parasites, everything went back to normal at Monika's place. Jim slept alone, scratched his itching stubble of pubic hair alone, whiled away ninety percent of his waking hours alone; he had no illusions about how he would spend the coming, momentous, Fourth of July weekend.

All day Tuesday and Wednesday that week, he worked like a pack rat, busking in the subway, ransacking trash bins, collecting refundable bottles, selling them in supermarkets, stocking up on beans and rice, till he figured he'd gotten enough to hole up for the entire four days.

On Wednesday night, he boiled the rice and beans, stirred them together in a giant pot, and dined at the kitchen counter amid the plants and fish tanks which had become his responsibility.

And while the rest of New York City spent a long, wild, weekend, with fireworks and a parade of tall ships, Jim passed his days in tranquility, practicing the flute, reading through Monika's paperbacks, listening to her Swedish rock, bothered only by a woman named Shelley Friedman who kept leaving urgent messages for Monika on the answering machine.

Then on Saturday afternoon, someone came around banging on the door, knocking for what seemed like ten minutes. Intrigued, and with nothing but time on his hands, Jim crept to the kitchen window and watched through the curtain.

Out there on Monika's mossy, crumbling brick steps, in the shadow of the rose tree and the iron portico, stood a beautiful lady in a creamy linen suit.

As Jim watched, she pulled a pen and a notebook from her handbag and bent her head to write, letting her lush, black hair fall across her large, up-slanting eyes, her roman nose, and full lips. She then shook her head, blowing at her hair unconsciously when it got in her way.

Finished, she tore the leaf from her notebook and sunk down on her heels, neatly scissoring her long, silky legs in her tight skirt. Folding the paper, she slipped it under the door, rose, spun on the balls of her feet in one graceful motion, and made her way back up the stairs with the dignified, straight-backed posture of a former ballerina.

She had barely disappeared beyond the stoop before Jim, mouthing the word "Wow," rushed over to the door, snatched up the note, held it to the light, and managed to make out most of the first couple of sentences: *Dear Monika: My name is Shelley Friedman. I'm a journalist seeking information on the death of . . .*

Obeying an impulse, Jim grabbed one of Monika's paperbacks off the shelf, propped open the front door with it, vaulted up the steps and took off down the street after Ms. Friedman.

He had some vague notion of approaching her as a friend of Monika's, asking how he might be of service. But when he caught up with her on Seventh Avenue, and saw her up close, he was reminded of how shabby and ill-kempt he looked in comparison, and his courage failed him.

Following her at a discreet distance, trying to recover his nerve, he kept expecting her to hail a cab and head uptown. Instead, she turned left into Waverly Place and left again into West Eleventh Street where she disappeared into a large gray apartment building halfway down the block.

A few minutes later, when he stepped warily into the empty vestibule of the building, he was delighted to find her name on a mailbox marked 8C. Consoling himself with the thought that he'd at least discovered her home address, and that sometime in the future he might possibly summon the audacity to make use of it, he raced back to Monika's before someone discovered the propped-open door and cleaned the place out.

For the rest of that day and night, and most of Sunday as well, Jim amused himself by fantasizing a meeting with Shelley Friedman. Finally, on Sunday night he was driven out of the apartment and into the garden, on account of the heat wave, and the stench of his own bean farts.

An hour or two before dawn, he was awakened from an odd and familiar bad dream—the toolshed behind his parents' old clapboard house, a dark figure blocking the light from the door, a stifled scream that might have been his own—by the sound of muffled voices coming from inside the apartment.

It was Monika and someone else, a man with a Brooklyn accent so strong that its cadences seemed almost foreign.

"... fuckin' reporter ..."

"... lucky Mike came to you ..."

"... boss finds out ..."

"... should've done her when ..."

"... cops everywhere ..."

"... do it now, man ..."

"... 'never touch a cop or the working press' ..."

For a minute or two, Jim lost the drift of the conversation, which until that point had seemed quite casual in tone. When he picked up on it again, however, there was a pleading note in Monika's voice, unlike anything he'd heard before.

"... who's Al to cast stones ..."

"... ain't just the crabs, per se ..."

"... friend of mine ..."

"... the fuck is he ..."

"... dunno ..."

"... lie to me ..."

Then came some smothered cries, and someone got slammed up against a door. Furniture fell over. Glass broke.

Startled from his torpor, Jim considered heroics for an instant, but he had a sense that he might only make things worse for Monika. Rolling off the deck chair, he slipped behind the bushes and over the mossy garden wall just as a man appeared at the French window.

A large, pot-bellied man with a smudge of black goatee, a Mets ballcap turned around backwards on his head, and long kinky hair pulled back in a ponytail, he switched on the outside light, slid the window open and stepped into the garden, breathing hard. His coffee-colored body—clad in only a loose black tank top, white thigh-length shorts and white loafers—gleamed with sweat. Loosely in his right hand, pointing downward, he grasped a slender, silencer-equipped, automatic pistol. With his left he reached for a handkerchief to wipe his eyes and his large aquiline nose, while at the same time he swiveled his head around, searching the shadows.

"You out there, boy?" he rasped. And then, shaking the handkerchief rather daintily for a large man, he folded it and replaced it in his back pocket. "You out there?"

Monika appeared behind him in a long, white, cotton dress of Swedish peasant design, ripped at the bodice. Blood ran from her mouth and nose. Her blue eyes glared wide and bright.

"Jim," she pleaded, slipping past the man into the garden. "If you're out there, come out!"

Standing on the roof of somebody's old doghouse, peeking over the wall through the shrubbery, holding his breath, Jim went over his options and decided that he had only one.

Monika continued, "Please, Jim, he only wants to talk."

"Goddamnit, what is this shit? Ain't nobody out here," the man grumbled. Then in a more conversational tone, leading Monika into the apartment and out of earshot again: "Too much heart, girl, takin' in that bum."

". . . I swear . . ."

". . . he's the one that deserves . . ."

". . . you and me, Ray . . ."

". . . wag your tail at me . . ."

". . . begging you, man . . ."

"...tempting, but..."

The answering machine came on loud, in a babbling, high-pitched, high-speed reverse, and in the middle a low *bap-bap* resounded, like a couple of ladyfingers going off.

The machine stopped. The man Monika had called Ray sniffed, cried out in sorrow and rage, and banged his fist against a wall to punctuate his sobs.

The radio came on.

"Isn't she lovely?" Stevie Wonder sang. *"Isn't she won-der-ful?"*

The front door clicked shut.

Sitting on the dewy, tarpaper roof of the doghouse, gripping his knees tight, Jim tried to make sense out of what had just happened. Yet there could be no question of what happened. The only question was whether to disappear immediately or stick around to confirm a forgone fact.

Across the garden he ran, over the wall and up the side of the house next door, up the fire escape like a human fly, over the rooftops to the old folks' place.

If someone had called the cops, they'd be there in a minute. The precinct house was only three blocks away on West Tenth Street. And there was no doubt whom their primary suspect would be.

Jim did not cry for Monika that night. Already, she was something other than herself. And it was like ... he'd had this flash before. In a certain way, she'd been dead all along, and everything that had happened in between was like a dream.

In the evening, there was an item about it on page nineteen of the *New York Star*.

WOMAN FOUND DEAD
IN GREENWICH VILLAGE APARTMENT

"Police responding to an anonymous phone call last night found a twenty-eight-year-old woman shot to death in her Greenwich Village apartment. The victim, a Swedish citizen named Monika Thorssen of 76 Charles Street, was shot twice in the back of the head, execution-style, and pronounced dead on arrival at Saint Vincent's Hospital. The gunman was apparently known to the victim, according to police spokeswoman Kim Royster, because there was no sign of breaking and entering and neighbors report overhearing an argument shortly before hearing what sounded like firecrackers. Drugs found in the apartment are suspected as a motive in the case. Police are seeking a tall, white man in his late twenties who spent the previous three weeks with the victim in her apartment," Officer Royster said. "The suspect has been identified by fingerprints found in the apartment as Jim Range, a California man sought by federal authorities on a Vietnam-era desertion charge and unlawful flight to avoid prosecution. An all-points bulletin has been issued for the fugitive's arrest."

Unable to go to the police and confess what he knew about the crime, unable to flee, holed up inside the old folks' place for days on end with nothing to do, Jim felt compelled to occupy his mind with something other than his own terror. He spent hours reliving his years of freedom at sea and on the road. When he'd had a bellyful of the that, he tried to summon an interest in the place where he lay in hiding, or its sometime tenants. But it was useless. He couldn't even be bothered to learn their names, or look through their letters in the bureau drawer, or the pictures in their six, hefty, family albums, or the documents in their desk. Indeed, he barely noticed the walls around him or the floors beneath his feet.

The apartment was like a picture of the inside of his brain, empty of all purpose or reason, holding only fear and fantasy and a kind of indefinable inertia. For days he laid on the sofa, staring up at the fly-specked, brown ceiling, the green plastic chandelier, or read the yellowing newspapers that the old folks used as shelf-liner, retaining nothing of what his senses absorbed, drinking gallons of water instead, till hunger drove him again into the nighttime streets.

The injustice of it all was what got to him. Here he was a wanted criminal, hounded by the authorities, when from his own perspective he was guilty of nothing more than protesting an unjust war and trying to survive.

Then he thought of the reporter, Shelley Friedman, and suddenly one thing, at least, seemed clear . . .

"Excuse me, ma'am," he said, calling her at her newspaper one morning, "I'm sorry to bother you, but I've got some information about a crime, a murder. And I wanted to talk to you about it."

"All right. I'll be happy to listen to whatever you've got to say. But please speak slowly and distinctly, so I can get it on tape . . ."

Cupping the telephone booth's speaker with his hand, twisting his head back and forth to make sure no one was listening, he told her everything. He felt the need to confess to someone, and she would do fine. The only thing he left out was the crabs.

"Okay," she said when he was done, all business. "I think I might know this 'Ray' you're talking about, and his boss, Al Rakozi. Is there anywhere or any way I can get in touch with you?"

"No, I told you, I'm on the street. And I can't accept the berth I had on a ship because the cops will be onto me by now."

"Look, if I can fix things up with the cops, will you be willing appear before a magistrate and sign a deposition?"

"Yes, if you can get me a guarantee of immunity from prosecution on the murder charge."

"That won't be easy, but . . ."

"I'm starting to think I should just turn myself in."

"Are you kidding me? With Streetlight's grease? And the military after you? They'll just lock you up and throw away the key. I'll have a word with a friend of mine, an ex-cop. Get him to talk to an old pal of his . . . An Assistant DA . . . I might have something more by then . . ."

After his talk with the reporter, Jim was at first elated, but he quickly grew disheartened again when he began to question her motives. Once she got her story, he started to think, she was likely to just throw him to the wolves.

He considered running again, but in the end, he couldn't resist sticking around to see what this reporter lady would turn up.

The thing was, though, nothing turned up.

Three days, four days went by, and the story disappeared from the papers. Nor was it a topic of sidewalk conversation in the Village. Things quieted down so much, in fact, that Jim felt safe enough to forgo his nocturnal existence.

Meanwhile, he'd decided he wanted to meet this Shelley Friedman in person, look her in the eye and convince her of his innocence and sincerity, gain her sympathy and support. Yet when it came to phoning her or ringing the bell at her place on West Eleventh Street, he thought of how much he had riding on this person he didn't really know, and he froze.

After that, he took to lurking down the block from her place, especially in the mornings and late afternoons. Why he did it, he wasn't sure, because he still didn't dare approach her. All he knew was this: When he looked at Shelley, when he watched her coming and going with her little boy and her nanny, when he imagined her apartment, her job, her life, she was everything he'd ever dreamed of. Everything he couldn't touch.

One afternoon, Jim discovered that he was not keeping his vigil alone. A slight, pale, surly, young man in dirty blue jeans, torn sneakers and a hooded sweatshirt spent a lot of his time watching 67 West Eleventh Street as well. His purpose was not, apparently, to follow anyone, perhaps merely to intimidate by his presence, for he passed the hours leaning on a fire hydrant across the street, listening to a Walkman, and never failed to stare at Shelley openly when she came out of her apartment building. One time, he even accosted her nanny on the street and sparked fear in her eyes.

Feeling protective, Jim decided to force the intruder's hand. He filched a notebook and pen from the old folks' place and took to dogging his footsteps, jotting down notes on his movements, pretending to phone "headquarters" every half hour from an open booth, trailing him even into the subway, even to his L Line home station at First Avenue and Fourteenth Street, across the street from Stuyvesant Town, where he always somehow managed to give him the slip.

One day, fed up with trailing him around, Jim walked up to the hydrant and said, "Hey, why don't you buzz off, man?"

"Whazat?" the guy replied. He had Johnny Rotten and the Sex Pistols on his Walkman, turned up so loud you could hear it ten feet away. "Whazat?"

"I said fuck off," Jim shouted into his face, "before I haul your ass into the precinct!"

After that, he disappeared without a trace.

Feeling good about himself, and his first real victory, his first good deed in longer than he liked to think, Jim got into the habit of spending his mornings in the kiddy park in Abingdon Square, watching over Shelley's little boy and his nanny.

With time on his hands, he noticed everything. Like the fact that Shelley's nanny was different from the other nannies. She was a redheaded, white girl, for one thing, and younger than most of them; and though she seemed friendly enough, she kept her distance. While the others chattered together in their various Caribbean dialects, Shelley's nanny stayed silent, contenting herself with the boy—a feisty, dark-eyed toddler who reminded Jim of his little brother, Dougie, at the same age. When the kid got hurt or cried or came to her for a hug, she showed genuine warmth, while the others—with the look of women with a brood of their own at home—seemed merely perfunctory. And she wheeled him to the park in this enormous, fanciful, Italian-style stroller, with polished stainless steel storage racks, bulging canvas saddlebags and elaborately spoked wheels like those on an ancient Bugatti, while the others made do with cheap, fold-up McLarens.

It wasn't long before Shelley's nanny noticed Jim's attentions. And once she got used to the idea, she seemed to enjoy it. It had been so long since anyone looked at him twice—except in fear or loathing—that it took him a while to get it through his head that she'd taken a fancy to him.

After that, whenever he caught her glancing at him from under her long heavy lashes, he took out his flute, gave her a big theatrical wink, and played something for her, usually something light and airy, like Mendelssohn's "A Midsummer Night's Dream," or Dvorak's "Humoresque." For some reason, she found his flute-playing hilarious. And her laughter was something to see. She had the sweetest, smallest, reddest mouth, with teeth like shiny, little, bowling pins, all in a perfect row. She was not exactly pretty, and a bit overweight besides, but he found her fresh pink skin, her tousled-red hair, her turned-up nose, her mild gray eyes, her pointed chin and even her frumpy foreign-looking clothes, immensely appealing. Aside from that, she looked the type who might feel inclined to ease a poor stranger's way. And this was nothing to sniff at either.

Late one morning, sitting on a park bench under the maple trees, halfheartedly fingering his flute, waiting for Shelley's nanny and her plump, little, charge to arrive with their sporty Italian stroller, Jim was struck by the fact that in this whole park full of pigeons, children, old folks, and women, he was the only able-bodied young man. And suddenly, he felt sick to death of himself and his own squalid existence.

It was a hot, humid morning, full of smog and the smell of Hudson River water and sickly, white light. His eyes were burning, his tongue felt dry and thirsty. With nothing better to do, he ran an idle finger into his watchpocket, and was amazed to find a crumpled dollar bill that he thought he'd lost a week or two before.

Suddenly, it was great to be alive again!

The serendipity of it was what grabbed him. Because this dollar bill had a history. Driven by hunger one night, he went through Monika's wardrobe closet from end to end and found a five-dollar bill in the pocket of one of her winter coats. Just as he was about to holler "Whoopie!" and race out to his favorite greasy spoon, she came home and caught him in the act. Sheepishly he proffered the fiver, admitting the truth, but she only laughed.

"Finders, keepers," she said in her charming, Old-World accent. "Go on, Jim, go out and get yourself some supper."

This dollar bill that he now held in his hand was the change he'd received from the toothpick-sucking, counter man after a meal of chicken-fried steak, white bread, dehydrated mashed potatoes and canned succotash at the Busy Bee Diner on Hudson Street at Fourteenth. And the thought of Monika's incredible generosity, generosity that extended from the grave, overwhelmed him now to the point of tears.

Marveling at how little it took to change one's perspective on life, he debated whether to use his windfall for food or drink, and decided in favor of the latter, on the grounds that an earthshaking stroke of fortune such as this should not be used on anything so mundane as lunch.

So, he sauntered across Bleeker Street to The Shamrock. Got himself a table out in the garden, under the trees. There were speakers in the trees, playing songs by the McGarrigle Sisters.

The waitress stepped over.

"A pint of Guinness, please."

The beer was thick and dark, almost edible in texture, and came in an enormous, Imperial-size mug, frothing over the brim.

Trembling, he reached for it, ran his tongue over the frosted rim, sipped it, swished it around in his mouth, swallowed it slowly, lovingly, felt it descending in cool, wisping chutes to the shriveled pool in his belly, and filling the pool, spilling into his blood stream, spreading in waves to the very stub-ends of his being. Afterwards, his pocket was again empty, but his body and brain tingled with a pleasure he had rarely known before.

He pulled out his flute and began to play along with the McGarrigle Sisters.

As in a dream, to the wailing of an immemorial Irish air, the nanny from Abingdon Square walked in, pushing the child in its stroller, accompanied by the beautiful Shelley Friedman, all dressed up for work as usual.

Catching sight of Jim, the girl smiled and nodded, as if they were perhaps acquaintances, and she enjoyed his playing.

Shelley noticed, made some comment, and laughed at the girl's reply.

Ordering sandwiches, and Perriers with lime, the ladies sat chatting amiably for twenty minutes. Then Shelley stood up, laid some money on the table, kissed her sleeping kid softly on the head, and left.

The instant she was gone, Jim was up, strolling over to the girl's table with his flute in hand, as if he had all the confidence in the world. In a sense, he confessed to himself later, lying in the old folks' bed on Charles Street with his cock in hand, the girl was a substitute for Shelley.

"Hi, I'm Jim Haynes," he said, using his mother's maiden name.

"Molly McKenna," she replied, smiling, reaching up to shake his hand.

"Mind if I sit down?"

"Not at all."

"You're Irish."

"Now what else might I possibly be, do you think?"

"What brings you to New York?"

"Well, you see now," she replied, with a small disparaging shrug, "I'm a night student at Hunter College."

"So, days you do this."

"It's not so bad, you know."

"And the woman you were with?"

"My boss," she said. "Toby's mum."

"Toby?" he said grinning, waving a hand over the sleeping child.

Then a curious thing happened. He started to hallucinate. He looked down into the stroller and "Poof!" the little boy, Toby, went up in a cloud of smoke, reappearing as a scrawny pre-teen in jeans and a sweatshirt. Then, "Poof!" he was a high school football player. A grown man in a military uniform. A portly gentleman in a gray flannel suit. "Poof!" again, and he was old and dead, with skin white as marble, and a tag on his toe. It was all so vivid, so much like a movie of the kid's life, that Jim started to tremble and perspire despite himself.

"Tobias, Tobias Newhouse ... you know, like the writer ... his father, you see," Molly was saying. And then: "Sorry, but is there something wrong?"

"Uh ... to be frank, I haven't eaten much today."

"Thought as much," she laughed. She had an amiable, Irish attitude toward indigence. "It's the Guinness as well, you see. And the sun's come 'round. It's heating up in here."

She handed him a half-sandwich.

"My boss left this," she said. "Here."

He devoured it in an instant.

When he was done, she smiled and said, "Shall we go out for a stroll?"

Walking the cool, shady streets of the West Village, Jim cleared his head, and they ended up on a bench in the kiddy playground in Hudson Park, behind the Carmine Street Swimming Pool, munching on hotdogs that Molly bought off a Sabrett vendor man, talking of places they'd been, people they'd known, while Toby cavorted with other infants in the sand pit.

Molly was impressed by his travel stories and had a few of her own to tell. He asked her about the skinny, little, towheaded guy who accosted her on West Eleventh Street that time.

"Towheaded guy? No, no, don't recall anyone like that," she said, with that same frightened look she'd worn the day he saw her confronted in the street. And he wondered just how she'd been intimidated.

Later that afternoon, he walked her and the boy home to the apartment house he already knew so well. In the doorway, he kissed her politely on the cheek, and they arranged to meet the next morning in Abingdon Square.

Everything about Molly encouraged frankness, and in the coming days Jim told her as much of the truth as he thought safe. He was an Army deserter, he said, a fugitive from justice. Yet, the confession seemed to deepen her feelings toward him.

"You see," she said, admitting to him what he'd known all along, "I've this thing for strays." And she took to bringing him over to the apartment when Shelley was out, feeding him in the kitchen like a mutt.

"Are you getting enough fresh, green veggies, love? Can't live without them, you know," she lectured, and prepared him lavish chef salads which he devoured standing up at the counter while Teresa the cat purred and slunk up against his legs and Toby rolled little cars around on the floor and talked to himself— "Vroom! Vroom! Go, *coche*, go!"

Molly's attitude toward Jim was frank and friendly, rather than seductive, and because he'd become utterly dependent upon her, he hesitated to push for more intimate favors. Also, she was basically such a dreamy, goodhearted girl, so placid and generous by nature, that it presented a problem—for Jim was cursed with an attraction to the fiery, unpredictable type, and tended to measure love not by the contentment it provided, but by the aggravation it caused.

Still, there came a time . . .

"I was beginning to wonder when you'd ask," she said, and led him into her room one afternoon when Toby was having his nap.

"I've fixed the room up myself," she said, but it didn't say much for her taste. The walls were bare, the floor untidy, strewn with women's magazines, nursing textbooks, and crumpled Kleenex. Her Indian bedspread was faded, stained and common, and she had Waylon Jennings and Loretta Lynn on her tape deck.

She stripped without preamble, pulled the covers back, and spread her ample, pink-and-white body on the sheets to watch him strip. He undressed slowly, watching her as she watched him. She noticed the stubble in his pubic area, and he could see that she wondered about it. But she said nothing, and it seemed not to alarm her. On the contrary, she calmly, sweetly, smiled.

He climbed on and she lay back and appeared to be enjoying it, but she made no sound, and her eyes had this heavy-lidded, glazed look. Her apparent inattention to the act had the paradoxical effect of carrying Jim far beyond the point that he would have normally reached with such limited emotion involved. And at the end he flopped like a dead man on her, heaving up great sighs of exhaustion.

All the while, he had pretended that she was Shelley, his cool, cruel mistress, unresponsive to all his greatest efforts to move her.

Later, when Molly fell asleep, Jim got up and crept into Shelley's bedroom, a sunny, white room with blue trim. Prying shamelessly into her personal affairs, he was able to piece together quite a lot about her in the little time that he spent there. Most importantly, he found out that she was not rich or well-connected, as he had imagined. Learning this about her and confirming that she was working on a story that seemed based on intelligence he himself had provided, a serious and important story that might be dangerous to her personally, Jim loved her even more, felt even more protective of her and her little family, and resolved to do everything he could to help her. Someday, perhaps, she would learn of it, and be grateful. For the kind of love that he felt, gratitude was almost enough.

After that, Jim and Molly fell into a routine. They met each morning at nine in Abingdon Square. They headed home for lunch at noon. From one to two they had their cuddle and nap. Jim played with Toby all afternoon. He left the apartment at five, because Shelley got home at six.

At six thirty, if it was a school night, he met Molly at the subway stop, accompanied her to Hunter College, waited for her in the student lounge until her class let out at ten, and saw her home. She insisted on it. "It's the least you can do," she said, "after all I've done for you."

If it was a free night, they'd go out. They'd go to one of two places, never varying. They'd go to a movie at the Waverly—it didn't matter what was playing, Molly liked them all; Jim had no say anyway, since he wasn't paying—or they went to have a drink or two at Bobby Day's, near Sheridan Square. There they met the same old crowd every night. Beery, red-faced, Irish Americans for the most part, unwinding after a long day at work. Jim retired to a corner with a borrowed book as soon as he got his Guinness Stout. Molly sat at the bar sipping a Shandy, chattering with the regulars till she lost interest and drifted off again into the void.

Sometimes, after she had spent ten minutes staring into space, Jim felt a twinge of pity for her, an obligation to go over and talk to her, amuse her in some way, coax her back to reality.

Beneath her placid surface, he understood, she concealed a perpetual state of panic.

Once, at Bobby Day's, she leaned across the bar at Jim and confessed that she was failing her nursing course at Hunter College.

"If I get a 'D' or an 'F' on the final," she said, "as it looks now, I'll be out on me arse. They'll cancel my student visa and send me back to Ireland. My aunt in New Haven could fix it in a jiff, of course. All she'd have to do is sponsor me."

"Will she?"

"Bloody unlikely."

"Why not?"

"Says she can't afford the responsibility."

"So, what'll you do?"

"Dunno, thought I might arrange a marriage with some likely Yank. Someone like yourself, Jim. Not for love, mind you. Only for the green card."

"Oh, you wouldn't want to do anything like that with me, Molly. I'm a wanted man."

"Aw, but you never know, things might get straightened out sooner than you think," she said, and to Jim it sounded like a threat.

CHAPTER FIFTEEN

Beyond Ecstasy

A bright, windy noon hour in mid-July. Clicking along the cobblestones of Nassau Street, on her way to lunch at the Bridge Cafe, Shelley heard a protest rally a couple of blocks away. Drawn toward the noise by instinct, she followed it across Beekman Street and Park Row to City Hall Park, where she found a thousand or more people clustered around the steps of the Mayor's Office, waving signs, and thundering for their rights in front of a couple of network TV cameras and a dozen or so bored-looking police.

END GAY BASHING!
GAYS NEED POLICE PROTECTION TOO!
FREE CHRISTOPHER STREET FROM FEAR!

At the top of the steps, facing the motley crowd of gays, straights, blacks, whites, freaks, and radicals, stood several distinguished personages in dark suits, sport coats and tribal dashikis, one of whom she recognized as Al Rakozi.

And what struck Shelley most about Al was that he had changed so little since she'd last met him. Short and bandy-legged, with a barrel chest, a great leonine head, a flat squinty mug, a Pancho Villa mustache and shaggy, tawny-colored hair, wearing his trademark desert boots, jeans, open-necked white shirt and bush jacket, he bounced up and down the stage like a rock star before a concert, socking the palm of his hand with a fist.

Her stomach rumbling in protest, Shelley lingered among the crowd, enduring the platitudes of small-time liberal politicians, the campy posturing of local gay activists, until she'd missed her lunch entirely.

At last, red-faced, and hard breathing, with the look of a renegade friar, Al leapt up to the microphone and was greeted with thunderous applause, which he acknowledged with a wide, gap-toothed grin and a raised fist.

"Hey, you know what? I hate prejudice," he began. And his voice—crude and gravelly, booming over the park without subtlety or finesse—was just as she remembered it. "I hate black-baiting, Jew-hating, queer-baiting, woman-hating. Yeah, I hate prejudice. I hate it in South Africa and Cuba, and I hate it here. In all its horrendous forms. I've known it all my life, in one way or another. And I have been its victim. But I'd be a liar if I didn't tell you that in my ignorance I was also, at a certain point in my life, one of its most vicious practitioners as well.

"When I grew up in this town everybody had his own space, his turf, where everyone knew everyone else. Anyone who didn't belong, he stuck out like a sore thumb. Well, it was my misfortune to grow up Hunky in a neighborhood full of Sicilians. You can imagine what happened to me when I started hanging out on the street. But, you know, my reaction was—I tried with all my heart to be more *paisan* than the *paisans*. And after a while, believe it or not, they began to accept me.

"So, when we'd spot some new guy on the block, someone who maybe didn't look like us, you know what we did? We chased him. We beat him. We hit him over the head with baseball bats. And I want to say to you now that I am deeply sorry for having once in my life been part of the cruel and faceless mob, part of the mindless, murderous beast of the city that takes perverse and bloody pleasure in cruelly attacking its brothers for the mere reason that they look or talk or act or make love a little bit differently.

"And so, I've come here today in sincerity, in righteousness, and in repentance, to lend my voice to the chorus, to join my hands with yours in support of our friends and neighbors in the gay community in their quest for equal protection under the law. And I come in anger, to demand why it is that the poor, the weak and diverse are victimized in this the two hundredth anniversary of our great rich nation, on the very week of the Democratic National Convention in Madison Square Garden, as they have always been, without end . . ."

Al spoke rhythmically, his voice never less than an indignant roar. But for his thick Brooklyn accent, he might have been an old-time tent revival preacher, completely out of place in this assemblage of cosmopolitans. Yet, he was a persuasive speaker. His power—worlds beyond that of the hysterical amateurs and bumbling party hacks who had preceded him—derived from his apparent sincerity, his irrepressible energy, and the aura of frank good-humored benevolence, of selfless, no-bullshit idealism that beamed from his lumpy, grinning face.

For all that, Shelley was not particularly impressed with the speech. Not only did it seem to her predictable, but it had been very carefully crafted to appeal to the audience on a purely emotional level. To a certain extent, she thought, it even stood in defiance to reason, for later in the speech Al went on to encourage his listeners to affect a compromise with the authorities that might not be to their best advantage:

"Now when I say you gotta bang on doors, you gotta bang on desks, I don't mean you gotta burn down the whole damn store ..."

Fundamentally, then, Al's speech was full of hot air, and, at least so far as Shelley was concerned, he had become nothing more than a smooth, hip apologist for the powers-that-be.

But tell that to the crowd. Surging up to the platform when his speech ended, shouting his stage name—"the boss, the boss, the boss man!"—they had to be forcibly restrained from carrying him away on their shoulders.

As Al pressed through the throng, flanked by a pair of hulking bodyguards, ducked inside his Streetlight van, and seated himself alone in the back seat, the crowd of reporters and supporters surged forward—"Boss, Boss, Boss Man!"—and swept Shelley along with it.

Al glanced out his window and went big-eyed with astonishment when he recognized his old lover among the crowd of onlookers.

"Hey, hey, hey!" he laughed, and rolled down his window.

She leaned in toward him without thinking, searching his battered streetfighter's mug, his slanty, little, black eyes and puffy lips for some clue as to her suspicions.

"Hi ... hi, Al," she murmured tremulously, grabbing the door latch for support.

"Goddamn, long time no see, girl."

"Yeah."

"Liked your story in the *Star.*"

"Thanks."

"'Cept for the bullshit that old faggot priest laid on you."

"I don't know. When he told me what you went through as a kid, Al, it kind of ..."

He reached out, grabbed her by the arm, and pulled her up close.

"Put things in perspective?"

"M-maybe," she muttered, evading his bright, hypnotic eyes.

Al opened his door and tried to pull her inside. She resisted at first but was no match for his strength and he dragged her in beside him.

"So, hey, what's the next installment?" he demanded, as his driver geared off through the crowd.

"I ... uh ... haven't written it yet."

"How 'bout an exclusive interview?"

"Wait a second, Al. What's this all about?"

"You still scared of me, Shell? After all this time?"

"Damn right I am."

"Hey, we were just kids, you know? Acting out."

Shelley sniffed, shook her head, and regarded him more

closely.

Al was jowlier in the chops than he'd looked on stage, his skin coarser, his crow's feet more numerous, but he exuded health and self-confidence and smelled of *Vetiver* cologne.

Until now, Al had been an abstraction to her, a hazy memory, and she'd been able to ascribe the most horrendous actions to him without much thought. But here beside him in the van, recalling their nights together on the road, and later, she went stiff with fear and clutched at the handle, ready to leap out at any pretext, for it seemed to her that Al would be able to see right through her, that he would become—and not without some justice—incensed with her.

The van pulled up in front of Streetlight. Unlike most of the rest of New York City, the sidewalks and gutters outside seemed squeaky clean.

The bodyguards jumped out and accompanied Al and Shelley to the front gate.

As they passed through a security check, she felt like she might jump out of her skin.

A large hanging slogan above them said:

"YOU ARE EITHER MOVING IN
OR MOVING OUT
YOU CAN'T HAVE IT BOTH WAYS"

Al's office was halfway up a little, winding, metal stairway, in the tallest turret of the Streetlight armory, with a three-hundred-and-sixty-degree view through tall, slit windows of long, narrow swaths of the East Ninety-Sixth Street, Central

Park, and the East River. Though the room was large and comfortable, with fine old leather furniture and framed photos of Al with his addicts, Al with smiling show biz celebs and city officials, it seemed to Shelley curiously anonymous, and bore the unmistakable stamp of some competent professional decorator working on donated time . . . The one thing that seemed out of place was an enormous, hospital size refrigerator standing in a corner.

Al took a seat in his desk chair and motioned for her to sit across from him.

She reached into her bag and pulled out a camera and notebook.

"Do you mind if I take a photo or two, Al?"

"Naw. Just make sure they're flattering."

"You were always photogenic, and you know it. Have you got a tape recorder around? I want to make sure I don't misquote you."

"Sure," he said.

Reaching into his desk, he pulled out a recorder and handed it across his desk.

She looked at him for permission, and when he nodded, she turned it on.

"Okay, lemme see," he began. "Why don't we just start with me? Here, at Streetlight."

She nodded, raised her camera, and snapped a black and white photo Al with an incandescent grin, a photo that captured his warped yet powerful essence.

"Back in the day, Synanon sent me to New York to set up their first East Coast chapter. On the way though—remember,

Shelley?—I got to thinking, 'Hey, why not start up my own program?' I could've felt guilty, you know? Synanon changed my life. So, I asked myself, 'What's this all about? Guilt trips? Ego trips? Or is it about curing drug addicts?' There was no question in my mind that by using my own ideas plus some of the techniques I'd picked up at Synanon I could do better with New York addicts. I mean, I'm a native; I been there, right? The proof in the pudding was when I went to Synanon's New York backers to angel them off? I told them I was gonna call it 'Streetlight' and they fell into my hands like ripe plums."

So then, Al went on, he started thinking again. There was this old, five-story brownstone in Park Slope, Brooklyn. The place had been derelict for years, and it was going for a song. But it was in an upscale neighborhood and wasn't zoned for an outfit like Streetlight. He went to his backers, and they hit him with the down payment, no questions asked. They even pressured the city to look the other way on the zoning issue. The neighbors took him to court but his high-priced lawyers, working pro bono, won the case hands down.

Now, all he needed was some patients. So, he combed the boroughs, went through every public and private rehab program in the city, and found twenty-five addicts. These were not easy fixes; these were people no one else wanted, the dregs of the earth. All of them were ex-convicts. The women were whores; the men were pimps, thieves, drug dealers and worse.

Calling in some old pals from Synanon to work as staff, Al shaved the junkies' heads. Locked them in for ninety days with no phone calls, no visits. Cut them off from everyone they had emotional ties with. Stripped them of their name, their private identity. Made them question their basic assumptions of reality. It was cruel but necessary, he said. They had years of substance abuse to leave behind, ingrained patterns of life that were not easy to shake. He ruthlessly destroyed this former self because it was the disease, the root cause of all their problems. Meanwhile he was running constant attack therapy sessions on them. And within a few months they were starting to shape up.

Now what he needed was a business, something to support the program on a permanent basis, because he couldn't keep borrowing from his backers all the time, and he wanted to stay clear of government grants and bureaucracy.

On the ground floor of the original Streetlight brownstone there was an old Chinese laundry. Al had it cleaned out, acquired some surplus laundry machinery from the Kings County Hospital for nothing—through one of his doctor backers—and opened for business. Immediately he was underselling all the local competition and turning a handsome profit.

"If you pay no wages," he said, "and you're tax-exempt, and you pool all your resources, and go around getting people to donate all your clothes and food, and you pay off your debts, pretty soon you've got excess cash. We take that cash and put it to work. We're constantly expanding, so there's always room at the top. Out in the world, all these junkies can do is steal or die. But here, everyone's an ex-addict, so they've got a fighting chance. Here they can still be a rebel, keep their cool, and come out a winner."

Shelley raised a hand, like she just wanted to get a word in.

"Now, you don't have to answer this next one," she began, "and correct me if I'm wrong. You've got this multi-million-dollar corporation. It does a lot of charity work, helps a lot of people out, does a lot of good. Almost nobody disputes that. But it's tax-exempt, unregulated by any local, state, or federal authority, and—because of its political clout—virtually immune from prosecution. This corporation employs hundreds if not thousands of people for no wages, makes a tremendous profit, and owns acres of New York City real estate. Is that right?"

"You got it!" he roared, clapping his hands as if it were the greatest joke in the world. "That's the beauty of it."

"And all of this is controlled by one man."

"Myself."

"You know the old dictum, 'Absolute Power Corrupts Absolutely.' Do you ascribe to that?"

"Of course," he replied impishly, rolling his eyes. "For everyone but myself."

And then she said it. She didn't mean to. It was premature, and probably against her own best interests. But she suddenly found Al's arrogance so galling—and felt so annoyed with herself for having once succumbed to his counterfeit charm— that it just popped out.

"Oh, and one last thing, Al," she said, letting her hand hover over the tape recorder, as if she were about to turn it off.

"Shoot."

"What do you think about the murder of your wife, Penny?"

Al's mouth flew open, and he shook his head like he'd just been slapped across the face. He leapt up from behind his desk, knocking over the chair behind him. "Huh? What'd you say?"

Shelley took a deep breath, preparing herself for a danger that she would have to face head-on.

"Penny was murdered with someone called 'Bobby O' on the island of Ibiza. The police there found prints of your old friend, Ray Pagano, and your secretary, Monika Thorssen, at the crime scene. Then Monika turned up dead. There's also a 'Tina Bowran.' An old friend of Penny's. She's disappeared as well. Got any theories?"

Bug-eyed, breathing hard, furious, Al hurtled around his desk and jerked her out of her chair, nearly snapping her neck in the process.

"The fuck is this, you bitch? Somethin' personal?"

"I . . . I'm a reporter, Al, and you're news. I'm only interested in the facts."

"Facts, huh?"

Al leaned in closer to her, but she darted her eyes about to avoid his hypnotic gaze and made a break for the door. He laughed, mocking her, then leapt across the room and slammed her against the door.

"Yeah," he whispered into her mouth. "Facts are important. I mean, you and me, we were a kooky little butt-fucking item once. Right? And that's a fact. What I'm trying to convey here, Shell, there are higher objectives now, and more lives at stake, than just our own. You understand what I'm saying?"

"I . . . I think so. And believe me," she mumbled apologetically, secretly gratified that he had so neatly absolved her of any guilt that their brief coupling might have inspired, "I really didn't mean to give you a shock, Al."

"Your apology is accepted. Now let me tell you something," he said in his official voice, opening the door to let her out. "And you can quote me on this. I'm sorry to hear about Penny's death, but I don't know anything about it. We're estranged, and I haven't heard from her in months. As for Monika, she left Streetlight recently. The word around here is she went back on drugs and was murdered by some other dope addict, some guy who was living at her place. And Tina Bowran? I do remember the name, but I swear I couldn't tell you a thing about her. Remember, we've got a lot of very rough trade coming through this place. Now, a good percentage clean up their act. But others, they commit crimes, they do time, they die, they disappear. That's the name of the game."

"Thanks, Al."

"You're entirely welcome," he said, leading her out the door, down his spiral stairs, past his office help and into the waiting elevator, smiling his public smile. "Any time at all. Come again and I'll give you a tour of the place."

"I'd like that," she replied, holding the closing elevator door with her hand. "Oh, by the way, I forgot the tape. Can I have it?"

"Sure, I'll send you a copy," he sneered, and she let the door slide across and squeeze him into nothingness.

When Shelley returned to the *Star* newsroom that afternoon, she stepped into Ben's office without knocking.

"Ben, I'm starting to have second thoughts."

"The fuck you talkin' about?"

"How about letting me interview Richard Burton? I did one before. And I hear he's in town."

"Come on. Get outta here! This Streetlight story's got legs. Oomph. And you wanna interview that old has-been?"

"You don't know how ... how manipulative, controlling, how evil that man Al Rakozi can be."

"Thought you said he was nothin' to you."

"I was desperate for a job, Ben. Just didn't think it through."

"So 'fess the fuck up."

Shelley zoned out, saw young Shelley lying stoned beside sleeping Al on his filthy, sopping, bathroom floor. Scratched and bleeding, covered with love bites, she rose like a ghost from his body, and peered into his cracked medicine cabinet mirror. Big-eyed, shocked by her battered image, she picked up his can of shaving cream and sprayed these words into the mirror: "BEYOND ECSTASY ONLY DEATH."

When she returned to the present, Ben was snapping a finger in her face.

"Hey Shelley. Shell! Are you with me?"

She shook her head.

"So lucky," she murmured. "To get away ... when I did. Otherwise . . ." Ben aimed a puzzled look at her.

"The fuck that guy do to you?"

She shrugged, distraught.

"Come on!" he said.

"He took . . ."

"What? What?"

"He took my mind."

Ben reached across the desk to grab hold of her hands.

"He took my body," she moaned. "He took my blood. He took my soul!"

"Listen!" Ben squeezed her hands in his, banged them on his desk, stared into her eyes. "All the more reason to bring the bastard down. Down!"

She shook her head and took a long, deep breath, as if to buck herself up. Then she shut her eyes and nodded with resolution.

"He wouldn't let me keep the recording I did of our interview. Lucky I always have..." She grinned and pulled a tiny tape recorder from her skirt's waist band. "Backup."

Ben laughed and slammed the table with glee.

"That's my girl, Shell! That's my girl!"

Yet later, on the way home, cheek by jowl with the other passengers in the rush hour crush, jostled in the turns, squeezed half to death at the stops, she felt her knees start to quake again, just as they had in Al's office. Her heart raced, the sweat budded up at her hairline, tracked down her made-up face. And she thought she might lose it again, might start to kick and flail and scream for air.

Casting about frantically for some thought that might have a soothing effect, she started composing a long mental list of tentative supper menus and food purchases that she would make on her way home.

Later, letting herself into her flat with an armload of groceries, welcomed as always by Teresa the cat, she heard a sound like the whinnying of a horse, and Toby shrieking with pleasure. Setting off down the waxed, wooden hallway unsteadily on her high heels, trailed by Teresa who had now begun to meow for her supper, she halted in the kitchen doorway and found a strange man on the floor, prancing about on his hands and knees, with Toby bouncing on his back, slapping his buttocks, hollering, "Gideeyup! Gideeyup!"

Kicking her shoes off, dropping her plastic, Food Emporium bags on the floor outside the door, she watched unnoticed until the "horse"—the same long, lean, craggily handsome, young man whom she and Molly had seen playing the flute in the Shamrock Garden—rolled over and collapsed on the floor in a fit of giggles and Toby started tickling him under the arms, going, "ticky-ticky-timbo, ticky-ticky-timbo!"

Shelley could guess how this little scene had come about, and she was furious at Molly for inviting a stranger into her home without permission. But she could not be angry at this young man. And it was not simply because of the rapport that he had established with her son.

Face to face with Al Rakozi only a few hours before, Shelley found that all her other terrors paled into insignificance by comparison. And now the sight of this distinctly less fearsome male provided her with an odd kind of relief.

"Hi," he said when he noticed her there, as if it were the most natural thing in the world that he should be beaming up at her from her kitchen floor, with Toby now seated on his tummy, pounding him on the chest, going, "Va-voom! Va-voom! Va-voom!"

"Hi," she replied, with a hand on her hip and one toe cocked, acknowledging with a little sigh and a grin her grudging approval of the proceedings.

"*Mamá! Mamá!*" Toby bellowed and toddled toward her on his little bowlegs.

"Hello, baby, hello!"

Flinging her handbag on the kitchen table, she scooped him up in her outstretched arms, whirled him about, smelled him, felt the excitement and happiness in his plump, warm, squirming body.

Yet, she was still acutely aware of the stranger in the room, the tall, smiling, young man who had now risen off the floor and stood leaning against her kitchen counter, smiling at her and Toby in the most benevolent yet proprietary manner.

"I'm a friend of Molly's," he said, when they'd stopped their spinning about the room. His voice was low and smooth, and sounded vaguely familiar. "She's not feeling well. Says it's her 'Auntie Flow.' So, she asked me to . . ."

"I figured it might be something like that," Shelley replied, bouncing Toby up and down on her hip while Teresa weaved in an out of her legs, still meowing.

And, when he looked like he wanted to shake, she shifted Toby to her left hip and reached out a hand to him. He took it and held it in his long, calloused hand firmly, the way she liked.

Toby stretched out toward the young man, and Shelley released him into his arms. Instantly, he threw the child into the air. His tee shirt rode up, and his belly showed for an instant—rippling abs with dark hair growing in a narrow straight line to his deep navel.

Toby crawled like a monkey over his shoulder and sat himself behind his neck, holding his mop of black hair like the mane of a horse.

"Gideeyup! Gideeyup!"

"So," Shelley sighed, bending to scoop Teresa up in her arms. And she wanted to say something, but she didn't know what it was. She scratched Teresa's head, ran her fingers down her spine, making her arch with pleasure.

The truth was, she craved a drink, a stiff sundowner, like the ones she used to have on Ibiza.

Instead, still holding Teresa crooked in one arm, she fished around in her handbag and found her cigarettes and lighter.

Lighting up, inhaling, blowing smoke at the ceiling, Shelley looked at the young man again, at the dark circles under his deep-set green eyes, the humped, broken nose, the thin, cracked lips, the stubble of beard on his fine jaw and chin, and decided that he looked hungry—really hungry. Like he wasn't getting enough to eat.

And she was about to invite him to dinner, or at least for a drink, when she remembered where she had heard his voice before.

"Well, I guess Toby's just about tuckered you out," she observed, as calmly as possible. "Guess you want to be on your way."

"Not really," he said, and looked across the kitchen at her with a peculiar intensity, as if he wished very much to say more, but couldn't bring himself to do it.

"So, tell me. You're the one who phoned me, right?"

"Yeah," he replied with immense relief, as if happy to get it off his chest. Yet he hastened to add: "But don't be afraid. I'm harmless, believe me."

"I'm not so sure about that," Shelley said, and paused to regard him very carefully for a moment, trying to reconcile his physical reality with the disembodied presence she had become acquainted with on the phone.

The fact was, she had gone through some ups and downs in her attitude toward Jim. When she first talked to him, she liked his tone, which struck her as sincere and undaunted. The calm way he explained his predicament to her, the way he tried to reason his way out of it, seemed to her noble and courageous.

She even romanticized him a bit when she wrote about him in her notes, recreating him as a kind of absurdist hero, firm in the face of a terrible, random fate.

Then in the van this afternoon, she had begun to doubt that her suspicions about Al were justified and wondered if for some reason Jim wasn't lying.

Later, leaving Streetlight with her suspicions reconfirmed, she had put Jim through a kind of wringer in her mind; he and his story came out smelling much nicer on the other side.

Now, with him standing before her, she recalled again her first sighting of him, and it added still another dimension. For that tall, handsome, young man in the Shamrock Garden, with his haunting Irish music and his Orpheus curls, reminded her of other lean young men—hippies, wanderers, sailors, musicians— with whom she'd had brief and often rapturous flings on her Spanish island, while her older husband was traveling the world on publicity tours.

"Tell me something," she asked. "Does Molly know about any of this?"

"No."

"How'd you get involved with her in the first place?"

"It was the only way I knew to get through to you in person."

"Why didn't you just . . . ?"

"I was . . . afraid," he sighed, the gravity of his tone belied by the fact that he was simultaneously removing Toby's little hands from over his eyes, folding them around his index fingers and amusing the child by shifting them back and forth like the gears on a caterpillar tractor. "I didn't feel I could trust you, unless I got to know you first."

"How do you feel now?"

"I think you're all right. But I'm a little worried about you. Did you know there was a guy watching your place?"

"Sure. I even know his name. It's Mike."

"He's working for Al, right?"

"Actually, I think he's working for Ray," she responded. And when Jim looked puzzled, she added, "Their interests don't always coincide."

"Anyway, you haven't seen him snooping around lately, have you?"

She shook her head.

"I took care of that."

"No kidding?" she said, laughing despite herself. And then, letting Teresa down on the floor, stooping to pick up her bags, setting them on the kitchen counter: "I should still be more careful about you."

"Why aren't you?"

"Instinct, I guess. Tool of the trade."

"Never fails you, huh?"

"Oh, it fails me," she said, reaching for the cat food, opening the can, setting Teresa to rearing on her hind legs and sniffing the air. "But I'm not going to get into that."

"Why not?" he asked, coming up behind her.

"Because then you'll know my secrets," she murmured, turning to glance at him over her shoulder. "And we can't have that, can we?"

CHAPTER SIXTEEN

Bum Heaven

Jim had just been to the late show with Molly. They were standing in the doorway, about to say goodnight, when suddenly her eyes went big and round, as if reflecting some vision of imminent peril.

He wheeled to face the danger and spotted "Mike," the skinny little guy with the hooded sweatshirt and the Walkman, leaning against the fire hydrant across West Eleventh Street.

A moment later, when Jim turned back to Molly, he found that she had already pushed through into the lobby.

He waved at her as she stepped into the elevator. She waved back; her look of terror replaced by a foolish grin.

"Hey, what is this shit?" Jim shouted, striding across the street to confront the man.

"Whazat?" Mike responded. He had the "Bay City Rollers" on his Walkman, so loud you could hear them up and down the block.

"I thought I told you I didn't want to see you around here anymore."

"Who the fuck you think you are, tellin' me what to do?"

"What've you got to do with that girl?"

"What girl?" Mike inquired, squinting as he removed the speakers from over his ears. "The one that just went inside? Hey, we got an understanding, man."

"What kind of understanding?"

"That's for me to know, and you to find out."

"Go on, get out of here, you little prick," Jim growled, shoving him down the block.

"*Fuck* you, man, *fuck* you!" Mike hollered. Then, quick as a weasel, he whirled and hit him a glancing blow on the shoulder and neck with a heavy piece of metal that he'd hidden in his sleeve.

Jim saw stars and fell to one knee. But he was up and running after the kid in a moment, around the corner onto Seventh Avenue, up the block, into the subway station at West Twelfth Street, through a token-operated turnstile and down the stairs two at a time.

Out on the platform he hesitated for an instant when he found the station deserted of passengers, but kept after him anyway, too pissed to care, until there was only the echo of their running footsteps bouncing off the slick, sweaty walls.

Up ahead now Jim could see lurking behind gummy metal pillars, behind scummy tile abutments and recesses, wearing sneakers, jeans, hoodies, and baseball caps turned around sideways on their heads, a whole big crew of evil, young, black dudes, with the lean, furtive look of drug abusers.

As he ran by, they fell in behind him.

Vaulting up the exit way toward the empty ticket office, Mike slipped around a large, dark figure standing at the top of the stairs and disappeared.

Hot on his heels, Jim looked up and saw that it was Ray, Monika's murderer.

"Hey," he said, smiling, blocking his way, "where you think you're goin', man?"

"Excuse me?" Jim replied, hesitating, with one eye on Ray and the other on the brothers coming up the stairs. "I don't think I know you."

"Well, I know you, Jim, and I don't like you."

"Why . . . why not?"

"Fuckin' hippy bum like you, hangin' out, havin' a ball with the ladies, and Monika in her grave. She was worth ten of you, motherfucker, and I blame you for that."

"Blame *me*?"

"Yeah, you, scumbag," Ray said, making eye contact with the boys down the stairs. "Crashin' where you don't belong, passin' crabs around, stickin' your nose where it don't belong. You know what I'm sayin'?"

Jim heard them come up behind him and started to turn, but before he could get halfway around, they hit him over the head with something. He felt himself sinking, weightless. Getting caught and hefted up on to somebody's shoulder. Carried down the stairs. Out to the edge of the platform. Felt himself gripped by the arms and legs. And then swinging out over the tracks.

As if in a dream, from a long way off, he could hear Ray

counting, "One! Two! Three!" Everybody laughing. A train coming down the track.

In the dream, Jim guessed they were only fooling, trying to make him shit his pants, trying to get some information out of him. Then he was screaming, hurtling through space. And suddenly his head was clear again.

Maneuvering like a panicked cat, he landed on his feet between the rails just as the train came wailing out of the tunnel. In the split second he had to decide, he could see a westbound train stopped on the other side of the station, loading passengers. With the eastbound train bearing down on him, only yards away, whistle shrieking, brakes screeching, sparks flying out from under its wheels, Jim made his choice.

Hot footing it over the electrified third rail and through the steel pillars as it flashed behind him, he dipped under the bar between the stopped cars of the westbound train, leapt for the brakeman's steps just as it started moving, and crawled slowly, painfully upward.

With the iron wheels whizzing by inches from his flailing sneakers, Jim heaved himself up on to the corrugated iron landing between the cars. He rolled to his feet, slid the heavy steel door open, reeled into the light, and fell into an empty seat.

Running his fingers gingerly over the bloody lump on his skull, blinking and shaking his head and trying to bring his surroundings back into focus, he looked across the aisle and read his own near fate in the wide and disbelieving eyes of the passengers.

Shelley opened the door in a white, terrycloth bathrobe, her thick, wet hair pulled back into a ponytail, and stood gaping for half a minute before she could say a word.

"Molly!" she managed at last. "Come quick, something's happened to Jim!"

They brought him in and tended him gently in the bathroom, exclaiming in horror and indignation as he told his story.

Nurse Molly opined that he might have suffered a mild concussion and prescribed three days of bed rest.

He spent the night on the couch in the living room, with Teresa curled up at his feet, and Shelley and Molly rustling in every couple of hours to lean over him, feel his brow, check his bandage, feed him some painkillers, murmur words of encouragement, and run their hands through his sweaty hair.

It was bum heaven.

In the morning, after popping another couple of Ibuprofens, he felt well enough to hobble into the kitchen for breakfast.

"I . . . I really don't know how I'll ever be able to repay you," he sighed, easing himself down to a plate of Belgian waffles and café-au-lait. "I only hope . . ."

"Enough already, you said all that last night!" Shelley laughed, raising her hands up like a traffic cop, with Toby looking on from his highchair, amused at his mother's antics, and Molly running in and out, gulping coffee, preparing to rush off to a meeting with her college advisor. "Will you stop thanking me, Jim, and start thinking about what we do next?"

"Ta!" Molly called, as she headed out the door. "See you lot in a bit!"

"Now listen," Shelley continued, barely noticing Molly's departure, "this is serious. It's only a matter of time before we're going to face this kind of thing again. So, what do you say we just put a stop to it, right now?"

"Sounds good to me," Jim responded, his attention not fully fixed on the subject at hand, what with all the pills he'd been taking, and his mouth full of waffle and maple syrup, and the proximity of Shelley's fragrant white bathrobe that kept slipping open in her excitement to display a luscious half-inch of olive-skinned cleavage. "But how're we gonna do it?"

"Just listen to this," she said, grabbing the phone off the counter, dialing a local number.

"Western Union? I'd like to send a telegram to Mr. Al Rakozi at the Streetlight Foundation, 105 East Ninety-Sixth Street, New York. I want it hand delivered, and I want it to read exactly like this:

"'RAY SECRETLY TESTIFYING TO PROSECUTORS IN RETURN FOR IMMUNITY. STOP. LITTLE MIKE PROVIDING CONFIRMATION. STOP. THEY CLAIM RAY DID PENNY, BOBBY O, AND MONIKA AT YOUR ORDERS. STOP.'

"Now, could you please read that back to me? Good. I want you to bill it to my American Express credit card, but I do not want you to put down my name or my return address. Is that clear? Thank you."

"Jesus, Shelley, do you realize what you've just done?"

"I know damn well what I've done," she replied, calmly

replacing the phone on the counter, and reaching over to spoon feed a grimacing Toby some more of his Cream of Wheat. "Would you rather it be one of us?"

"Oh, you are bad," he said, shaking his head admiringly.

"Only when it comes to protecting my own," she said, wiping Toby's smeary, little, red mouth with her napkin.

"Well, if Ray and Mike turn up dead, there won't be any doubt who did it."

"You think I haven't thought of that?" Shelley asked, untying Toby's bib from around his neck, lifting him out of his highchair. "Upsy-daisy!"

Later, after Shelley had left for work, Molly came in, fed Toby his lunch, put him to bed for a nap, and crawled under the sheets with Jim.

"Look," he said gently, as she lay quietly, yet expectantly, by his side, "I don't think we ought to do this anymore."

"And why not then?"

"Well, I don't love you, Molly, and I doubt very much that you love me."

"What's love got to do with it?" she wondered. And then, after a moment had passed: "It's Shelley, isn't it?"

"Why do you say that?"

"I've got eyes, haven't I?"

"We're just friends."

"Oh, just friends?" she sniffed, and propped herself up on an elbow to search his eyes. "You know, I'd not mind it so if you told me straight. What I can't stand is lies. Don't diddle me about, Jim. I may not look like much, but once I get me Irish up . . ."

"You talk about lies. And the guy who did this to me, Mike, you know what he said? He said you had an understanding with him."

"Understanding?" she asked, blinking. "What kind of understanding?"

"I don't know, why don't you tell me?"

She smiled, shut her eyes, and shook her head.

"What I couldn't figure," Jim went on, "that big fat guy, Ray? He knew my name, and he's never seen me before."

"Dunno . . . dunno what you're talking about, love."

"See, Molly? Honesty's a two-way street."

"What do you want from me, Jim?" she demanded. "Before you came along, Mike and I had a little thing. It wasn't much because he wasn't much. Not much for the ladies at all, I shouldn't think. And then he started his threats."

"What kind of threats?"

"Said he'd call on Shelley and get me sacked. Said he'd ring the immigration office, have me deported for working on a student visa. Said he'd 'break my face.'"

"What'd he want?"

"Shelley had come snooping round at his mum's flat, he said, and he was keen to find out why. But it seemed he wanted more than just that. Wanted me to look through Shelley's papers and stuff."

"How much did you give him?"

"As little as possible."

"Did you give him my name?"

"What's in a name, Jim?"

"Sometimes it can mean a lot."

"Go on with you now, it's all written in the stars," she said, smacking her hands with finality. "Your name comes up, that's it."

CHAPTER SEVENTEEN

Prime Suspect

Shelley high-stepped into One Police Plaza, turning heads as usual, took the elevator to the sixth floor and wound up at Manny's desk.

"So, what's up, Manny?"

He leaned in close, looked around to make sure no one was listening, and whispered, "Okay, there's good news, bad news, and the very worst."

"Gimme the good news first."

"I got some more hits on this Ray Pagano character, and on that Monika Thorssen lady you mentioned."

"Who just turned up conveniently dead."

"Turns out she was associated with Streetlight, too," he said, nodding.

"As if we hadn't guessed."

"Now, the bad news is, this Tina Bowran lady? Penny O'Riley's friend? She's totally off the radar. No one's seen her in weeks. Her friends and her roommate know zip about any plans to move, and they're all worried sick. She quit her job without giving notice, and she didn't even bother to pick up her check. She ain't in jail. She ain't at the morgue. She ain't overseas 'cause she ain't got a passport. Word on the street is there's a hit out on her."

"Now gimme the worst."

"Okay, this Jim Range dude? No one in the NYPD or the DA's office is interested in hearing his story. They don't wanna take his deposition, and they ain't about to offer him immunity in return for his testimony. As a matter of fact, he's still their prime suspect in the Monika Thorssen case."

"You mean to tell me that no one in Homicide except you has put two and two together?"

Manny shook his head.

"Streetlight, right?" she said. "The juice is working."

"No doubt about it. But tell me somethin', Shell. I never seen you follow a story so hard. You got an axe to grind with this Rakozi cat? Or what?"

"Hey, my brief in this case . . . and my job as a journalist . . . is to find the truth and record it. Nothing more, nothing less."

Her edgy little speech came across as something less than convincing, and Manny picked up on it.

"Yeah," he said. "But you know? I think you're gonna find . . . I mean, this is what we find in police work. Sometimes the truth, it ain't black, it ain't white. It just kind of blends into different shades of grey."

"Where you going with this, Manny?"

"That dude you got stayin' at your place . . ."

"What?" she said, eyes flashing. "You following me?"

"For your own good. Listen. That AWOL motherfucker? He's got no kind of honor. He's playing you, Shell. Kick him out."

"Bullshit. He was anti-war. That's all."

Just as Manny was about to react, Chief Inspector Ron Nelson suddenly appeared above them.

Leaning over the cubicle's wall, he looked Shelley over, and flashed an insincere smile.

"Don't believe I've had the pleasure," he said.

"Shelley," Manny replied, looking up, "this is our Chief Inspector, Ron Nelson."

"Nice to meet you."

"You wouldn't be Shelley Friedman, would you?"

She nodded.

"Wow, I used to follow your stories in the *Star*. And now, I see you're back working for them again."

"Yes, I am."

"Caught that story you wrote on the early life of that Streetlight guy, Al Rakozi? Well done."

"Thanks."

Ron's smile turned to a grimace.

"But just for your information, Ms. Friedman," he said. "It's expressly forbidden for members of the press to enter this room and cage information from detectives."

He turned to glare at Manny.

"And you, Detective Rivera, should know better."

"Now, just a—"

"After you escort Ms. Friedman from the building,

Detective, I'd like to see you in my office."

He turned to Shelley and assumed another fake smile.

"I look forward to reading your next installment on the Streetlight story, Ms. Friedman, and I trust it will be as positive as the first."

As Ron walked away, he stopped at a cubicle to talk to one of his other detectives.

So, Shelley whipped her camera out and snapped a photo of him in profile, looking smart, confident, yet somehow phony.

Shelley and Manny left One Police Plaza together and huddled together for a moment on its gum-splattered, paper-strewn front steps.

"Looks like I may be out of a job," he said.

"All my fault."

"Naw."

"You kidding me?" she said. "But don't sweat it."

"Huh?"

"I already talked to Ben. You got a job with the Star. Any time you want."

"No shit. What doin'?"

"Private Investigator."

"What's the pay?"

"Hell of a lot more than you make here."

"I'll take it."

"You're shucking me."

"No way. Just what I been lookin' for."

"Really?"

"Hey, I already done my twenty here. So, on top of my pension? That gig of yours at the paper is just gonna be cream on the cake."

"Got it all figured out, huh?"

"Yup. Can't wait to see the look on that asshole Nelson's face!"

CHAPTER EIGHTEEN

Water Under the Bridge

"I don't like to start off the day with bad news," said Ron Nelson, the boss' (ex-officio) NYPD liaison. "But you know that reporter who wrote the story about you in the *Star*? She's been schmoozing with someone in the Narco Squad on the issue of your late wife. And I don't—I mean, we haven't seen Installment Two yet, have we?"

"Who's the cop?" the boss demanded. He was pissed now, his eyes darting about the room from one Board member to another, as if one of them might be at fault, which set them all to fidgeting in their chairs. "Who is he? I want his fuckin' badge number."

"I . . . I convinced him to retire, so he'll be out of your hair as . . ."

"Good work, Ron." he said, and pointed across the table at his fat, little, City Hall man. "And Greg, I want you to facilitate this dick's departure. Okay? Make it quick. Meanwhile, the rest of you, I want some action on this. Who's got juice with the *Star*? Let's nip this shit in the bud."

What the boss didn't know, though, Ray was thinking, he wasn't going to nip shit, because he wasn't playing with a full deck. But you couldn't say a word to the fucker, even to save his ass. Tell him what Shelley knew, what Mike got from the nanny, and he'd blow *you* away, leave her free to go around doing her thing. Do her yourself and you'd take the fall; the press would be all over you like Gangbusters.

Yeah, that Shelley, she was a trip. Had her own private agenda here. And there was more to this than either one of them was putting out. Two days on the road, back in the day, and they got so tight, they squeezed Ray out entirely. All he could do was fucking *watch*, with a big, leaking hard-on in his hands. Then when they got to New York, they were an *item*. 'Shelley this, Shelley that,' for days on end.

Later, after the meeting, when they were alone in Al's office, he turned on Ray and said, "Lemme tell you something, man, something you are not going to fucking believe; I still got nits. I tried the cootie stuff, right? But I guess it's not strong enough. That fucking cunt, it's her revenge from the grave."

"Jesus, Boss, you probably infected half of Streetlight by now, half of New York."

"You think it's funny?" he said, bounding up to glower in Ray's face. "And what's this I hear about you and that guy who's staying at Monika's place?"

"I don't know. I guess we could track him down, though. All

we gotta do is follow the crabs."

"You think it's funny? What're you trying to whack him for, you fuck?"

"Where'd you hear that?"

"I thought we agreed, man. He's the perfect suspect."

"He's still a suspect, but he fell in front of a train."

"You sure he's dead? He's not dead, pretty soon he's gonna start putting two and two together."

"You don't believe me?" Ray said. And then he took a calculated risk: "Ask Mike."

"Mike? What's that little punk got to do with this?"

"I needed help."

"Help? You know his mouth. He'd sell his own mother, his sister, for a gram. And he's going to think you did this on your own? No way. He's going to think I *told* you to do it. You disappoint me, man. Now we got business to do."

"Damn, boss, when is this shit gonna stop? I mean, he's your own fuckin' brother-in-law."

"I don't care who he is. Now tell me where you got it."

"Got what?"

"Come on, you know what. I want it. I'm gonna to whack the little fairy myself."

And at that point, Ray smelled a rat. The boss had never been into guns. Always liked to have someone else handle that end for him. So, it was kind of funny, he suddenly gets pistol happy. But the boss was the boss Man, and an order was an order.

So that night Ray went out and dug up the gun where he had it buried out back, handed it over, and phoned Mike to arrange a meeting.

"This is a big one, Mikey!" he raved. "There's something in it for you, too, but keep your fuckin' mouth shut for once, okay?"

Then he threw a pick, a shovel, and a spade in the back of a Streetlight van and he and the boss drove downtown. They picked up the kid at his new digs at Monika's place and headed out through the Bronx past Tarrytown and Peekskill and wound along the east bank of the Hudson for almost an hour.

The Boss was driving—he insisted on it—and he kept strictly to the speed limit.

"Where we goin'?" the kid kept asking from the back seat. "What's the deal?"

"Never mind," the boss said, "you'll find out when you get there."

Meanwhile Ray was thinking, 'Let's face it, he knows more than he ought to; he's got plans for you too, man.'

People would think that Ray was holed up somewhere, hiding from the law. Same with Mike. A fuck-up, a junky, he was the type who could easily drop out of sight and never be heard of again.

For that reason, the boss would want to bury the bodies deep. But he was lazy. So, he'd do Mike first. He'd have Ray get the pick and the shovels out, and they'd both dig a great big hole in the ground.

Then Ray would go in there with Mike.

The boss would do this to him, his oldest friend, with regret, because he knew what Ray knew: If and when the shit hit the fan, there was no one on this earth who wouldn't cop to save his own ass.

Yep, the boss was playing cat and mouse.

But Ray was no mouse.

So, Al pulled off onto a rough dirt road in the woods, somewhere near the Bear Mountain Bridge. Drove way up to the end, his headlights bouncing off the beech trees and maples and evergreens, till he was high on a ridge above the river.

The moon was bright and almost full, but it was partially hidden behind these wispy, low clouds that clung to the branches of the tallest trees; so, when he switched off his lights it went all eerie white.

"What's goin' on?" the kid kept asking. Though by now he was only fooling himself. "What's the deal?"

"Come on, Mikey," the boss said, almost sympathetic, it seemed, "come on, boy, get out of the car."

Mike got out, but already he was starting to sniffle and whimper. What else was he going to do? He was frail and pretty as a girl, and there was something in the boss man's voice, something he'd always had, something you couldn't refuse.

"Sit here, Mikey," he coaxed, pushing him down on a log.

And then, while the kid looked up at him, helpless as a kitten, he pulled out the gun, its barrel long and dark with the silencer on the end.

The kid's eyes went wide. His mouth dropped open. He drew in his breath to scream.

And "Bap!" his face lit up for an instant.

A little dark hole appeared between his eyes.

His head jerked back.

He rolled off the log and landed with his neck bent under his chest, his feet around his head, like a skinny acrobat.

"He was dead before he hit the ground," Al observed, checking his pulse. And Ray could swear there was a catch in his voice. "See what you got him into, man? I hope you learn a lesson from this. Now let's get the fucking pick and shovels out."

So, they started digging. But it was tough going. The soil was rocky and gnarled with the roots of trees. They dragged the body—pathetic little body, couldn't have been more than a hundred and twenty pounds—to another place, down in a hollow, and then it was easier going.

Ray bided his time, and when Al had his hands full with a shovel-load of dirt he wound up and swung the sharp end of his stubby little spade at him.

Hit him square across the face.

His nose disappeared in a spray of blood.

He spun and fell into the shallow grave like a ton of bricks.

Ray thought he was dead meat, but he popped right up with the pistol in his hand.

There was another flash and a "Bap!" and Ray lost half an ear. But already he was swinging the spade, and he hit him again with the sharp end, just above the wrist.

Al dropped the gun in the grave, started groping around down there for it with his left hand.

Standing above him, finding him almost pathetic, Ray brought the flat of the spade down on the back of his head with all his might.

The Boss was still breathing, but he was on his face in the dirt and very, very quiet.

Ray was tempted to reach down and grab the gun, if not the keys to the car. But it was dark and spooky down there, and . . .

he didn't trust him. The fucker had such a powerful life force, he'd come back from hell just to haunt your ass.

So, Ray grabbed the pick and threw it at his head.

"Thwonk!" it went, breaking bone.

And he just turned around and walked off. Left them both lying there.

"You shoulda learned, boss, you shoulda fuckin' learned," he snickered, as he hot-wired the car. "Let sleeping dogs lie."

On the way back to the city, though, he was bleeding all over the van, and the thrill of victory turned to anger and vexation. Smacking the steering wheel with one big, hairy paw, trying to steer with the other, he snapped at the air: "Shoulda *killed* the motherfucker! Shoulda killed him and buried him deep!"

Still later, drifting over the Henry Hudson Bridge in a fog, dizzy from loss of blood, he let up on the gas and rolled the window down to let the cool night wind blow in his face.

The fog, it turned out, was only in his head. Far below, in Spuyten Duyvil Creek, he could see the lights of the Bronx and Inwood reflecting off the swift, swirling black waters of the outgoing tide.

And it occurred to him what a waste, what a crying shame it all was. Ray and Al. Playmates, church-mates, schoolmates, teammates, job-mates, cellmates, bunkmates. Asshole buddies and crime partners for thirty years. And it all came to this. Water under the bridge.

CHAPTER NINETEEN

The Monster Lies in Chains

Sometimes, catching Jim staring at her as she went about some household chore, Shelley felt that this peculiar emotion, love, had a kind of magnetic attraction all its own, quite apart from its author and agent.

Jim was not the sort of man she'd have imagined for herself. Especially not at this juncture in her life, when maturity, stability, financial security—if not for her own sake, then at least for Toby's—seemed infinitely more logical goals.

Yet *being* loved, she found, was a powerful aphrodisiac.

In the evenings when Molly was out to class and Jim and Toby sat playing Lego at the kitchen table while she made supper, she felt so content, so natural and *right* somehow, it was almost like being a wife again . . . in the first happy days of her marriage.

Other times—on nights like tonight—at one o'clock in the morning, alone in her bed, still sleepless with fear and worry after three stiff vodka gimlets and a couple of valiums from her stash in the cupboard under the bedstand, she found herself unreasonably tempted to tiptoe out to the living room and crawl under the covers with him.

God, if it weren't for Molly, she thought, letting her fingertips stray under her cotton nightie and softly over her thigh, into the warm tangle between her legs, I might go in there and see him right now.

And she wondered again about Molly's curious relationship with Jim. Were they really just friends, as they claimed? Considering their youth, and human nature, and the number of hours they spent together, it was hard to believe.

Yet, why shouldn't they be taken at their word?

Thinking this, caressing herself, Shelley had begun to tingle, and she'd gone all wet.

There's something missing in you, Jim, she thought, and something else that hurts, but it's nothing I couldn't . . .

Just then the phone rang beside her bed.

She picked it up.

"Hello," she said, and she could smell herself on the hand that held the phone.

She liked the smell. It made her smile. It smelled of love. She wanted love.

"I wake you up?" Manny asked.

"No," she said. "I couldn't sleep."

"Sorry to call so late, but this couldn't wait. Now, listen to this. They just filed a Missing Person report on Al Rakozi."

"Holy fucking shit! Who filed the report?"

"Lemme see here. It's a Ms. Syreeta Brown, special assistant to the director, The Streetlight Foundation, at 12:47 this morning."

"How'd you find out so fast?"

"I got this computer guy at HQ who owes me a favor, right? Couple of weeks ago I told him, 'Anything comes through on Al Rakozi, lemme know.' So, he put this little warning message in. Strictly illegal. Nelson finds out, it's his *culo*. But it came up a few minutes ago and he called me at home. I figured you'd wanna be the first to know."

"What's in it?"

"In what?"

"The report."

"Nothing much. Missing about twenty-four hours. Checked out a Streetlight van last night about midnight. Nothing unusual for him, they say. Except, I happen to know that he's usually got his bodyguards with him. Anyway, when he didn't turn up in the morning, they phoned all their other branches. No one had seen him. So, they sent out a posse of ex-junkies to comb the ghettos. Nothing. They waited another few hours; then they phoned the police..."

"You think it might have something to do with my telegram?"

"What do you think?"

"You told me the shit was gonna hit the fan, but I didn't see it going this way."

"Maybe Ray and Mike fought back. You thought of that?"

Hastening out to the darkened living room as soon as she'd

rung off, guided by Teresa's bright green eyes, Shelley bent over the couch where Jim slept and whispered to him urgently, "Wake up, Jim, wake up."

He awakened instantly, while she still had her mouth pressed to his ear, and instinctively slid his arm around her. All up and down her hip and waist she could feel his hard calloused hand on her skin, running over the light cotton material of her nightie.

"No, no, I have to go," she moaned, when he pulled her close and kissed her throat. "That's why I woke you up. Al Rakozi's disappeared . . ."

Arriving at Streetlight by cab, Shelley found Al's new executive assistant, Syreeta Brown, waiting downstairs at the security desk.

"Hi, I'm Shelley Friedman from the *New York Star*," she said, smiling, flashing her press tags. And Syreeta, a tall, amiable, young, black woman with close-cropped hair and beautiful, Hamitic bone structure, filled her in on the details of Al's disappearance.

As it happened, she had little to add to what Manny had already said.

While Shelley stood around debating whether to go back home and take up where she left off with Jim, a call for Syreeta came in. She kept her voice low while she spoke, and when she hung up, she claimed the call had nothing to do with Al, but it was obvious that she was nervous and agitated about something.

Shelley thanked Syreeta and caught a cab downtown to

the *Star.* After signing in at the security desk, she headed up to the newsroom, which was still brightly lit and humming with activity even at this late hour.

She consulted the large, detailed map of New York and vicinity that hung on the wall and asked herself where she would go if she wanted to kill someone and dump the body.

Then she sat down at her desk and started phoning rural police stations in the Catskills and Hudson River Valley.

On her eleventh try, she connected with the Cold Spring Police Department.

The dispatcher was a nice young man with a slight Polish accent, who confessed that it was his first night on the job. And his inexperience became evident when Shelley, identifying herself as a reporter from the *New York Star,* asked if he had anything on a Mr. Al Rakozi.

"Mr. Rakozi was gravely wounded in an apparent murder attempt," the dispatcher replied, reading off a police report, and releasing so much information that his boss would surely have his job in the morning.

"His companion, a Mr. Michael O'Riley, was killed outright. Left for dead, Mr. Rakozi remained unconscious for several hours, but eventually managed to drag himself through the woods to State Highway 9, near Garrison, New York, where he was able to flag down a car.

"Now he's on the critical list at Cold Spring Community Hospital. No visitors, not even police, are allowed. That's why information on the crime is at present so sketchy."

Thanking the dispatcher, Shelley bypassed the night editor and dialed Ben directly at home with the news.

"Goddamn, this is hot stuff!" he exclaimed, when she told him the story, then instantly turned irritable. "Only trouble is, that sonbitch Corvo's gonna want to know how come I sent *you,* the newbie, out there, 'stead of one of our Big Guns . . . But alright, just make sure you write this thing up as a straight news story, you hear?"

"Sure, but what's up?"

"I'm gettin' shit from the publisher. Seems his wife's got this friend, Dorothy Dayton Lewis, who's on the board of the Streetlight Foundation, and she's convinced them that only good should be heard about the place."

"This isn't going to affect my series, is it, Ben?"

"You shuckin' me? You don't write another word, honey, till you got iron-clad, confirmed documentation, and our lawyers have gone over it with a fine-tooth comb."

Back at home, Shelley crept past the living room entrance—the last thing she needed was a scene with Jim right now—and slipped around to rap softly at Molly's private door.

Sleepily, the girl let her in, and Shelley gave her instructions on what to do in case she came home late.

"Don't be afraid to leave Toby with Jim," she said, "if you have to go out before I get back."

"I shall do just as you say then, Shelley . . . I've been invited up to my auntie's in New Haven, you know. So, he might come in handy at that."

"Oh, Molly, by the way," Shelley said, when she was heading out. "Have you still got that nurse's uniform they made you wear at your other job? Yes? Can I borrow it?"

An hour and a half later, Shelley exited the Taconic State Parkway in her rented car and drove over a low-wooded ridge into Cold Spring, New York. The town—made of old brick and wood and cast-iron facades—had grown up a gentle slope from the Hudson River, on the opposite bank from West Point. The community hospital, a rambling one-story, brick building, was situated at the high end of town, near the woods, with a splendid view.

Pulling into the parking lot, Shelley looked out across the town and the broad river to the lofty and romantic precipice on the other side, where the military academy shone like a vast gothic castle, its battlements reflecting in the water below.

Dressed as a nurse, Shelley felt no fear or compunction about scouting the premises in search of a way into Al Rakozi's room.

What she found, in a surreptitious ten-minute excursion around the grounds, was that Syreeta and eight or ten other Streetlight people were already there, crowding the visiting room, clamoring to be let in to see Al.

Security police were stationed at the front entrance and the emergency room entrance, but the service entrance out back had been left completely unguarded.

Entering the hospital brazenly through the rear, wending her way through trash-compacting rooms and storage rooms and kitchens, Shelley noticed that everyone on the staff wore a white plastic ID plate with the name of the hospital printed in bold black letters.

Grabbing up a clipboard and pencil that happened to be

lying on a table, pressing it to her breast, she walked rapidly, with an intent expression on her face, as if preoccupied by some very pressing and important duty.

Several of the staff, encountering her in the hallways, did double-takes, as if to say, "Hey, you must be new here!" But no one presumed to challenge her.

It was not a large hospital, and within five minutes she found Al Rakozi's name and health chart hanging on the door outside Room A56.

Grabbing the health chart off the door, she slapped it onto her clipboard and stepped inside Al's room as if she had every reason to do so.

The patient, his head and much of his face swathed in bandages, his eyes blackened and puffed shut, was lying on his back, in the room's only bed, with his head raised. One of his arms, in a large, white cast, lay suspended above and before him on a pulley device. The other was hooked up to an IV unit. Various other tubes and wires appeared to link him to an array of beeping, flickering machines that measured his vital signs and provided the room's only light.

Well, the king has fallen, she thought, the monster lies in chains. At the same time, she was wary. And recalled another time when he fell—stoned, drunk, naked—on the kitchen floor of a roach-infested pad in the East Village, his enormous, pulsating, blue-veined penis standing above him like a marble tower.

"Now slap it," he lisped, in an eerie falsetto. "Slap it, slap it, slap it. Now suck it. Suck it and make it better."

And she did. Did she? Yes, she did . . .

"Al, can you tell me what happened?" she whispered, feigning sympathy, reaching over to pat his shoulder. Then, when he licked his mouth and seemed as if preparing to speak, she quickly drew her hand away to switch on the cassette in her bag. "Who did this to you, Al? Who did it?"

"Pa ... Pa ..." he muttered, and she could see one brutally swollen eye open just a crack.

"Pagano? Did he fight back, Al? Is that what happened? Was it Ray?"

"... fuckin' Ray ..."

"So, he figured it out, huh? He turned on you."

"... turned on me ..."

"Then what?"

"Then," he said, and started to cry. "Why, Penny, why?"

"What happened to Penny?"

"... gone," he croaked, "gone ..."

"You loved her, right? But you had Ray kill her."

"... killed her ..."

"What for?"

Al opened both eyes wide and focused on Shelley for the first time.

"What for?" she insisted, hearing voices just outside the door.

"What have I ever done to you," he asked, "that you should do this to me?"

"You wouldn't believe me if I told you," she said just as the door opened, revealing a young Chinese doctor, and an older white nurse with dyed blond hair.

"Patient's looking much, much better; at this rate, he'll be out in no time," Shelley said cheerily, sweeping briskly past the astonished pair and out the door with her clipboard clasped tightly to her breast.

CHAPTER TWENTY

Sliding Inside the Dream

It was Sunday, Molly's day off, and she'd gone up to New Haven to see her aunt.

Shelley had returned from Cold Spring early that morning, only to change clothes and race out the door again, excited about her latest Al Rakozi story.

So, Jim and Toby were left alone.

The sun was out, bright, and warm, but the oppressive heat and humidity of the past few days had disappeared, chased southward by a high-pressure system from Canada, and the open-air beckoned.

Glutted on Lego games, Sunday morning kiddy shows, and Teresa's relentless affection, Jim and Toby left a note for Mom, dug a couple of ice cream bars out of the freezer, and headed for the beach.

Toby sat self-confidently atop Jim's shoulders, gripping an ear with one hand, dripping ice cream into his hair with the other.

Meanwhile Jim juggled his cone and the stroller, the seat of which was occupied by a large plastic Macy's bag filled with towels, sandwiches, pop-top cans of juice, a sand pail, a jug of cheap red wine and his battered old flute.

It was a long way to the beach. Their route down Hudson and Washington Streets took them through the Meatpacking, Printing and Butter & Eggs Districts, and Toby never ceased inquiring of his laboring mount, "Wuss dat? Wuss dat?"

Turning right at Chambers Street, they crossed under the overhead ramp of the corroding, derelict Westside Highway, wended their way through a maze of inhabited packing crates and stripped automobiles and finally came out at their destination, the great landfill beach which had been created ten years before, during excavation for the World Trade Center.

The sand was fine and white, and so inviting that Toby pounded on Jim's head with his fists to be let down immediately.

Deposited on the beach, he ran directly off toward the river, his fat little bare feet kicking up sand.

Jim, encumbered by the overloaded stroller, was slow to follow, and caught him only a yard or two from the oily, chemical-colored water.

"No, Toby, no, it's not that kind of beach!" he yelled, grabbing him up in his arms, throwing him over his shoulder.

Then, as he conveyed the kicking squalling child—"Wanna swim, *quiero nadar!*"—back toward the stroller, it seemed to him for a moment that the dome of the sky was the dome of a great blue eye. And the eye was open, looking up.

Then a wave of curved light flashed above. The eye blinked and opened again immediately onto the same cloudless sky.

Yet everything had changed.

This beach where he found himself now was no longer on the Hudson River, but on the murky Sacramento River Delta, near Rio Vista, California.

Back across the beach, it was not Chambers Street, but County Road 12, and the cars were late '40s brands, with chrome, Art Deco looks.

Up in the sky, the planes were not 707s and 747s, but Stratocruisers and Super Constellations.

And this was not Toby, flung casually over his shoulder, but himself.

"No, no, it's not that kind of beach," Jim said again, Jim's burly, young prison guard father said again, each voice echoing off the other, getting fainter and fainter, till they died away in the years.

"Look, Toby, here we play in the sand, see?"

Fishing out an array of toy cars, trucks, and planes from the stroller's side pockets, Jim dropped to his knees and showed the boy—speaking softly, patiently, yet with an edge of sorrow and guilt in his tone, attrition for some repressed memory of cruelty or negligence in the past—as his own father had once shown him, how to make roads and towns and airports, and move produce to market.

Toby picked up fast; within minutes he was impatient to carry on alone, and Jim could spread a beach towel, strip off his shirt, pull out the jug of wine, sit back on his elbows, have a leisurely sip and a look around, and ride his time warp back to the present.

With the sun beaming down from its Canadian High, the

tugs, barges, and excursion boats floating by, the nude and half-nude, straight and gay couples swapping spit and smoking shit on their beach blankets all around, and Bob Dylan's "Rolling Thunder Revue" playing on three boomboxes at once, there could be no doubt that this was Lower Manhattan, in the summer of '75.

An hour later, Jim caught sight of Shelley tripping across the sand in a sleeveless off-white blouse, a long, tie-dyed summer skirt, and a pair of espadrilles, swinging a big straw Spanish bag.

"Hey, how come you're not home in bed?" he asked, as she trotted up. "You couldn't have got much sleep last night."

"I don't need much sleep," she responded. And he figured she was right because she looked sensational.

"Wow!" Jim exclaimed, rolling his eyes, when she slipped out of her clothes. And she laughed and posed for him, long-legged and voluptuous in her black bikini.

Then, while Shelley set out their lunch on the towels, Jim took off Toby's clothes and left him to run around naked.

At one point, the child made a break for the water again, and Shelley took off after him like a retriever.

Catching him just as he was about to stick a toe in, she swept him up in her arms, drew him to her breasts, and started blowing on his neck and cheek, going "blubba-blubba-blubba!"

And the vision of them coming back—plump laughing boy, beautiful laughing mother, the river behind them, the sun in their hair, the reflection of a million World Trade Center windows spangling over their brown naked flesh—was something that Jim would take with him to the grave.

After lunch, he shook out the towels and he and Shelley lay

down, side-by-side, smoking cigarettes, with the jug of wine sitting an easy distance in front of them, while Toby played happily beside them, fingering pebbles, talking to himself.

"Dass a wock? Dass a wock?"

"Yes, that's a rock!" Shelley laughed, raising up, taking a swig of wine.

And then, flopping back down on her belly, she whispered to Jim confidentially, "He's right at home here, you see? In Ibiza, the two of us spent most of our time at the beach."

"What about his dad?" Jim whispered back, just to make conversation. He was dizzy from the wine, the scent of Shelley's dark, sun-warmed hair, the touch of her skin on his arm, the flash of her teeth when she smiled.

"What *about* him?"

"Where was he when you were at the beach?"

"Writing, mostly, or holding court. He wasn't much for picnics, or any outdoor stuff."

"Why not?"

"Well, Tobias is a funny kind of guy. He wants to look young, tan, and fit, but he's sixty-five years old and he's afraid of skin cancer, so he avoids the sun, uses Man-Tan and an exercise bike instead. He likes to cultivate this reckless, hard-drinking air, but he waters his drinks, and he never drives his Alfa Romeo over sixty miles an hour. Deep down he's a frightened and worried person. When you think about it, he's a lot like Al Rakozi."

"How you figure that?"

"Well, he's a self-made, bigger-than-life character; he's got a large following, and he's developed this public pose of complete self-confidence. But under it all, he's on very shaky ground. When Tobias left Poland, after the war, he reinvented himself, so he's not sure who was originally there. I think Al's pretty much the same."

"Has it ever occurred to you," Jim observed, sniffing, shaking his head, "how often this guy Al crops up in your conversation?"

"For Christ's sake, I'm doing a story on him. What do you expect? I'm involved. And there's a moral issue here that I feel very strongly about. I mean, there's something especially slimy about a crook, a murderer, posing as a do-gooder, don't you think?"

"Of course," he replied, anxious to smooth things over now.

"But you know, up there in Cold Spring," Shelley went on, "I didn't get anything out of him that I didn't already know. Didn't push hard enough, I guess. I mean, he was hooked up to all these machines, and so pathetic, I caught myself feeling almost sorry for him.

"Then ... listen to this ... on my way back to New York I had this fantasy where I got a chance to go through the whole thing again. I went back to the hospital, back into Al's room just like before. This time though, I pulled the plug on his life-support system, jerked the IV out of his arm, and let him die. I just stood there watching him, with no remorse, because there was no question in my mind; as soon as he gets out of that hospital, he'll be a lethal weapon again, pointed at everything I hold dear. And get this, in my fantasy, I got away with it! Nobody knew me in Cold Spring. No one could identify me, especially in Molly's nurse outfit that's way too big for me.

And the crime went unsolved until I made a confession on my deathbed."

"Shelley, you are so trippy!" Jim said, tipping the wine. "I thought reporters were supposed to be the factual type."

"I *am* the factual type. I just have a rich fantasy life."

"Oh yeah? How do I figure in your fantasy life?"

"Wouldn't you like to know."

"Well," he said, changing the subject to hide his confusion, and the hard-on that was digging a trough in the sand beneath him. "I hope you left off your fantasies when you wrote up your story this morning."

"Oh, there's no danger of that. My editor drove all the way in from Westchester, killed his Sunday golf match, just to make sure I did the right thing."

"He like the story?"

"Loved it, of course. 'DRUG GURU NEAR DEATH IN MURDER ATTEMPT.' It's a tabloid dream, and we got it out before anyone else. It would've been a whole lot better though, if Corvo, the top editor, hadn't killed all the details. 'Too speculative,' he said, and I lost the first big exclusive of my career."

"They still feeling the heat on the other thing, the series?"

"I tell you, if it gets any worse, I'll have to think about going somewhere else."

Later they packed up and stood by the river to watch the sun go down.

Just as it slid behind the lopsided Jersey skyline, the wind stilled. The water glassed off. The sea birds—which only a moment before had been swooping and shrieking and squabbling over refuse in the wakes of homebound sailboats and motor cruisers—lighted on the river and fell silent. Traffic noises, drifting over from West Street and Chambers Street all afternoon, suddenly wound down. Even the jetliners, gliding along the Hudson River flightpath, seemed to throttle back and hang in the air.

And the three of them stood there together for the longest time, watching the sky go from red to pink to palest blue.

Strolling back uptown in the twilight, pushing a sleepy Toby out in front of them, Shelley and Jim held hands. At one point, crossing the vast, gray, brick, industrial plaza at the entrance to the Holland Tunnel, she let her head fall on his shoulder. And Jim, looking down at her, with no idea what would come out of his mouth next, said, "I crave sincerity, don't you?"

"Yes . . . yes, I do," she murmured, looking up at him, as if startled by the question. "More than anything else."

At home, they were delighted to find that Molly hadn't come in from New Haven yet. Bathing Toby, dressing him for bed, feeding him, they fondled each other shamelessly.

Toby, groggy from his day at the beach, accepted it all with complete equanimity.

After he'd been put to bed, they stood listening for a moment outside his room with the door ajar.

The moment Toby's breathing settled into a steady rhythm, Shelley smiled at Jim, took him by the hand, and led him down the hall toward her room.

"Wait . . . wait a second," he protested, as she shoved him backwards, and none too gently, through her door. "Molly's gonna be home any minute now."

"So what? I thought there was nothing between you two."

"There isn't, from my point of view."

"Let me get this straight," she said, kicking the door shut behind them. "We're supposed to put everything on tap until we straighten out how Molly feels?"

"That," he replied, trembling as her fingers slipped under his tee shirt, "would probably be the most reasonable course."

"I tell you what. I'm not feeling too reasonable right now, are you?"

"I'm not sure we ought to do this," he said, balking at the edge of the bed. "I'm not sure you want it the way I want it."

"How do you want it?"

"I want love. I want sincerity."

"Oh, Jesus, don't be so corny."

"I mean it."

"All right, sincerity you get. But love I don't know about yet. Why don't we just see what develops?"

"I'm sorry, Shelley . . ."

"My God, I can't believe this. You want a certificate of intention or something? I mean, I'm not such a good catch myself, you know. I'm over my ears in debt. I smoke too much, drink too much. I'm an insomniac. Why don't you just try to get to know me first?"

"I know you better than you think."

"How is that?"

"I looked through your things."

"You did that?" she said, drawing away. "You looked through my things? When?"

"When you were out. Before you knew me. When Molly

used to bring me around."

"So, tell me."

"What?"

They circled about each other like boxers.

"Find anything interesting?"

Jim moved to the window and looked out at nothing.

Shelley stepped up behind and turned him around to face her.

"What'd you find?" she asked, and an expression of anguish crossed her face. "The beatings?" She started to sob. "The bondage? The blood-sucking? The two and three at a time?"

Jim grabbed her, pushed her down on the bed and leaned his head against hers.

"Hey, you think I haven't done some bad shit in my time? Things I regret? Maybe you don't know it, Shelley, but we've got a lot in common. It's the way we look at things. As soon as I read your stuff, I knew."

"Hey, you know, Jim, you overwhelm me," she said. And then all at once she was angry again. "So, what do you want from me? What? You want to move in, help support the family? Shit, you can't even support yourself. The way I see things now, if you're up for a one-night stand, fine. Otherwise, really, let's just say fuck it."

"Okay, fuck it," he said, heading for the door.

"Wait!" she cried. "Wait."

"What?"

"I didn't mean it."

She caught him by the hand and kissed it.

"I want you to love me, Jim, I do. I want to love you too. I just don't know if it can happen."

"It can happen, all right."

He took her hand and lead her to the bed.

"What ... what do you want first?" she asked, falling back, breathless, pulling him down on top of her.

"This," he said, and, slipping the blouse down over her shoulder, he drew a nipple up into his mouth and sucked.

Later, sliding inside her, he felt himself sliding inside the dream he'd had of her. It was all around him now. He was right where he wanted to be.

They had no idea when Molly came in that night. The next thing they knew it was ten o'clock in the morning and someone was pounding on the front door.

"Police, open up!"

"Hurry, baby," Shelley whispered, reaching for her robe. "Get your clothes on and go out the back way. I'll try to stall them at the door."

Hastening down the hall to Molly's room, Jim found the apartment oddly silent for a Monday morning and assumed that Molly and Toby had gone to the park.

He peeked out through Molly's door, found the coast clear, tiptoed to the stairway door, eased it open, and was just about to close it behind him when he spotted a big, ruddy-faced man with wiry red hair, stick his head around the corner at the far end of the corridor.

"Stop, police!" he shouted, groping for a pistol under his sport jacket.

Jim bolted down the stairs, taking them three at a time. Yet he'd only gone a flight and a half down when he could hear the guy pounding after him.

"Freeze, freeze, or I'll fire!"

Bursting through the door on the next landing, Jim raced to the end of the corridor, squeezed through the open window, and started clattering down the fire escape.

Two flights down and he glanced up just in time to see the cop leaning over the railing, aiming a snub-nosed .38 at him with both hands.

"Freeze!" he hollered, and Jim ducked inside an open corridor window again.

Sprinting back down to the stairs, he hurtled through the door and ran headfirst into another plainclothes cop, a chubby little black man with muttonchop sideburns, sending him head over heels down the stairs with his pistol hand banging off the wall. The gun went off. A chip flew off the brick wall just above Jim's head, and a bullet ricocheted up the stairwell. The cop ended up on the third-floor landing, cold-cocked.

With the devil above and the devil below, Jim took the stairs, hurdled over the comatose cop, and reached the ground floor a few seconds later. About to burst through the door and take his chances with anyone who might be lurking on the other side, he remembered from his nightly forays to take out Shelley's trash that there was a rear exit from the basement.

Bounding down the stairs and out the rear door, he hit the garden wall running, scampered up, and was about to leap over when someone above him on Shelley's fire-escape screamed, "Stop or I'll shoot!"

Jim didn't even hesitate but rolled off just as a .38 slug plowed into the wall beneath him, followed by the sound of a shot.

Landing stiff-legged in the rather formal back garden of a four-story townhouse, he now confronted a little, old, gray-haired lady in a straw hat and a blue smock who was working on her geraniums. She had apparently stopped her work upon hearing the commotion, and now sat poised on her knees, big-eyed, mouth wide open, with a pair of clippers in one hand and a straw basket in the other.

Behind her, the door to her kitchen hung open.

Whispering "Sorry, Ma'am," Jim rushed past her into the house, through her kitchen, dining room and living room, and out the front door onto Perry Street without pausing to look one way or the other.

He tore across the street regardless of traffic and found himself facing a schoolyard surrounded by a high fence. He jumped before he hit the fence and was already halfway up when his hands and sneakers gripped the chain link. He vaulted over and hit the ground just as a police car came wailing up the street with its red lights flashing.

Lighting out like a rabbit, Jim crossed the schoolyard, raced around the side, clambered over another chain link fence, and found himself on the familiar cobbles of Charles Street again. Spurting six doors down to Monika's ex-pad, he climbed her wall, swung onto the fire-escape, made it to her roof, rolled onto the hot tarpaper beneath the brick parapet for a moment to get his breath back, and crawled across the rooftops to the old folks' place.

CHAPTER TWENTY-ONE

Cop a Plea!

With nowhere to run, nowhere to hide, Ray figured the one place to go was Monika's. Mike was long gone. And Syreeta Brown, knowing the fate of its last three tenants, most probably avoided it like the plague, though she had residency rights as the boss' current number one. The boss himself was superstitious, and highly unlikely to visit the scene of even one of his proxy crimes, assuming he was in any shape to travel.

So, Ray let himself in with his key, which he had thoughtfully pocketed on the night of Monika's demise, and holed up, amusing himself with the stash of coke under the floorboards that the cops had missed when they did their search of the premises.

Then one morning, he chanced going out to cop a paper at the corner Mom & Pop. Skimming the headlines as he padded down the littered sidewalk, he was relieved—but not particularly surprised—to find that though Al Rakozi was still page three news, there was not a word about Ray Pagano.

Back at Monika's, he seated himself at the kitchen counter, amid her fetid fish aquariums and dying plants, with a pencil and paper and a little mound of coke in front of him and tried to plot out his options. After working at it for an hour, reducing the mound to a smear of white, he concluded that he had only one: cop a plea.

Only thing was, with the D.A. in Streetlight's back pocket, it would have to be the Feds. For that he needed a lawyer, the best. And then there was the bail money. Plus, maybe a little retainer for living expenses. Therefore, it was obvious. He had to get through to Shelley, and through her to the power of the press.

Next morning, he rose late as usual, popped in at the corner for a *New York Star*, stopped at Lanciano's, on West Fourth Street, for a take-out *capuccino* and a ham and egg sandwich on a croissant, meandered up Bleecker Street to Abingdon Square and found a bench in the sunshine.

Vainly scanning the playground for Shelley's kid and his nanny—who little Mike, God rest his soul, had once pointed out in this very place—Ray opened the paper and started on his breakfast.

A minute or two later, he looked up and who was sitting down next to him on the bench? The very person he'd been looking to meet.

"Ah, but that's a nasty cut on your ear," she observed, in her companionable Irish brogue. "Whatever happened to it?"

"Love play," he replied, with his mouth full of coffee and egg.

"Really?" she said, her eyes going big and round.

"Nah," he grinned, swallowing, wiping his mouth with the back of his hand. "Let's put it this way. It was a work-related accident."

"I see," she said, keeping an eye on the kid, who was playing cars with another urchin in the sandbox. "And what line of business might you be in, then?"

"Nightclubs."

"Really? I used to work in a pub once, in Dublin."

"You ever need a job in New York, lemme know."

"Why, thank you. As it happens, I may be in need rather soon."

"Johnny Di Dio's the name," he said, grinning wolfishly.

There was something about this girl that he liked. Something fresh and sweet that he wanted to bring to earth.

"Pleased to meet you, I'm sure," she responded, placing her plump, dimpled little hand in his. "I'm Molly McKenna."

A couple of hours of chit-chat and he ferreted out everything he needed to know about the situation at Shelley's ... That fucking flutist, who was supposed to be dead, was hanging around there, screwing things up again.

"Here's my address, sweetheart; you ever need anything, just pop on by," he said, after treating her and the kid to lunch at the Shamrock Pub and making his way back to Monika's for the afternoon dog nap which had become his recent habit.

First thing next morning, the doorbell rang. Scared the living shit out of him. He was halfway out to the garden with his tail between his legs before he realized the only one who knew his whereabouts was the girl.

So, he opened the door and there she was. She had the kid

with her in a stroller, and she'd been crying.

"Come in, doll, what's a matter?" he said, sniffing opportunity.

The moment she was inside though, the kid started acting up. So, Ray grabbed him up out of his stroller, slung him over his shoulder like a flour sack, and set him out in the garden with a can of orange soda pop and some of Monika's pots and pans and wooden spoons.

Pretty soon he was happy as a clam, doing a percussion number that was enough to wake the whole neighborhood.

On his way back, Ray stopped in the kitchen to get Molly a cup of coffee and a box of Monika's Kleenex. Then he sat her down on one of the futons, patted her tenderly on the knee, and said, "Now what's up, sweetheart? Anyone fuck with my girl, I'll break his balls."

Whereupon she poured out her tale of woe.

"That Jew bitch, she's somethin' else, ain't she?" he said, when she was done. "And that boyfriend of yours! You just gimme the word, babe, and I'll . . ."

But she didn't want to hear that, and she started to cry again, like she had the whole world on her shoulders.

"Wait a second, I think I got just what you need!" he said and hurried out to the kitchen again.

Snorting up the residue of cocaine that he'd left on the counter the night before, he made a quick, furtive call to 911, grabbed the pot of coffee off the stove and a bottle of Sambuca Romana from the liquor cabinet, hustled back into Molly, refilled her cup, and dumped in some Sambuca.

"Here, have some of this, it'll do you good."

"Why thank you, Johnny, I think it might."

"Now you know what I want you to do?" he said, in a soft, persuasive tone he learned from the boss. "I want you to start at the beginning. You say you feel alone in this country. You got no one to turn to, no place to go. Even your aunt, like she don't want you around no more, right? So, think of me as your Father Confessor. A sympathetic ear. And try to look back in time and lay it out for me, how you got to this place where you're at right now."

"Well," she said, in this high sing-song that she put on, like she was enjoying the sound of her own voice, "I came over here to this country, Johnny, because Ireland's a cold dead-end. But after all I've been through, I can tell you, New York's been cruel consolation. I'd hoped to be a nurse, you see, although now it seems I've little talent for that. I've not a clue what I'm to do next. It's all up at Shelley's, and I'm scared I'll be deported."

"What if you had your wish?" he asked when she was done. "What if you could get anything your heart desired?"

"Oh, that's easy," she answered, brightening up. "Get married and move to the countryside. A wee bungalow with a bit of garden in back, not too far from the city. A dog, a cat, perhaps a pony. Keep house for the hubby. Raise up some little ones. It's not much, I admit, but it's my dream."

"Well, lemme see, sweetheart," he said, with sudden inspiration. "Maybe that's not so far fuckin' out as you might think."

He poured her some more Sambuca, had a pull himself, and started petting the back of her neck and her hair. Her neck was soft and fleshy, her wavy, red, Irish hair very fine. His hand looked dark against her white, freckled skin.

The petting got heavier. She laid her head on his shoulder. He poured out some more Sambuca. And soon they were lying side by side on the futon.

He kissed her rosy little mouth. Nipped her lower lip. She didn't respond, but she didn't resist either.

Meanwhile, the kid was still out in the garden, banging on Monika's pots and pans.

Ray kissed her again, ran a hairy paw up under her blouse, over her big, soft, titties, and across her hard, little nips.

He hadn't felt this good in months.

He rolled her onto her tummy, hoisted her skirt up over her hips, slid her panties off her feet, dropped them on the floor, and she just laid there with her eyes shut.

So, he figured he'd wake her up.

He started with her toes. Sucked on each one for a minute, then started licking—up the sole of her foot, her Achilles tendon, her calf, the bend of her knee, the back of her thigh, her ass and the thin line of long, fine pubes that grew around behind, going snuff-snuff like a basset hound.

She was still just lying there, but suddenly she was all wet.

He parted her legs with his face, slid his long, rough tongue inside from the rear, ran it around to her clit, and lapped it off.

She was moving now. Not much. But she was moving.

So, he jerked his zipper down, whipped it out, and plunged it in to the bone.

She sighed and settled, and he worked at her, nipping at her shoulders and the back of her neck, till he came.

Whether she got off or not he didn't know. She was sound

asleep before he pulled out. But he could care less. She had this talent for making him happy.

The thing was, she reminded him of others he'd known, down on their luck, that he'd cared for at his club and other places, who paid him back in this way or another. If it had been up to him, none of them would've come to any harm.

Sure, he was a crook, but the truth was, he had a little soft spot in his heart. He'd followed the wrong star, was all. If he could go back and do it all over now, he would play it a different way.

So, maybe this one, he figured, she was like a last chance.

CHAPTER TWENTY-TWO

The Possessed

Only after it had been established that no one was seriously hurt during all the alarms and excursions up and down the halls and stairways, only after the police had interrogated Shelley, threatened her with prosecution for harboring a fugitive, and then left her alone, did it occur to her that Toby and Molly were nowhere about.

Assuming they'd gone out to play, she dressed and went tramping around the neighborhood to the kiddy playgrounds in Bleecker Park, Abingdon Square, Washington Square, and Hudson Park. Finding them nowhere, yet still only mildly concerned, she returned home to check Toby's room, and then Molly's room, for some clue to their intentions.

And it was there, in Molly's room, on her dresser, under a pile of stained and dirty underwear, that Shelley found a second-hand, paperback copy of Fyodor Dostoyevsky's THE POSSESSED, with Jim's name written on the inside cover.

Leafing through it, she found a torn, crumpled piece of brown paper sack filled with his childish scrawl. It was as if at some point, he'd felt the need to write his thoughts down, grabbed the nearest paper at hand, then stuffed it into the book to be forgotten:

"The instant I see my benefactress, Molly, I'm plunged into the deepest despair. I can't spend a minute with her without churning up bile, inflaming my stomach lining with the bitter juices of frustration. And though she's my sole support in the world, my only access to Shelley, I'm sometimes tempted to scream at her that she drives me to tears, that our days are an endless bore."

Shelley imagined Molly coming in last night from New Haven, glancing at Jim's empty bed on the living room sofa, and then hearing sounds of love through her bedroom wall.

She saw her creeping back out to the living room, going jealously through Jim's things, seeking some clue to his behavior.

She watched her find the note, imagined what she felt then, what she must be feeling now, and her mild concern for Toby's well-being instantly turned to terror.

Frantically, she dialed 911 and reported her son as a kidnapping victim.

"Kidnapping is maybe too strong a word for what we got here," said the desk officer on the other end of the line, after identifying himself as Sergeant Ryan and hearing her story. "Has this Irish girl got any relatives in this country?"

Following the sergeant's suggestion, Shelley called Mrs. Neal, Molly's aunt in New Haven.

"They're not here," she said. "Molly didn't tell you they were coming, did she? After all, she's just barely left."

"Give 'em a few hours," Sergeant Ryan said, when she phoned 911 again. "You file a kidnapping complaint, it's serious stuff."

Finally, at eight o'clock that night, when Shelley was at her wit's end, Molly and Toby danced in the front door together, laughing.

"Molly! Where have you been?"

"Right here in the Village. At my friend Johnny Di Dio's house, over on Charles Street. Right Tobes?"

"Johnny! Johnny!" Toby squealed, running into his mother's arms.

"Where on Charles Street?" Shelley demanded, squeezing Toby to her as if he might suddenly slip through her fingers.

"You mean the address? Seventy-six, I think."

"What?" she gasped. "And who the hell is this 'Johnny?'"

"Johnny Di Dio," Molly said, grinning delightedly, triumphantly, as the Italianate vowels rung out. "Sounds like a Mafia Don, doesn't he? Mind you, he looks the part as well. But he's ever so nice."

"Why didn't you give me a call, for Christ's sake? You knew I'd be frantic."

"Would you like to know the truth then, Shelley?" she replied, looking her straight in the eye. "I wanted you to hurt, as I've been hurt."

"Wait a minute, you and Jim are supposed to be just friends, right? That's what you told me."

"Oh, I think you knew better than that."

"I'm not going to stand here and argue about it. Whatever

the case, your behavior is inexcusable. I could never let you go out with Toby again. I'd be petrified."

Molly sighed and laid Toby's things on the kitchen table. "Well, I s'pose that's it. I shall just gather my things, then."

"I hope you'll wait till Toby's in bed. It's going to be enough of a shock as it is."

"As you like."

"By the way, are you the one who called the police on Jim?"

"The police? Whatever for?"

"Anyhow, he got away, in case you're interested."

"I'm not," she said, going in to pack her bags. "And I shall not shed a tear if he rots his bloody life out in jail. After all I did for him. And I'll not forgive you for what you've done to me either, Shelley. Not ever."

"Well now that we're assigning blame," Shelley said, following her into her room, "I doubt if I'll forgive you very soon either. And when you have a child of your own, I think you'll understand why."

Later though, while she was putting Toby to bed, Shelley started feeling guilty. It was just as much her own fault as Molly's, she thought. And if anyone bore primary responsibility, it was surely Jim, who'd lied to them both shamelessly. And the girl's anger was so righteous, so genuine, so totally remote from her normal placidity, there could be no doubt that she felt seriously wronged.

Looking at it that way, Shelley was on the point of going in and apologizing. Then, when she recalled how Molly had blackmailed her with Toby, all pity vanished.

Lying in bed that night, drugged and sleepless, long after

Molly had gone, Shelley heard footsteps on the fire escape stairs outside her room.

Holding her breath, expecting the worst, she saw Jim's face appear in the window.

"What're you doing here?"

"No place else to go," he said, out of breath, sliding the window up and leaping into the room. "The old folks finally got back from Florida. I heard them rattling at the door, trying to get in. But I'd latched it from the inside, so I had time to sneak out through the window."

"When was this?"

"This was only two or three hours after I left here," he went on, slipping out of his shoes and making himself comfortable on the bed beside her. "I figured the cops would still be lurking around the neighborhood, so I went over the roofs to Monika's place, and you won't believe what I saw."

"Don't tell me, I bet I can guess."

"I heard this big racket and peeked down over the parapet and there was Toby, out in the backyard, banging on some pots and pans. I figured Molly was with him, hanging out with whoever lives there now."

"You know who lives there now? Guy named Johnny Di Dio. Looks like an Italian mobster. Sound familiar?"

Jim looked blank.

"What if the name's an alias?"

"Ray Pagano?"

"Now," she said, locking eyes with him, "imagine that my son was in there with Ray Pagano, and you looked down on him playing in that yard, and you left him there."

"For Christ's sake, how was I to know? Toby looked happy enough to me. It seemed wiser to just leave him right where he was, stay up on the roof till dark, rather than cause some big commotion, have the cops breathing down everyone's neck again."

"Let me tell you something, Jim. What we've got here is more than just a little disagreement. I mean, we'll leave Toby out of it for now. Let's just talk about the lies you told, and the way you treated Molly . . ."

"I'm sorry," he said when she's done with him. "I had no intention of doing anybody any harm."

"Sorry isn't quite good enough, I'm afraid."

"No, you'll see. I've been thinking. You know what I'm gonna do? I'm gonna turn myself into Streetlight as a drug addict."

"What? Why would you ever want to do that?"

"You could use an inside source, right? And I need to prove myself."

"Prove yourself to whom?"

"To you," he murmured, reaching out to touch her shoulder . . . "and to myself. See, I've always been the kind of guy . . . I'm always flying apart, blowing along with whatever wind comes along. I've got nothing I can latch onto and say, 'Hey, that's me, that's the meaning of my life.' Now I want to do something that *counts.*"

"Just stop it now," she said, shaking him off. "Stop romanticizing everything. It's bullshit. Tell me what's *really* in it for you!"

"Okay, I've got to disappear for a while," he replied, grinning sheepishly. "And I thought, what better place than Streetlight? It's the *last* place anybody'd think of, right? The only thing I worry about is, who's going to look out for you and Toby when I'm gone?"

"Oh, don't worry about us," she said. And then, after observing him very carefully for a moment, and deciding that his contrition was genuine: "Look, Jim, I agree that you could be useful in Streetlight. But it's a very bad place in there. You don't know how bad. I just can't let you do it."

"Hey, not to worry!" he shouted, leaping from the bed, pacing up and down the room, full of bravado again. "I've got it all planned out. When I go in there, I'll have myself in such a state, I'll actually *believe* I'm strung out.

"See, there's no way you can fake this. To get accepted by these guys, I'll have to be the genuine article. I'll have to forget about you and Toby and everything else. I'll have to invent a phony past and convince myself that it's real. I'll have to actually *become* the person I'm pretending to be."

"You can do that?"

"You bet I can, I'm the best!" he exclaimed, then stopped in the center of the room and—as if to offer some concrete physical evidence in support of his flimsy assertions—spun gracefully around on the ball of one foot, pointed at her, and smiled photogenically. "I've been doing it all my life."

The gesture was so innocent of vanity, so practical and uncomplicated in intention, yet so devastatingly effective in execution, that it nearly won her over again despite herself.

"There's . . . there's no way then," she said, flustered, "no way I can talk you out of it?"

He shook his head.

"But how will you get information out? You'll be locked in for ninety days, incommunicado."

"I'll find a way."

"Well, if you really want to do it, and I can't talk you out of it . . ." she said. And a moment later, remembering something Mike had told her: "All right, I think maybe there *is* a way to get word out of there."

The next day, not twenty minutes after Jim had left the apartment, Shelley got a phone call from Ray Pagano.

"Hey, babe, izzat you?"

It was the first time she'd heard his voice since their journey across the country back in the '60s, when they sang "Walk on By" with Dionne Warwick on the radio. For an instant, she found herself unable to reply.

Back when she'd known Ray the first time, she had thought the high, tinny quality of his voice, his Damon Runyon accent, rather quaint and charming. Now she found it sinister.

Her problem with Ray now, however, was not so much fear as shame and embarrassment. Here was this gangster, this cold, slimy killer, and he had once known her intimately, had done things to her with the help of his friend, Al, that no man had ever done or ever would again. And he felt perfectly comfortable now, addressing her with the most horrid familiarity.

Of course, Al Rakozi had done the same, and he was no better, perhaps even worse. But at least Al had charisma.

A guy like Ray Pagano though, how could she have ever

let him touch her? It was inconceivable. It was like she'd read it somewhere, like it had happened to another person. It was so awful she didn't think she could ever forgive herself for it.

"Izzat you, Shelley?"

"Yes."

"You ready to deal?"

"Depends on what you've got to offer."

"How about exclusive rights?"

"Possibly."

"You want to know the price?"

"I'll leave that to my editor."

"Alright, you do that, and I'll get back to you tomorrow," Ray hissed. Then he sighed, as if tired of the whole nasty business. "And meanwhile, remember, I know where you live."

"Well, if it comes to that, I know where you live too, Ray. You're at Monika's place."

"Jesus, you're quite the sleuthhound, Shell," he said, laughing as if it were the best joke he'd heard in months. "Reporter like you, the boss ain't gonna stand a chance."

CHAPTER TWENTY-THREE

The Unsavory Truth

In the drug supermarket behind the Union Square subway station, Jim lined up with a bunch of other skinny, shaky-looking, city folk in front of a plump, moon-faced, black kid in a baseball cap, blue-tinted granny-glasses, and a New York Yankees warm-up jacket.

Into his role now, enduring without flinching the stares and whispered asides of his fellow shoppers—"Yo, who dat new bubba be?"—he patiently waited his turn. When it came, he submitted to a body search from the kid's hefty lieutenants, copped a nickel bag of smack and a clean syringe for a sawbuck and change, sat himself down on a decrepit bench beside a couple of other customers, broke the seal on the syringe, cooked up in a tablespoon from Shelley's kitchen and, while squirrels scurried and pigeons strutted amid the drug litter at his feet, shot up just enough to show on a blood test.

With some experience of the drug—in Amsterdam he'd

skin-popped once or twice—he expected little or no rush. He was surprised when he stood up, therefore, to find himself suddenly grasping the bench's armrest to prevent himself from reeling to the ground.

Later, checking in at the front desk of the Streetlight armory on East Ninety-Sixth Street, declaring himself to be an addict in need of instant assistance, he assumed he would be taken immediately inside. But he was made to sit in the waiting room with four other funky newcomers for more than an hour, under a large black and white sign that said, "YOU ARE EITHER MOVING IN OR MOVING OUT: YOU CAN'T HAVE IT BOTH WAYS," watching more seasoned patients getting buzzed in and out with impunity by a uniformed security guard who sat behind a desk at the other end of the room.

With nothing better to do, and still riding the slippery slope down from an infelicitous high, Jim sized up his bench-mates from the corner of one drooping eye:

... A painfully thin, short-haired, little, part-Asian woman in a holey tee shirt and dirty jeans who kept fidgeting all the time, rubbing her fingers, scratching her scalp, standing up and sitting down, swiveling her small narrow head around from side to side, focusing with round bulbous eyes on something very distant, far beyond the cool redbrick walls of the armory.

... A short, stocky, goateed spade cat in a dirty wrinkled suit, wrap-around sunglasses, and a white fedora, drumming his rough, splintered fingers on the bench seat between his legs to a monotonous conga beat.

... A pretty, fortyish white woman, a suburban housewife down on her luck, in a ratty blond pageboy, a wrinkled paisley blouse, a soiled tan skirt, and scuffed penny loafers.

... A beautiful, golden-skinned Puerto Rican, little more than a boy, who never once moved, never blinked an eye, and seemed almost catatonic.

Finally, a short, square-jawed, athletic-looking, black man in a tight Blood Bros tee shirt, jeans and immaculate white sneakers was buzzed out through the heavy steel door, and bounced across the room toward them, smiling officiously.

"Hiya!" he piped out, while he was still ten feet away. "I'm Eljay, and I'm gonna take you inside now, okay?"

"Sure, let's go," Jim volunteered, but the others stayed glum and silent, and merely followed him through the door that he'd left open behind him.

On the other side of the door, there was an enormous open space, the former parade ground of the armory, full of scrawny, yet cheerful-looking, patients in gray shorts and black Blood Bros tank tops. Some of them were lifting weights, some playing basketball and volleyball, others doing an aerobic routine to a loud, hard-driving Otis Redding number, still others jogging around the perimeter.

Every few minutes, some inspirational message, evidently pre-recorded by the director, would boom out over the public address system: "Remember what our Latino brothers say, folks, 'El Pueblo Unido, Jamas Sera Vencido.' In English, loosely translated, that means, 'United We Stand, Divided We Fall.' And it's just as true here as it is south of the border ..."

Eljay led the newcomers off to a corner, where a nurse gave them all a blood test. Then he sat them down around him on the hard cement floor and gave them a little orientation talk that he'd apparently memorized by heart.

"Couple of years ago, I was an undercover agent for the Federal Drug Administration," he began, in careful white diction that inadvertently lapsed into black from time to time. "Started using some of my own confiscated goods. Got hooked. Lost my job. My home. My wife and kids. Only way I avoided prison was by talking the judge into letting me come in here.

"When I got here, I was strung out, fucked up, totally at odds with myself. And, to make things worse, I had a chip on my shoulder. It was rough for me at first, because I was an individualist, and I fought against the tide. But in the end, I learned a lot from the teachings of the boss man.

"The boss had been involved in crime and drugs, just like everyone else in here, and he came out the other side. So, he was just passing on what he'd learned himself, from hard-earned experience. And he made me see that true bliss cannot be found in the self, but in submitting oneself to the will of the clan. Alone, I was lost in a formless void. As a member of the clan, I'm now part of a real world, with very defined limits. Suddenly there's a structure to my life.

"The boss man's message is as old as time, but nowadays folks tend to forget," Eljay continued, and then he turned and pointed to a sign on the wall above his head:

"IN LOSING YOURSELF, YOU FIND YOURSELF"

Eljay went on to explain how their stay in Streetlight would begin. They would start with nothing, he said. They would start literally hairless and naked, and then work themselves up.

"Shit we did on the street," the hipster wanted to know, "that count against us in here?"

"The boss is not interested in what you did before you came in," Eljay explained. "We assume it was bad or you wouldn't be here. And by the same token, we don't want you blaming your problems on what happened to you before."

After a tour of the immaculately clean premises, including the kitchen, the cafeteria, the infirmary, the offices, workplaces, and dormitories, where they were greeted pleasantly and politely by patients and staff, Eljay conducted them to the Streetlight main office.

There, beneath a mammoth black and white sign that read, "ENVY IS IGNORANCE, IMITATION IS SUICIDE," they sat at a long worktable and filled out questionnaires.

Under the category of Education and Work Experience, Jim wrote that he had majored in Pre-Med in college, worked for Emergency Medical Service, and had some hospital experience.

He lied in this way at Shelley's suggestion, so that he might eventually gain access to the infirmary, where Al would most likely be staying when he got back from Cold Spring Hospital.

After they finished up with their questionnaires, Eljay handed them a legal document.

"Think carefully before you sign," he warned, "because it states that you're gonna be locked in here with no visits, no phone calls, no nothing. This is an alternative lifestyle rehabilitation program, so you'll be subjected to some non-conventional treatments and experiences that a straight or square person may not be prepared for. You're not ready for that, you might as well turn your ass around and walk out the door right now."

When they'd signed the document, Eljay led them downstairs to the bathroom where they had their heads shaved, had them run through a shower, a delousing spray, and out the other end to a wispy, androgenous, little Filipino who awaited them with freshly laundered, surgical gowns.

Finally, Eljay herded them down to the basement and lined them up outside a large white door with a sign that said 'FISHTANK.'

The door opened and a plump, pretty, Hispanic woman with a butch haircut stood there smiling, holding a pile of coarse gray blankets. Behind her stood an older, almost toothless, white man, holding a neatly folded stack of gray coveralls.

"Take one of each," Eljay instructed. "And then I want you out in the center of the room, on the double."

Inside, the room was large and brightly lit, with no furniture or windows. Its smooth cement floor was painted glossy black, its walls flat white, and its only discernible features were a pair of water faucets, a drain and a bucket in one corner, an open toilet in another, an elaborate track lighting and loudspeaker system on the ceiling, and several huge signs hanging on the otherwise blank walls. The largest of the signs said:

"STREETLIGHT CHECKLIST

1. Examine yourself.
2. Be honest with yourself and others.
3. Seek responsibility.
4. Trust yourself.

5. Understand rather than be understood.
6. Love rather than be loved.
7. Give according to your abilities.
8. Take only according to your needs.
9. Observe the Honor Code."

"Welcome to the 'Fishtank!'" Eljay shouted, laughing heartily. "This is where all our newcomers spend their first week. We call it 'Hell Week.' It's gonna be rough, there's no denying that, but it's all part of the boss' three-point program, which has proved over the years to be the most effective treatment for recovering addicts.

"If you all pull together, you can survive it. Alone, you'll go nowhere. In this room, you will become one Mutual Support Unit among many at Streetlight, all of them operating in perfect harmony.

"From this moment on, you'll live together, work together, sleep together, do everything together until you leave Streetlight. And none of you will leave till all of you leave.

"You got it? You're in for the long haul, people, for better or worse, so you might as well get with the program."

Next, he introduced them to their "trainers," the pretty Hispanic woman, the tall toothless white man, and a husky, young, black man, with narrow oriental eyes.

The Latina woman seemed to be in control.

"Okay, people, I want you outta them surgical gowns," she commanded, in the tones of a WAC drill sergeant. "Fold 'em up real neat, stack 'em on the floor, and get into your jumpsuits.

Soon as you do that, I want you to lay your blankets in the corner. Then you gonna have dinner."

Dinner—salad, boiled potatoes, hamburger patties and milk—was served all jumbled up in one big bowl. No utensils or napkins were provided. The Hispanic woman simply walked up to where they were standing in the center of the room and slung it down at their feet.

"How're we supposed to eat this?" Jim asked the white woman beside him.

"Hey, asshole, listen up!" the Hispanic woman yelled. "I'm gonna tell you this once, and once only. You got something to say, you say it to everyone. No private property here. No secrets. You don't report your friend's transgression, you get the same punishment. That's the Honor Code. You got it?"

"Uh . . . yeah, I guess."

"You guess? You better know, buddy. Ain't that right, people?"

"Right on!" the trainers shouted.

"Ain't that right, fish?"

"RIGHT ON!"

"That's what I like to hear. Everybody agrees with me. Now, I want you to help me in correcting White Boy here. Listen and repeat after me—asshole, asshole, asshole!"

"Asshole, asshole, asshole!!" everyone shrieked, their spittle flicking over Jim's face and clothes.

When they'd all had their fill of that, the Hispanic woman—whose name, it turned out, was "Toot,"—indicated that now it was time to eat.

"I leave it up to you how you're gonna do it," she sneered.

"But I'll give you a tip. And then she turned and pointed to a sign on the opposite wall:

"DON'T AGITATE, COOPERATE!"

Somehow, they managed despite their trainers, who hazed and ridiculed them through the entire dinner. Immediately afterwards, Toot switched off the lights and ordered them to go to sleep, though it was only nine pm.

In darkness, they made their ways to various corners to roll up in their blankets alone. Just as they were getting to sleep, the lights flashed on again, and Toot and the other trainers descended upon them, shrieking, "What the fuck you think you're doin'? We told you to do everything together. Get up! Get up! Everyone to the center of the room!"

After enduring a twenty-minute harangue under bright lights, they were made to throw their blankets down at their feet.

"Now get down, get down!" Toot shrieked. "I want you butt to butt and belly to belly. You are not alone in this room. You are one! You are one!"

The lights went off, and Jim instinctively made for the white woman. She sought him out as well. Heedless of the others, who enclosed them on either side, they began to whisper to each other.

The woman started to shiver and cry, and Jim attempted to comfort her by putting his arms around her and patting her smooth bald head. Her body was soft and round and warm, under the rough fabric of her overalls, and a great comfort to him.

Again, the lights came on.

"The fuck is goin' on there?" Toot demanded.

She had slipped up on them in the darkness and now stood directly over them with the other trainers. "You think I don't know? Listen to me now. Sex is not against the law at Streetlight. You can fuck anyone you want, any time you want, any way you want, any number you want, long as the party or parties is willing and ready, and it don't interfere with your work. And you don't have to worry about whether it's somebody else's old lady or old man, 'cause no one here is anyone else's property.

"But exclusion is against the law. You wanna make it with someone, you talk it over with your MSU. Bring it out. For example, these two white breads here, they seem to want to get it on. Maybe some of you others, you might wanna ask 'em why that is, and on what basis you others are bein' left out. You understand what I'm sayin', people?"

"RIGHT ON!" everyone yelled, including Jim and the white woman, whose name, he'd discovered, was Donna.

"Now," said Toot, addressing Jim, "you wanna make it with this lady, or not?"

"I . . . I was just trying to comfort her," he replied. "She was scared and cold."

"'I was just trying to *comfort* her,'" Toot drawled, mimicking Jim's California surfer dude inflection. "You're just trying to fuck her, man, so why don't you 'fess up to the clan?"

"I wasn't!" Jim insisted.

"He wasn't," Donna seconded. "Really not."

"What we got here, I think, is a minor insurrection," Toot sighed, shaking her head. "And how do we deal with insurrection at Streetlight?"

"WE BLOW IT AWAY!" the trainers shrieked in unison.

"How we gonna do that?"

"GIVE 'EM THE LIGHTSHOW, THE LIGHTSHOW!"

"All right, the light show it is. Now lemme tell you something, fish. You fuck up, everybody fucks up. You get punished; everybody gets punished. You asked for it, now you gonna get it."

So, the lights went out again and they had *son et lumiere*: bright colored spinning reflectors blinking on and off in time to weird atonal music turned up so loud that it shook the cement floor.

For a minute, it was a kick. In ten, it was beginning to wear. In twenty, it was unbearable. After an hour, everyone was screaming in pain.

"You had enough?" Toot cried out over the public address system, her voice reverberating throughout the vast room.

"YES, YES, YES!"

"All right then," she said, switching off the light and sound, "go to sleep."

An hour later, they were rousted out again.

"How you feel now? How you feel?" Toot and the others demanded, crowding around them.

"Like shit," Jim responded.

"Like shit? You hear that, people? A little while ago he felt like a little nooky. Now he feels like shit. Well, let's give it to him, whadaya say?"

The others ran out the door, came back with a bucket full of a smelly brown substance, dug their hands in, and pelted Jim with it. As it turned out, it was only simulated shit, made of wet clay and fishmeal, but it took a minute or two to figure it out.

Afterwards, everyone took to calling him "Brownie."

And so, it went. For a whole week they were locked in, deliberately disoriented, bombarded with multi-media light shows, deprived of a sense of time.

To make things worse, everyone including Jim—who had so thoroughly succeeded in convincing himself that he was a junky by now that he no longer had to pretend—was going through withdrawal symptoms, and they had to be constantly soothed and talked through their crises.

After a few days, they were all in a state of virtual hypnosis, incapable of making the smallest decision. Like children, they asked permission to go to sleep, to get a drink of water, to go to the bathroom.

"How you feel?" their trainers kept asking. "What you feel like?"

"I feel like a inseck," the Asian woman said once, and Toot had everyone buzz in her ears for an hour. After that, she answered to the name, "Bug."

Another time, Donna said she felt like people walked all over her, so Toot had everyone walk on her, bruising her black and blue. Thus, she became "Steps."

Toot asked the young Puerto Rican kid what his greatest fear was. "I'm afraid of being locked up," he replied, so she locked them all up in a closet in the corridor for twenty minutes. "You're locked up!" Toot had them all chanting, pounding him on the back with the flats of their hands. "You're locked up! Come out of your shell! You got the key inside your head!" And his name was "Key" from then on.

The hipster claimed he was afraid of the dark, so she kept everyone in the dark for twelve hours, comforting him in his pain. Thus, "Nightlight" was born.

Key was the fuck-up. He was the one who had gone through the most severe withdrawal symptoms. He was the one who always held them back. In the beginning, they pitied him. Then they grew to hate him. And finally, they saw that they'd do better as a team if they got behind him and took up his slack. At first Key took advantage of this, lazed while the others worked. But soon, encouraged by Toot and the other trainers, he started to pull with the group. He still fucked up, but now at least he tried.

In the end, Key was the most beloved member of the group, and they doted on him like a baby. Once, when his withdrawal symptoms seemed unusually cruel, they all laid hands on his beautiful suffering body at once and rubbed him to sleep. Another time when he had a seizure and screamed out for his mama, they all took to kissing him spontaneously, and continued to embrace him, every part of him, till he reached a state of blissful quiescence.

Astonishingly, they'd become exactly what Eljay had said they would. They were one, a single, Mutual Support Unit, each valuing the others above himself, each giving according to his means, each taking according to his needs, and all of them enjoying it.

As an honor upon graduating from the Fishtank, they were allowed to name their own MSU. It was customary to choose a land animal—a symbol of their transition from the tempestuous sea of their experience to the safe dry land of Streetlight—as their logo. But it turned out that most of the usual names had already been used up. With a choice between Aardvark and Zebu, they unanimously chose the former, though none of them had a clue what an aardvark might be.

Out of the "Fishtank" and into the "Zoo," or general population, at last, going through the rigorous daily routine at Streetlight, the Aardvarks felt that they had achieved a tremendous victory. They were clean of drugs. Their abode was immaculate. Their life was well-ordered. They had plenty to eat. And though they were made to work ten hours a day scrubbing bathrooms and toilets, they got eight hours of undisturbed sleep. Also, they'd been assigned to the same dormitory, and they found that deeply gratifying, for their strict regime during Hell Week had tended to inhibit romance, and now they suddenly rediscovered their primal urges.

It started off with Nightlight. Back in the Fishtank, he said, he'd found something in himself that he never knew existed before.

"Layin' hands on dat beautiful, little, brown motherfucker," he said, while Key gazed shyly up at him. "I find out what I dig. And if he dig what I dig, we gon' git it on."

That night, listening to Nightlight and Key heaving and moaning in the bunk above, Jim got so hot he couldn't contain himself. Leaping from his bed, he jerked the mattress off, threw it out on the floor, dragged Steps out of her bunk by the hand, flung her down on the mattress, hoisted her tee shirt up over her hips, and went down on her as if he hadn't eaten in days. Hearing the commotion from her bunk, and feeling a like urge, Bug came down and joined them, and they ended up in a spinning triangle, with every likely orifice and protuberance engaged.

Thinking about it later, Jim found it remarkable, and highly commendable, that he had enjoyed bony, pop-eyed Bug quite as much as soft, round, full-breasted Steps.

Never had he felt more loving and accepting, been more loved and accepted. When he thought of the interchange between him and the other Aardvarks, he imagined it as a great shining orb of positive energy, a star made of iridescent skin and bones, its light reflecting clean through his body to his soul, filling him with waves of well-being, and a peace past understanding.

Only rarely did it occur to him that he didn't need this kind of shit the way a real junky might, that he'd embraced the teachings of the boss not as a convert but a spy, that his impulse to conform proceeded not from a desire to rehabilitate himself but to preserve himself in a hostile environment. And when it did occur to him, he quickly put it out of mind, like his terrible recurrent dream, the toolshed dream, that sometimes returned to haunt him in the light of day.

His only fear now was of losing what he'd gained at Streetlight, of having to admit—to himself, his MSU and clan—the unsavory truth.

CHAPTER TWENTY-FOUR

A Billion Points of Light

Tied up with a sweet loving bitch, serious as shit for the first time in his life, Ray didn't know what to do with himself. All through the dog days of August, he lounged with Molly in Monika's apartment, with the doors and windows locked, avoiding the garden and its fresh air like the plague, pigging out on root beer floats, tootsie rolls, ordered-in hamburgers, french-fries, and milk shakes, leaving the dishes and cartons to rot in the sink.

Aswirl in the accumulated smell of food gone bad and much unventilated sex, he waited impatiently every evening for Molly to return from her special summer school class, snorting at Monika's rapidly diminishing stash of coke, swigging Budweiser by the six-pack, tossing the empties in the corner, half-heartedly glancing at the Mets or Yankees game on TV, pointing an imaginary .38 Super at the screen and popping off opposing team members.

All night, he strained and moaned at her on the futon, frontwards and backwards and upside down, rolling in great hot pools of melded sweat and pubic fur, so totally absorbed in her expansive, unresponsive flesh, her victim's face—a face in which he saw and suffered and sanctified a long procession of similar victims—that the outside world ceased to exist.

Then one morning, lying behind her on the futon with his large dark dick reposing contentedly between the broad pink cheeks of her ass, he heard the phone ring beside the bed and reached across her hip to pick it up.

"Okay, you got yourself a deal," Shelley piped up on the other end of the line.

"About fuckin' time."

"There were some complications. For a while, it looked like I'd have to take it to another paper. Then, when I finally convinced the publisher that we had a Pulitzer Prize in the making, the Feds started giving us crap about the Witness Protection Program. Finally, this morning our lawyers cut a deal I think you can live with."

"Well, that's nice to hear, but the truth is, I don't give a fuck how we do it, or who we deal with," he responded, feeling his member start to stiffen again, running deeper into the crack, as Molly shifted her haunches on the futon. "As long as we see the end of this. All I wanna do now is get married and settle down."

"You sure you haven't been drinking, Ray?"

"Lemme tell you something, Shelley," he said, slipping his throbbing loaf into Molly's wet, hairy red hole from the rear, recalling a time, not so many years ago, when he did the same to this uppity lady on the other end of the line. "I mean, you might laugh, but it's so fucking simple, so true. The life of crime, it's a dog's life, right? Without a bitch of your own, nothin' counts, nothin's real, nothin's worth all the danger you put yourself in. It's just you out there, on your own. And who are you if it's you alone? You're dogshit. You dry up and blow away in the wind."

"Well, congratulations, Ray! never would've suspected. And I bet I know the lucky lady, too."

"You *know* you do!" he roared, hoisting Molly up into the canine position, shoving it to the hilt. And then, pulling it out again almost to the tip, he pressed the phone to her lips. "Right, Molly?"

"Uh, yeah, uh, yes!" she grunted, as he socked it to her again.

"Wow," Shelley breathed, on the other end of the line. "I guess stranger things have happened."

"I don't know where," he replied.

And then way down in the dark, oily depths of his predisposition, he felt the lifeblood start to gather, felt it come flooding up the shaft, bursting into the hot, shiny, pinball, world on the other side, and caroming from one bright bonger to another till it hit the 1000 buzzer and exploded into a billion points of light.

CHAPTER TWENTY-FIVE

To Live Is to Live Outside Yourself

A ripple of excitement ran through the armory from end to end. At first no one could figure it out. It was like the charged atmosphere before an electrical storm. Everyone got the jitters. No one could work or exercise. Lovers quarreled. Fights broke out for no reason.

Then word came around that the boss was to be brought in from Cold Spring. No one knew when, or how. But it was assumed that he would arrive that night.

So, Jim—or "Brownie" as he thought of himself now—and everyone else in the infirmary, including ambulatory patients, stood silently, patiently, waiting at the emergency room door till the wee hours of the morning, hoping that HE would appear.

At last, after hours of vigil, a private ambulance pulled up to the Emergency Room entrance. The attendants got out and stepped around to the back. They opened the rear door, slid out a dolly and laid it on the pavement.

The boss' bodyguards, Jazeel and Tall Boy, in black cowboy boots, black jeans and black leather jackets, leapt out of the ambulance behind the dolly, shoved the attendants aside, and wheeled the patient into the Emergency Room.

Gaping down at the reclining form of their leader, the junkies in the receiving line ooohed and aaahed, trembled and swayed together like spindly young poplars in a blast of hot wind.

The boss man, his massive head and arms bound in bandages and casts, grinned, winked a catlike eye, and saluted them like some great post-nuclear warrior injured on the field of honor, his blanched, Hunnish face lit with pleasure. Then he was whisked off down the corridor and locked inside his room, leaving everyone wide-eyed and panting with disappointment.

That night, however, and in the nights that followed, Brownie could observe him at closer hand. Working in the infirmary on the graveyard shift, sweeping and mopping, soaping wash basins, changing bedpans, scrubbing walls, he sometimes lingered after cleaning the boss' room and gazed down in wonder upon his great leonine head, the thick mane of tawny hair spreading around him on the starched, bleached-white pillow, under a sign that read, "TO LIVE IS TO LIVE OUTSIDE YOURSELF."

One night, perched over him so, Brownie was startled to see one slanted eye pop open, and return his stare from under heavy lids.

"The fuck you lookin' at, asshole?"

"Uh, just resting here on my broom for a sec, boss."

"Who the hell are you, anyway? Never seen you around here before."

"Brownie."

"When'd you come in?"

"Month or so ago."

"Hey, you don't look like no junky to me. Where you from?"

"California."

"No shit? I was out there for a while. But I'll take the Apple anytime. Bad as it is, it ain't phony. What you see is what you get."

"Uh, yeah, maybe you're right."

"You bet your sweet ass I'm right. You get out there in Lotus Land with your fucking relatives, ex-old ladies, old crime partners, it's all negative energy. Get with the program, man. You know what I'm saying?"

Brownie started to answer; but before he could, the boss had already changed the subject.

"Just wait'll I'm up and out of here. I got me some bad plans for this place. See, the thing is, you build something up, right? Something good. Something that saves lives. And people get jealous. Don't ask me why. It's human nature, I guess. You raise yourself up and they want to tear you down to their level."

"I don't think I get what you mean, boss."

"Here," he said testily, kicking at the crumpled *New York Star* at the foot of his bed. "Read it for yourself."

Brownie picked up the paper as if it were a dead mouse. Newspapers were not permitted in Streetlight; it was the first one he'd seen since the day he arrived. And he found its reek of the outside world, of disorder and sorrow, profoundly disturbing.

"DRUG GURU ACCUSED OF MURDER," the headline reads, "RAKOZI PAL TALKS TO FEDS IN IMMUNITY DEAL." And a bit farther down, "Exclusive Story by *Star* Reporter, Shelley Friedman."

"I . . . I . . . uh . . . see what you mean, boss."

"Lies," he said. "The rankest fucking falsehoods you ever heard. I know that bitch, see? The writer? And she got a grudge against my ass. From back in the day. We had a scene once. You dig? But don't think we're gonna take it lying down!"

"No way!" Brownie managed, but the headline had sent him into a funk that would last for days, the origin of which was his continuing inability to sort out where his true loyalties lay.

The boss man, on the other hand, seemed to get stronger by the hour. And it wasn't long before he was able to issue orders to his lieutenants, tape fireside chats, receive petitioners, conduct board meetings, and even bring lovers into his bed at night.

His current main squeeze was the luscious, black, Syreeta Brown, his executive assistant, though there were several others, of both sexes, including his bodyguards.

What Brownie found odd about these interludes was not the fact that the boss made it with men as well as women, or that he bit their necks and sucked blood till they had big red hickeys, but that immediately afterwards he always yelled at them to get the fuck out of his bed and smacked them upside the head.

It happened again and again, till Brownie began to suspect that his male and female lovers—on some level, at least—enjoyed the rough stuff as much as the boss.

It was like a ritual, an unwritten, unspoken contract. Al felt impelled to exert his power by sucking their blood, perhaps to prove to himself that his power existed, and for this he required someone to humiliate. They felt a need to re-enact the drama of their crime-ridden, guilt-ridden youth, and for this they required a vengeful vampire of a father figure.

But with the boss, it was even more complicated than that. Because, as soon as his lovers left the room, he went "*Yuck!*" to himself, and shivered with revulsion. Then he rang for the head nurse, a stout black matron called Naomi, to come and sponge-bathe him from head to foot and remake his bed with fresh linen.

One night though, after he'd sent one of his lovers away, the boss called Brownie over to his bed.

"That fuckin' black bitch," he rasped, fretting in his sweaty tangled sheets.

"Who's that, boss?"

"Naomi, goddamnit. I've rung her ten times if I rang her once and she still don't answer."

"Want me to see what's up?"

"Nah, why don't you do it?"

"Do what?"

"Wash me down and change my sheets, goddamnit, what do you think?

"Uh ... whatever you say, boss," Brownie replied, heading over to the wash basin.

Feeling not at all comfortable in this new role, he returned with a towel, a clean washcloth, a brimming bowl of hot water, and set about his task, soaping around the boss' cast and bandages, over his hard, sweaty chest and belly and around his comey crotch and ass and all the way down his wounded legs to his feet and toes.

"Haven't you forgotten something?" the boss complained when Brownie was done.

And though he knew damn well what he'd forgotten; he let the boss man see his puzzled look.

"My cock, you silly sonofabitch!" he shouted, pointing to his member that stood up from amongst the rumpled sheets like some great Leaning Tower of Pisa.

"Sorry, boss, but I'm not into that."

"Get down here and do it, you fuck, or I'll make you lick it off."

"No way," Brownie retorted, shaking his head slowly, stolidly. "No way."

The boss must have seen that he was serious because a moment later he left off trying and washed it himself.

"Alright, asshole, now help me change these fucking sheets," he commanded, when he was done, and Brownie set to, feeling as if he'd achieved some small but important victory.

Despite his harsh words, the boss called for Brownie again the next night, and the nights after that as well. Whether it was because he'd had the guts to defy him, or for some other reason, was anybody's guess.

Whatever the case, Brownie was immensely pleased. And not just because of these signs of the boss man's favor. A man who could accept such implicit criticism, he figured, could not be all bad.

With this in mind, he spent hours and hours in the next few days, between his work assignments and his obligations of time and attention to the Aardvarks, trying to analyze his feelings, sort out what was right from what was wrong.

If the boss had come up with the concept of the MSU, and the MSU was essentially good, how could the boss be as bad as he sometimes appeared to be, as bad as Shelley and everyone else believed?

If the boss was fundamentally good, then appearances were deceiving, and what Shelley and the others had said about him were either outright lies or false conclusions based on flawed evidence or bias.

On the other hand, if the boss was as evil as he appeared to be, as evil as many thought him to be, then the concept of the MSU was inherently evil as well, and Shelley and the others were right.

At present, the most compelling evidence Brownie had before him was his own MSU. Noting its obviously beneficial effects upon all its members including himself, he concluded that the MSU was a beautiful concept, a model for all humanity, and that therefore it must be inherently good. Being good, it could have only come from good.

Still, this conclusion—in constant, unreasoning competition with the evidence of his own eyes, and the memory of a beautiful, bikini-clad mama striding across a white, New York City beach with her naked little son in her arms—remained entirely theoretical in Brownie's mind, and might never have been resolved at all, if events themselves had not forced the issue.

CHAPTER TWENTY-SIX

Brainwashed

"It's a family emergency," Shelley said to the Streetlight operator, phoning from her cubicle in the newsroom at the *New York Star*. "His father just died."

A few minutes later, a man called "Eljay" came on the line.

"Mrs. Range, I've just spoken to your son, and he wants me to say that he grieves for his father, and he wishes you his deepest condolences. But he feels that right now it's better not to talk to anyone from the outside. He's afraid it might disrupt his therapy, and that wouldn't do anybody any good, would it?"

"Now just a second here, I insist on speaking to my son in person."

"All right," Eljay replied, and she could hear him cup the receiver with the palm of his hand. "I've just spoken to your son again, Mrs. Range, and he wants me to tell you that he loves you very much, and he's disconsolate over his father's death, but he just doesn't feel able to speak to you at this moment. He'll write you today, he assures me . . ."

Ringing off, Shelley jumped up from her desk and ran for Ben's office, nearly upsetting the coffee cart in her haste.

"He won't talk to me, Ben!" she shrieked, flinging open his glass door. "You think he's been brainwashed? Is he under duress? Shouldn't we try to get a court order and bring him out of there?"

"Now hold it right there, hon," he responded, looking up from a pile of news stories on his desk. "A court order's goin' take time, 'specially with Streetlight's lawyers on the case, and that'll just make things worse for him."

"Damn, I was crazy to send him in there."

"The hell you mean? It was his idea in the first place."

"Yes, but I went along with it," she insisted, shaking her head. "And he's not the only one who's been hurt by this story."

"Hey, the truth is strong shit, Shelley; you stir it up, people goin' get splashed," Ben said, and then turned in his swivel chair and pointed out his picture window, into the teeming city below. "You want to 'redeem' yourself? You want to help that boy? You keep after this story. It's a good story. It's the right story. You go at it hard enough, the walls goin' come tumblin' down around that Hunky bastard.

CHAPTER TWENTY-SEVEN

The Abyss

"Listen up! Listen up! New policy statement coming down!"

The cook slapped his knife on the cutting block. Sweepers dropped their brooms, moppers their mops. The aerobics teacher paused her taped Hall & Oates cut and had everyone run in place. In the used clothing warehouse, the donated can goods warehouse, the cardboard box factory, the utensil factory, the tee shirt factory, the shoe shop, laundry and commissary, workers froze in place.

The Aardvarks and other MSU's, lounging in the dorms on an R & R break, poured out onto the floor of the gym and gathered in a spontaneous circle, holding hands, and swaying together like some lost prehistoric tribe, awaiting the hour of their deliverance.

For weeks now, the boss had been out of bed, hobbling around on a cane, while Streetlight, subjected to a daily barrage of insults by the press and the federal prosecutor, sank deeper and deeper into the abyss.

Three board members had resigned. Backers in city hall, in the tabloid press, in public relations and real estate were deserting in droves. Funding had dwindled to a trickle.

News from the outside world, defying the boss' longstanding ban, breached the fortress-like walls of the arsenal with impunity. Rumors of destruction abounded.

"Utopia is under siege," the boss kept ranting over the in-house radio. "The forces of darkness are gathering round."

But his pronouncements remained vague, and he'd done nothing to organize an effective opposition to his enemies.

He seemed stricken, paralyzed by the forces arrayed against him, and spent his days locked up in his room with his favored lover of the moment, the brown and beautiful Key.

Flattered that one of their own had been chosen as the master's paramour, and that their position in the Streetlight pecking order had thus risen dramatically, the Aardvarks had kept a judicious silence. But the rest of the clan had grown restless, and they muttered aloud about being trapped aboard a rudderless ship.

Then yesterday, a fresh rumor went the rounds. "A new concept's coming down," it was said. An immediate hush fell over the place, and for hours everyone sat waiting with bated breath. After twenty-four hours had passed, however, with still no new concept, they grew even more restless, and whispers of mutiny were heard.

Finally, only minutes ago, Eljay came over the wire with the news they'd all been waiting for.

"Listen up! Major policy statement coming down!"

"Jesus, the boss is really something," Steps marveled, breaking the Aardvarks' trance-like state at last. "He's got this incredible ability to get us all stoked up about something before we even know what it is."

"Yeah," said Nightlight, who seemed to be taking the departure of his lover boy, Key, with amazing grace. "Boss man tell us what we want, even before we know we want it."

"Well," replied Brownie, his head like a vast, dark chamber full of milling, groaning sinners, each of them crying to see the light, "we need *something*, I can tell you that."

And just at that moment, the boss' voice blared out over the speakers.

"Batten down the hatches, babies, 'cause this is the final fucking phase," he began without preamble, his strong masculine voice, his rhythmic rapping phrases, sounding through all the high fluted chambers of the arsenal at once, through all of Brownie's echoing head, shattering the darkness, spreading the light. "Any clan member who's been in the military, any expert in weapons training or martial arts, should step forward now, because we are gonna start forming militia units in here, people, and seek our enemies in their lairs.

"Any former clan-member who badmouths us, any board member who goes over to the other side, any fucking reporter who lies about us, anyone who accuses us of crimes we did not commit, is gonna be notified that they are subject to the retribution of the clan. And if they continue to issue falsehoods against us, we are gonna convince them to hold their peace. And if they refuse to be convinced, we are gonna intimidate them into silence. And if they will not be intimidated, then we are just gonna send 'em to perdition, for we are in deep shit here, and they are to blame, and now it's payback time.

And suddenly, "Now's when we start stripping for war," the boss went on, seeming to gather strength from his own incendiary words, and the repetition of certain key phrases. "Now's when we separate the men from the boys. It's martial law time, troops. And in the name of martial law, I hereby issue the following decrees.

"Number one: everyone, including myself, will shave his fucking head today. You heard me. Not just the fish. All of us. We're a nation of skinheads now, people, and if you don't like it, then get the fuck out.

"Number two: as of this hour, in the interests of military secrecy, no one leaves the premises unless on a mission of war. You got an outside job, then you just quit, soldier, 'cause the gates are closed, and no contamination from the outside world will be tolerated.

"Number three: as of this hour, celibacy is the order. Lovers will immediately cease and desist, as a sign of unthinking loyalty to the clan.

"Number four: all MSU's are hereby abolished. The concept of the Mutual Support Unit is as dead as the dodo bird, and I don't care how long you been a part of one.

"Now we're just one big-ass clan, people, a nation of warrior monks. And if you think that's not democratic, then fuck you, 'cause this ain't no democracy. It's tyranny, babies. And I'm the fucking tyrant."

The response to the boss man's speech was instantaneous and overwhelming. It was like he'd dangled them all this time on purpose, like, when he finally got off the pot, they were so relieved that they just plopped in his water, happy as pigs in shit.

Without a squawk, without a peep, without even a flicker of revolt, everyone—including Brownie—changed tempo at once and started boogying to the boss' new beat as if they'd known it all their lives.

That night, sitting up in the cab of a Streetlight half-ton truck with Jazeel, heading down Interstate 95 for the state of Virginia, observing strict radio silence, with a certified check and an itemized order in his pocket for enough guns and ammo to withstand a six day siege, Brownie reflected that this strong and noble collective action that he had witnessed today, this unthinking rally to the common defense, this instantaneous manifestation of a single will, was something beautiful to behold, and stood out as a great marvel when compared to the ennui, the inertia and cynicism that he'd observed in the outer world.

And though he still had very mixed feelings about the boss' ban, he concluded that the beauty of Streetlight lay not in the boss himself, not in the boss as a *person*, but in the world that he—like some random god—had created, perhaps by accident. As a person, the boss man was but an icon, a battered and imperfect symbol of that beauty, which shone more truly in the people of Streetlight, in the culture which had evolved there, in the love and self-sacrifice and communal spirit that flourished there as an example for all humanity.

So strongly did Brownie feel this way, so proud was he of his loyalty to the clan, his obstinate, unreasoning faith in its fickle, cruel, and greedy creator, that he didn't even drive by Shelley's place on West Eleventh Street to see if her lights were on, tempted though he might have been.

CHAPTER TWENTY-EIGHT

Tina the Ballerina

Shelley found Mrs. O'Riley standing in the doorway to her apartment in Stuyvesant Town, dressed not in mourning clothes, as she had imagined, but in a faded, flower-patterned housecoat.

"Sorry I took so long," Shelley said, taking her hand. "But the least I could do, I thought, was come over and tell you how sad I was to hear about Mike's death."

"That's alright, dear." Behind Mrs. O'Riley, through the door, Shelley could see two other ladies, apparently neighbors, sitting with coffee cups in their hands. "I hate to say it, but I'm kinda gettin' used to it by now. And I still got another one, you know. Marty. Owns his own medallion cab."

"If there's anything I can do . . ."

"I'll tell you what you can do," she replied, raising her voice, causing her lady friends to prick up their ears. "You can get that man. The one who's responsible for this."

"I'll do my best. I promise."

Shelley smiled, gave Mrs. O'Riley's hand a last squeeze, and started for the elevator. Halfway there, she spun around, as if something had just occurred to her, and popped out with the question which had brought her here in the first place.

"Say, I wonder. You know, Penny's friend, Tina? I've never been able to get in touch with her."

"Yeah, I figured. I didn't read about her in the *Star*."

"Got any ideas?"

"Well, lemme see." Mrs. O'Riley stepped out into the corridor, allowing the door to swing shut behind her. "Tina used to have this boyfriend, Lennie. Another damn junky. Died of an overdose a few years back. But Tina's stayed close to his mother, I do know that."

"What's her name?"

"Rose Martell. Lives somewhere out in Queens."

"Thanks, Mrs. O'Riley, and I'll let you know if anything comes of this."

"You don't have to, dear, I'll read about it in the paper," she replied, following her to the elevator. "But there is one thing I'd like to know. Is it true what Al's lawyers said about you in the *Times*?"

"What'd they say?"

"Said you and Al used to be lovers, and this whole story's nothin' but sour grapes."

"What do you think?"

"I think they're full of crap."

"Go with your instincts, Mrs. O'Riley," Shelley said, and stepped into the elevator.

Downstairs in the lobby, she borrowed the security guard's phone book and found that there was an R. Martell listed at 29-76 Ditmars Boulevard, Astoria, Queens.

Rushing out to her car, she leapt inside and shouted the address to Manny.

"Jesus, what's all the excitement about?" asked Manny, whom Ben had hired, on the heels of the Streetlight story's success, as her temporary driver, bodyguard, and factotum.

"Never mind, just go, go!"

And only much later, as he crept over the Queensboro Bridge in bumper-to-bumper traffic, did her roaring surge of adrenalin ebb sufficiently to allow for explanations.

"Manny, this is gonna give us what we've been looking for all month. That is, if Tina is still alive."

"Refresh my memory," he said, lighting up one of his acrid cheroots.

"Corroboration of Jim and Ray's testimony."

"How you figure that?"

"Tina was Penny's best *friend*, for Christ's sake. You know how women talk. And she's not wanted by the police. Readers will *believe* her story. A jury will too."

Mrs. Martell's apartment building—gray brick, six stories high, half a block long—was located near the corner of Ditmars Boulevard and Twenty-Ninth Street, a block from the overhead railway line, and right under the flight pattern for La Guardia Airport, with short-haul jets whistling over every few minutes. There was a patch of yellow grass and a withered rose tree outside. All the other buildings in the neighborhood looked the same.

Leaving Manny in the air-conditioned comfort of his company car, Shelley climbed the stoop and punched Mrs. Martell's button, 5G. No one answered, so she sat on the stoop and waited. Ten minutes later a young Hindu woman in a beautiful red sari came up the walkway, pushing a pair of dark, little twins in a double stroller.

"Can I help you with that?"

The woman returned her smile and nodded.

Shelley picked up the front of the stroller and the two of them hefted it up the steps.

"Thank you verry verry much," the Indian woman said, still smiling, tilting her head from side to side in time to her words. "Dunno how I am doing this every day alone."

"Don't mention it," Shelley replied. "And maybe you can help me. I'm trying to reach Mrs. Rose Martell. She won a raffle at our Church bazaar, and we haven't been able to contact her. It's a considerable amount of money, so we're anxious to get it off our hands. Do you have any idea where I could reach her?"

"Mrs. Martell is never, never staying round here at this time of year. She is taking a cottage in Atlantic Beach."

"You wouldn't know the address, would you?"

"No, but the lady upstairs, Mrs. Pappas? She is feeding Mrs. Martell's birds. You might inquire of her."

Upstairs, Mrs. Pappas was, if anything, even more cooperative than the Indian woman, especially when Shelley brought up "the raffle."

Jumping back in the car, more excited than ever, Shelley directed Manny onto the Grand Central Parkway, around Flushing Meadows, past Willow Lake, and the Maple Grove

Cemetery, down onto the Belt Parkway, and around Kennedy Airport on Rockaway Boulevard, constantly prodding him to go faster, faster.

"Two cars back," Manny observed, as they rolled off the Atlantic Beach Toll Bridge, "there's a white Ford van like the ones they drive at Streetlight. He's been back there quite a while now, I think. And I might be gettin' paranoid or somethin', but this ain't the first time it's happened in the last couple of days."

"I don't know," Shelley reflected, turning around. "I can't get a look at his side panel, so I can't tell one way or the other."

Just as they turned off Ocean Boulevard onto Mrs. Martell's street, the van pulled over to the curb and stopped.

"I tell you what, let's just go have another look," Manny said, but by the time he looped around the block, the van had disappeared.

Mrs. Martell had taken a brick bungalow, a block from the beach, at 165 Oneida Avenue, directly under the flight pattern for Kennedy Airport, with big DC-10s and 747s roaring overhead every three or four minutes.

"So, maybe she likes airplanes," Manny said, as Shelley got out of the car, and she laughed.

No one answered the doorbell, though Shelley leaned on it for three minutes. Figuring that Mrs. Martell had perhaps gone off to the beach, Shelley climbed back in the car, and they settled in for a long wait.

"You know what, Manny?" she said, after five or ten minutes had elapsed in silence. "I can't tell you how sorry I am."

"For what?"

"For making you lose your job."

"Oh, fuck, not that again," he moaned, rolling his eyes, shaking his dark-rimmed head. "Shelley, you're a broken record, you know that?"

A half hour later, a fat, little, old lady in peroxided hair, a pink, peddle-pusher outfit, and gold sandals came waddling up the street, accompanied by a slight, pretty, dark-haired woman in her late twenties, wearing black, Chinese sneakers, black shorts, and a black tee shirt.

Evidently, they'd been to the supermarket, for they were laden with plastic A & P bags.

Neither of them looked like they ever got near the beach.

"The young one walks funny," Manny noticed, when they got closer.

Shelley turned and verified that indeed the young woman had a curious way of walking. Though she moved swiftly and easily, even with her load of bags, she tended to set her weight on her heels, with her feet splayed out at a forty-five-degree angle.

"Oh, I see!" Shelley blurted out, after observing her for another moment, "she's 'turned out.'"

"Say what?"

"She's a ballet dancer."

"How you know that?"

"I'm a fan."

When the two ladies turned in at Mrs. Martell's gate, Shelley slipped out of the car.

"Tina!" she called, and the young one stopped, whipped her long neck around, and stared at her for an instant, big-eyed, expressionless, like a startled doe. Then she whirled to bound away, and Shelley was on her like a deerhound.

"Tina, I'm so glad to see you!" she shouted, talking a mile a minute, dangling her press tags in front of her like a hunting license. "I'm Shelley Friedman and I've been trying to locate you for the longest time. I've been doing a story on Al Rakozi and Streetlight. Maybe you've seen some of it in the *New York Star*? And I thought you might be the one person who could help, even though I do know you've got every reason to maintain your privacy and keep your whereabouts secret . . . and believe me I'm perfectly prepared to honor that. So, what I'm looking for, really," Shelley said, pausing at last to take a breath, "is background, especially on Al and his relationship with Penny O'Riley . . ."

"Penny's dead," Tina replied, dropping her bright, intelligent eyes, starting again for the house.

"I know that," Shelley pursued. "What I'm trying to do, I'm trying to get to the bottom of that. Can you help me?"

Tina hesitated and glanced over at the fat woman, who sighed, nodded at Shelley, and proceeded up the front steps.

"I'm Rose," she said. "Come on in outta the heat, honey."

Inside, while Rose prepared iced tea, Shelley took a quick photo of Tina and then sat with her on a sticky, plastic-covered sofa, facing a defunct fireplace lined with pots of artificial flowers.

"You're a dancer, aren't you Tina?"

"Yes, how'd you know?"

"Oh, there's no missing it."

"Come on," Tina protested, but she smiled and flushed in embarrassment, and her beautiful, porcelain face—deadpan till now—illuminated the shabby living room with her pleasure.

Studying Tina again—marveling at the way her small, flawless head perched atop her elongated neck, the way an unruly ringlet of black hair spiraled down her pale temple, the way her lips puffed out—Shelley snapped a close-up of the girl and decided that there was something childlike about her ... something unripe ... despite her bright, intelligent face and physical grace.

"I'm Penny's oldest friend," Tina said when the tea came, choosing her words carefully for the tape recorder that Shelley had placed on the coffee table before her. "We grew up together in Stuyvesant Town, and from the time we were six years old we were scholarship students at the School of American Ballet. We were good dancers, each in our own way, and by the time we were sixteen we were being courted by several important companies, including the Joffrey. It's not just me saying that. They even did a story on us in your paper. 'The Baby Ballerinas,' they called us."

"It's true, it's true!" exclaimed Mrs. Martell, her eyes lit with pride. "I read it myself!"

"Then we discovered drugs," Tina went on, smiling penitently at her benefactress. "Three years later we were both strung out, dancing topless, turning tricks on the side to feed our habits."

"God," Shelley groaned, and reached out to stroke Tina's long, limp, bird-boned hand. "I studied ballet too, Tina, for years. I even considered making it a career. And when I think of some of the crazy things I did later ..."

Though Shelley's expressions of empathy were heartfelt, and she was truly touched by Tina's story, there remained at the same time another, smaller part of herself, the greedy, professional part, that was positively rejoicing. For here, she knew, she had a tabloid story of—as Ben would put it—"heart-stoppin' poignancy." In her mind's eye, she could already see the photos, the captions, the headlines, the by-name the *Star* would bestow upon her that all the other tabs would swiftly imitate: "TINA THE BALLERINA."

". . . finally, it got so bad with the drugs," Tina was saying, in her high, precise, little voice, "that we went to Ray Pagano, the boss of the club where we worked, and asked for his help. Ray got us into Streetlight. Penny met Al there, and they got married a few months later."

"What kind of marriage was it?"

"For the first couple of years it was all right," Tina replied. "Al couldn't do enough for her. Got her involved in everything he did at Streetlight. Eventually, she was running the whole show, on a day-to-day basis, which left him free to organize and raise funds. But Penny had enemies in Streetlight—jealous people. And they kept badmouthing her, whispering that she was 'stealing his fire.' Al did nothing to stop it. In fact, he stirred it up. He was right up front about it. 'Divide and rule,' he said. 'How else we gonna keep these fucking junkies in line?' He was even hurt when Penny complained."

Penny never doubted that Al loved her, in his own way, Tina explained. It was his *definition* of love that got her down. He thought nothing of having affairs with other women, and men too, right before her eyes. And there was always the ego factor. "It's like trying to live with Zeus," Penny said once. When the end came though, it wasn't over anything personal. It was a disagreement over policy. Al wanted to have Streetlight declared a religion, so the government wouldn't hassle him. And Penny thought it was total folly. She told him so to his face, in one of the board meetings. All the board members agreed with her. But nobody else had the guts to defy him like that, in public. He was furious. He called her a traitor, said he never wanted to see her face again. "You won't," she said, and walked out.

Penny had given a lot of time and energy to Streetlight, and she thought Al owed her something to make a new start. She knew better than to ask him for money. But she also knew that he had a private stash; Streetlight funds that he shipped out to Switzerland every year on the sly. So, she got into his stash, took thirty thousand dollars, left a note saying that she'd expose him if he gave her any trouble, and skipped the country with a black dude named Bobby O who'd been one of Al's pampered favorites.

From Al's point of view, this was the ultimate betrayal. He'd had no inkling that Penny would actually leave Streetlight. He'd told everyone that she'd come crawling back to him on her hands and knees. So, it was a devastating blow to his ego. He locked himself in his room. Wouldn't eat. Wouldn't see anyone for weeks. One could hear him in there talking to himself all night. One minute he'd be calling her "baby" and "sweetheart," swearing he couldn't live without her, the next he'd be screaming for revenge. For a while, he'd looked like he might actually commit suicide. When Tina and others tried to force his door, he threatened to burn the place down, send everyone up in his funeral pyre.

Finally, one day he asked for food to be brought in, and

they knew it was over. But when he came out, he'd lost his sense of humor about himself, which had always been his greatest quality.

"What were *your* feelings, Tina, after Penny was gone?" Shelley asked.

"I felt like there was nothing holding me to Streetlight anymore. I'd been clean for a long time. And the place was just getting too weird for my taste. So, one morning I left for my outside job and never went back. Al tracked me down, tried everything under the sun to hook me in again, including threats and intimidation, but I wouldn't budge. Then he just gave up on me, I guess. Next thing I heard, Penny and Bobby O were dead."

"Did you hear anything specific about how they were killed?"

"Yes, my Swedish friend Monika told me. She came to see me one day and said there was something she had to get off her chest. She and Ray had gone to Spain, she said, and Ray killed Penny and Bobby O there. Ray didn't want to do it, but the boss forced him to."

"How'd he do that?"

"Ray was wanted on a dope charge, and Al said he'd turn him in. But it was more than that. Al's got this kind of power. It's hard to say no to him."

"Penny and Bobby O had cocaine in their blood when they were found. Why do you think that was?"

"It's something that Al doesn't like to get out. Actually, it's very common for people to go back on drugs, once they leave Streetlight."

"Tell me one more thing, Tina. Why'd you decide to go into

hiding?"

"A couple of days after Monika got killed, one of Al's bodyguards, Jazeel, came by my place and threatened my roommate. Wanted to know where I was. Luckily, I was out. No telling what they got out of Monika before they killed her. That's when I asked Rose for help."

"Thanks Tina, and thank you too, Mrs. Martell," Shelley said, rising to go, snapping a quick pic of the two of them together.

"Don't mention it, dear," Rose sang out, jumping up like a servant to see Shelley out the door. "Now, you be careful with that Al Rakozi, you hear?"

"Oh, I will, believe me," Shelley replied, glancing up and down the street, checking for a white Ford van.

Two nights later, curled up with Teresa the cat on the living room sofa, nodding off in front of the Eleven O'Clock News, Shelley had to blink and shake her head twice at the ten second video clip that flashed across the screen: Tina the Ballerina, wrapped in a shroud of petroleum-colored seaweed, yet pale and lovely as the drowned Odette in *Swan Lake*, being fished from the bottom of Jamaica Bay.

"The cause of Tina Bowran's death is still unknown," the female commentator said, in portentous tones. "But according to neighbors, she was last seen in the presence of a large, bald, dark-complected male, wearing a black leather jacket."

About to shriek, about to cry, about to fall to her knees and beat the floor with her fists and send Teresa up the wall in fright, Shelley brought herself up short with the thought that she was jive, that what she really wanted was a sideshow, fireworks, to celebrate the fact that she could feel remorse for her actions. When the truth was that nothing, absolutely nothing she ever did, no matter how right or noble or true, could make up for what she had done to Tina the Ballerina. And in the cosmic scheme of things there would be very heavy freight to pay for that one, beautiful, "unripe" life.

With her crime thus exposed, its ramifications self-evident, Shelley sought in a panic for some way to mitigate its effects, or at least contain the damage.

The first thing to do, she realized, was to make sure that Toby was safe. She had to speak to Ben tomorrow, get him to invite her and Toby out to his place in Westchester till the danger was over. He and Wendy had a servant's cottage that wasn't in use, and a nanny who rode the train out every day from the South Bronx to watch over their kids. Toby would miss his little day-care friends, but he'd soon get on with the little Hirschbergs, playing with them all day in their big backyard while Ben and Shelley commuted into the city to work. At night, they'd catch the 6:07 home and Shelley and Toby would sleep in the servants' cottage. It was the perfect solution. If Wendy didn't like it, to hell with her. This was an emergency. It was about time they made up, anyway.

Next, she had to make a concentrated effort to save Jim from Streetlight. Tomorrow she would call Ray at his safehouse. "Ray," she would say, "you owe me one, man. You've got to help me get Jim out of that place before it's too late."

And finally—if she was serious about this—she had to leave

off her relentless pursuit of Al Rakozi before she put even more lives in jeopardy.

It was then that Shelley understood she was still fooling herself, that she had no intention of giving up her story, no matter what the consequences, that she'd die and go to hell and take the whole world with her before she let up on Al Rakozi, that a cataclysm of this sort might even be a prerequisite to his destruction, for his evil was on a grand scale, and when his pirate ship went down, there would be many who would go along for the ride.

CHAPTER TWENTY-NINE

The Safehouse

Way the hell and gone over to Jersey on the George Washington Bridge, along the west bank of the Hudson on the Palisades Interstate Parkway, across the state line on Route 9W and up the ass-end of New York to Piermont, Ray's safehouse made him feel so safe.

Piermont was this rinky-dink, little burg that looked like a fishing village transported by magic from Nova Scotia and plopped down on the fringes of suburbia. Old brick and wooden cottages cascading over a high, wooded bluff and descending in green, terraced steps to a narrow, cobblestone main street along the water line. No quaint shops. No tourists. Just folks. Mostly Italians, as it happened. With a well-behaved suede cat or two for local color.

Ray's particular house was about halfway up the bluff. A little, white Colonial, two stories high, with green trim, a small, neat front yard with a picket fence, and a huge backyard with a

lawn, a flower garden, fruit trees, and a hedge for privacy. There
was even a little, round, plastic, swimming pool.

Next door, on either side, a place just like his own. A house
full of kids. Dogs running around in the yard. A station wagon
parked out front.

Inside, it was all fixed up like maybe somebody's grandma
might've done it. Wallpaper, throw rugs, overstuffed furniture,
doilies on all the armrests and tables. A large sunny kitchen with
a breakfast nook. Two bedrooms upstairs, each with a squeaky,
old-fashioned double bed.

The FBI men kept their sound and video equipment in the
smaller bedroom. Four of them on duty at all times, two inside
and two out. But they came and went in eight-hour shifts, so
there was no occasion for them to sleep on the premises.

In fact, Ray would have been displeased if any of them ever
nodded off, knowing the boss and his capabilities.

He and Molly had the master bedroom. Out their large,
shuttered window there was a view down the hill to the town,
the Hudson River, the Tappan Zee Bridge, and the towers of
Manhattan sixteen miles across the water. The leaves were
starting to change, and everywhere you looked, it was green and
gold and rust. Sunny and warm in the daytime, cool at night.

Mornings, Ray got debriefed by the prosecutor's men in the
living room, in front of the video cameras—like a fucking movie
star!—while Molly soaked in the pool, sunbathed on the lawn,
strolled downtown with an FBI escort, or dusted the house just
to pass the time.

There was an hour break for lunch. Coffee and sandwiches
that Molly prepared on the run, during commercial breaks in

her favorite soap opera.

Then Ray and the Feds headed back to the living room for four more hours while Molly did the dishes, took a siesta, and watched her game shows on TV.

So, this one day, Ray was sitting at the dining room table facing two FBI men, young Agent Flynn, and middle-aged Agent Brown. A large tape recorder lay on the table between them.

"Hey, tell me, Ray," Agent Brown asked, "why'd you and Al head out to Synanon, back in the day?" Ray was about to answer when the phone rang. Agent Flynn turned off the tape recorder. Agent Brown rose, crossed the room, and picked it up.

"Yeah?" he answered. "You sure? Okay."

He stepped over and handed the phone to Ray.

"Hello? Yeah."

Shelley was on the other end of the line. Wanted him to tell her the easiest way to get someone out of Streetlight.

"Who you wanna get out?"

"Jim Range."

"You mean the dude who was fucking Monika and gave her the crabs and caused all this shit? Is that who you're talkin' about?"

"Listen, you owe me one, Ray. Come on!"

"Awright, awright" he said, just to get her off his back. "But gettin' someone outta that place? It ain't easy, you know?"

He hung up.

"You gonna do it?" Agent Brown wanted to know.

"I doubt it," said Ray.

"Why should you?" Agent Flynn put in.

"I mean, what is this Range? A fuckin' coward. A Vietnam

deserter."

"What you ought to do is this. Tell Rakozi what she wants. And that crazy sonbitch, he'll tear the place down looking for the apostate."

"Apostate?" Ray asked. "The fuck's that mean?"

CHAPTER THIRTY

An Unmanned Missile

"Hey, have you heard the latest?" Steps wanted to know, when bald-ass Brownie got back from his gun run to Virginia. "There's a spy in the clan, working for the *New York Star*."

"But how . . . how do we know that?"

"Some anonymous caller."

And suddenly it was like he was regarding her for the very first time in his life, as if he had not been looking at her from inches away, touching her, feeling her, smelling her every day and night for weeks.

What he saw now was a plump middle-aged woman with a lumpy shaved head, a furrowed red face, and crazy blue eyes, on her knees in the infirmary lobby beside a pail of soapy water, making quick nervous circles on the vinyl floor with a rag, her coarse gray sackcloth jumpsuit ballooning around her body like a clown costume.

"But why . . . why should we believe an anonymous caller?"

he asked, turning to glance at himself in the shiny infirmary window—*That guy in there, that extraterrestrial with a head like an unlit lightbulb, that's Brownie, that's me.* "Maybe it's just someone stirring up trouble."

"His information was totally convincing," Steps replied, bent over her work, her tone sharp and metallic, pinging off the hard white vinyl in a rigid party-line that managed at the same time to sound spacey and all-accepting. "There can be no mistake. He knew all about us. He wouldn't divulge the informer's name, but he did say that he was a recent arrival, he was white, and he was not from the New York area."

"Jesus, there's twenty people in here who fit that description."

"Including yourself," she reminded him, then paused in her work and sat up on her heels to take his measure.

A day later, Brownie was standing in a line of twenty scalped and stripped white men with pink shriveled dicks on a stage set up at the far end of the armory gym.

The boss strutted up and down in front of them on his stumpy legs like a bald-pated, tin-pot dictator, waving his cane in the air.

And the clan behind him filled the great resonate space with their hissing voices like some mighty confabulation of angry insects.

The boss man raised a hand.

The room went silent.

"Now it's Brownie's turn. His old MSU knows him best, right? Steps, what do you say?"

"He didn't have any real withdrawal symptoms when he got here, boss. I mean, he went through the motions, but it wasn't very convincing. He didn't suffer the way we did."

"Nurse, can you give us a rundown on the suspect's physical status when he got to Streetlight?"

"Trace of heroin in blood. One recent skin perforation in lower left forearm. No sign of chronic addiction."

"Now this is getting interesting. Is there anyone else in the audience who's willing to come forward?"

"Yo, boss! He got a call from the outside not too long ago. Some woman. Said she was his mama. Said his dad had just died. But she sounded too young to be his mama."

"Thank you, Eljay. Now, is there a chance, Brownie, that I'll recognize that voice? Because, you know, we record all incoming and outgoing calls."

Brownie bowed his head like some small furry animal, dragged in by the cat and set down before the master, still alive.

A moment later, he lay stretched out on the floor of the gym, while the clan cried out for his blood.

"Death to the traitor! Death to the traitor!"

Yet, the boss stood firmly beside him, warding them off.

"Don't listen to them, man, don't listen. Let it go. Let it all come out. Everything you been holding back."

And then like in a dream, he poured out the whole long story of his life, starting with a crystalline memory from the age of three when he was molested by a prison trustee who worked mowing the Range family lawn, and ending with his pact with the she-devil, Shelley Friedman.

When he coughed up his last confession, the crowd went

silent.

"See?" said the boss, in his compassionate mien. "You don't blame the victim, people. You don't blame the one who was used and abused. He confessed. He repents. Now's the time for redemption."

And then the loving hands. All over him. Waves of them, pulsing up and down his spine like electric charges. Till he was an unmanned missile again, primed and loaded and buzzing with encoded instructions, waiting to be fired.

CHAPTER THIRTY-ONE

A Caricature of Evil

"Okay, I'll cry 'Uncle,'" said Al, standing with Shelley under the Brooklyn Bridge, the only neutral place they'd been able to agree on, while evening rush hour traffic roared over their heads, and their bodyguards—one apiece, according to the ground rules—hovered behind them, smoking cigarettes. "Why don't you call off the dogs?"

"'*Uncle*?'" Shelley laughed, wondering why he'd suddenly decided to shave his skull. Bereft of his tawny, luxuriant mane—about which he had once been so vain—it turned out to be pointy-eared and misshapen, with bulging blue veins and jagged white scars. "You think that'll do it, huh? That's all justice demands."

"You don't like it? I'll up the ante. You stop all the trash, and I'll let your pretty boy go."

"Which of my pretty boys are you talking about, Al?"

"We call him 'Brownie.' That's because he's always getting

himself into shit."

"What's his real name?"

"Jim Range."

"Never heard of him," Shelley replied, glancing over her shoulder at Manny her bodyguard to make sure he was on his toes.

"That ain't what *he* says." Al turned casually, leaning on his cane, to check on his own bodyguard, an enormous black man named Jazeel with a head like a polished coconut. "He claims he's working for you."

"He's lying."

"Alright, let's put it this way. If you did have a guy in there working for you, would you be willing to make a deal to get him out?"

"Why would he want to get out? I thought you had a workers' paradise in there."

"That's true, but he hasn't been too comfortable since we found out he's a traitor to the cause."

"Just for the sake of argument," Shelley said, feeling sweat beading up under her arms, in the crease beneath her breasts, "if I had a guy in there, and you wanted to make a deal with me to get him out, I'd say he's not yours to keep. We have laws about holding people against their will."

"What if he likes it where he's at? What if he gets a kinky, little thrill, suffering for all his crimes against us?"

"Then he's got no reason to come out, has he?"

"He might, if I brought him around to it. Let's put it this way. Old Brownie, he's kind of leaning on my every word, these days. Just don't seem to have a mind of his own."

"If in fact your prisoner were an employee of mine," Shelley said, watching a police helicopter hovering over the choppy, gray East River, just over Al's shoulder, and wondering what poor drowned soul it might be searching for, "I don't think he'd want me to compromise my principles, even to get him out of your clutches."

"You haven't seen him lately. If you had, you might talk different."

"What've you *done* to him?" Shelley cried, losing it, causing Manny to shift nervously behind her, and Jazeel to frown and pat the gun under his black leather jacket.

"Woo, now we're hittin' close to home!" Al crowed, smiting out with his cane at the Fulton Fish Market debris—soggy cardboard boxes, bloody plastic wrappers, scaly newspapers— that littered the ground around them. "You're so fucking concerned, why not make a deal?"

"What deal is there to make?" she said bitterly. "The fifth installment of the story's already gone to press. The federal prosecutor has forty-six hours of video-taped testimony from Ray Pagano, not to mention the two hours I got from Tina Bowran, before you had her blown away. And next Monday, the prosecutor goes before the Grand Jury seeking an indictment charging you with thirty-eight counts under the RICO statutes. That's enough to put you away for about a century and a half.

"Meanwhile, we've got informers coming at us out of the woodwork. There are a million termites gnawing at your foundations, Al. Streetlight's so rotten, it's collapsing from within. I mean, why not give up the ghost? Let the guy go. Call up the Feds and try to work out a plea for lesser charges. It's your only chance."

"I'll see you in hell," he said softly, his voice for the first time registering something approximating true feeling, "before I give up everything I've worked for, leave those poor junkies out there all alone, with no guidance, no hope for the future ..."

"I'm afraid you're not going to have much choice, Al. If I were you, with your 'deep' concern for Streetlight, I'd go gracefully, start arranging for my own succession."

"Don't gloat, Shelley, don't gloat," he sighed, shaking his head. There was no longer much animosity in his tone, only a kind of wistful, world-weary quality, with a touch of self-pity. "It ain't over till it's over."

"You're right there," she retorted, wishing she'd packed a wire—their ground rules included a pat-down by their armed bodyguards before the meeting. "Is there any statement you'd like to make now to the press?"

"Sorry, but my lawyers tell me I oughta keep my big mouth shut."

"Sound advice."

"Whoa, you got me there," Al laughed, but he wasn't really hearing. "I'll tell you what, though. There is one thing, Shelley. You never answered my question. And before this is over, I'd really like to know. Why have you gone so far, worked so hard to destroy me, when I never did anything to you, except maybe show you who you really are?"

Shelley skipped a beat before answering. Al's aggrieved tone, coming now, after all she had learned about him, was hard to bear.

"I guess I'm just old-fashioned," she replied at last, looking back at Manny again to assure herself that he was on the alert, and then letting fly with everything she'd been holding back: "None of this New-Age, Buddhist shit for me, man. I see a fly, even if I knew him way back when, as just a tiny maggot, I pick up a swatter!"

"Ooooooh, the lady is bad!" he rapped, smacking his desert boot with his cane, playing to the bodyguards, getting all excited about himself again. "But really, Shelley, tell me the truth. Did I knock you up or something? Is that it? You had to face the knife alone? Or like maybe I left you with a dose of the clap? Or maybe, like a lot of young girls with bad motherfuckers, you thought you could domesticate my ass. And then when you couldn't, you got all resentful and shit. Wouldn't be the first time, I can tell you."

"Like I told you before, Al," she said, marveling that he'd hit so close to the mark. "I'm a reporter. I'd forgotten your existence until you became a story."

"Oh yeah, is that right?" he responded, puffing up his chest, narrowing his eyes at her. And it was such a caricature of evil that it would have been funny if . . .

But Al was wrong about her; she'd never yearned to change him. It was his dark side that turned her on in the first place. And for its sake, she has stayed on for days in that East Village pad they called home, enduring his perversities with shrieks of pleasure and pain, till some residue of self-preservative instinct kicked in one night while she lay stoned with him on his sopping bathroom floor and—scratched and bleeding, carrying his venomous spawn—she rose like a succubus from his body, peered into his cracked medicine cabinet mirror, saw her crazy

'British War Bride' mother staring back at her, understood at last that beyond ecstasy there was nothing, only death, and walked out of his flat, out of his life forever, she thought.

"Is that right?" Al went on. "Well, I'm telling you for the last time, Shelley, back the fuck off."

"And if I don't?"

"You got a kid, right?"

"Come on, Al, you've been watching too much TV."

"You think I'm joking?"

"No, I just think you're full of shit," she said, and instantly regretted it, because he hawked up a big one and spat full in her face.

Wiping it off with the back of her wrist, she was vaguely aware that he'd wheeled around and was hobbling back toward his bodyguard.

Then suddenly he dropped his cane, jerked forward, and fell flat on his face.

At first, she thought he'd had a stroke or a heart attack. But then she saw Jazeel with a gun in his hands, a huge heavy-looking thing, a .357 Magnum by the looks of it.

He fired over Al's prone body, a great jet of flame and smoke flaring from the muzzle, and Shelley thought she'd been hit, because she was lying on the ground with Manny on top of her.

She heard another shot, and Jazeel stumbled backward, with the pistol still in his hands, and Al was up and limping off toward his waiting van, bent over low, stumbling over trash, trying to keep balance with his cane.

Manny fired again, the noise deafening her ears, and Jazeel fell in the river.

"You alright, Shell?"

"I . . . I think so. How about you?"

"Not . . . not so good," he rasped. "That chopper still flyin' around?"

"I don't see it."

"Then I think you better get to a phone," he murmured. But he made no move to rise, and she could feel something wet and warm soaking through her jacket and blouse, puddling up beneath her.

"Manny?" she whispered, as Al barreled off in the Streetlight van. "Manny?"

CHAPTER THIRTY-TWO

Every Dog Has His Day

In the evenings, after Ray was done with the FBI, he and Molly would sit together in the window of their room, sipping Irish whiskey, munching on Fritos and potato chips, tossing the wrappers in the corner, not saying much. Not snorting much either, though Ray still had a gram or two from Monika's stash. Not feeling the need to, for the first time in longer than he cared to remember. Just taking the breeze. Smelling the new-mown grass and burning leaves. Listening to the kids playing in the yard next door. Watching the sun go down behind the bluff, and the colors—red and purple and blue—it makes on the wide Tappan Zee below. And then the dog star, his star, Sirius, the brightest fixed star in the firmament, rising above the big maple tree in the front yard.

The nights were full of flying fur, of licking and panting, sniffing in private places, of nips, yelps and growls, and the squeaking springs of their bed.

From downstairs the sound of low voices came floating up. The slap of cards on the kitchen table. A Mets game on the radio in the unmarked police car out front.

And from farther off, the whine of diesel engines in the railroad yard outside of town, the hoot of the whistle in the pet food cannery down by the water.

Neither of them had a care in the world, though they'd not a clue what they'd do, where they'd go, how they'd make a living, once they were out on their own.

They had even considered moving to Ireland, where no one knew Ray as anything but an upright citizen. Open a kennel, maybe, raise bulldogs for a living.

Molly had missed her period, and they were both so sure she was pregnant, and so blissed out by the fact, they hadn't even bothered to get it verified by the medical profession. It was like: Hey, not to worry, the Feds will take care of it all.

Every dog has his day, and this was Ray's.

CHAPTER THIRTY-THREE

The Second Story Man

One night, the boss took Jim aside and whispered in his ear. "An admirer of mine with connections in the federal prosecutor's office has provided me with the address of the traitor's safehouse. Only trouble, they got it so over-guarded, it'd take some kind of . . ."

"Second story man, right?"

"Right."

"That's me," said Jim.

So, the next morning at dawn, he tied a sheet to the leg of his bed, dropped secretly from the infirmary's second story window, and made his way from Manhattan to Piermont by public transportation.

Checking into the town's one motel under an alias, he spent the next few days sleeping in the daytime and sneaking out at night, climbing backyard fences, walls, and trees, crawling over roofs on his belly, sussing Ray's safehouse.

The Feds were lax, he found. Spent all their time playing cards in the kitchen or listening to the radio in the squad car out front. None of them ever went out to check the yard, and they'd gotten rid of their police dog because—he overheard them say—Ray's old lady complained that he shit on the grass where she liked to sunbathe.

Jim waited for a cloudy, rainy, moonless night. Packing all his equipment on his back and in his belt, he approached the safehouse from the rear. Sprinted across the floodlit backyard. Climbed the rain drainpipe. Tied on a rope so he could rappel back down. Bellied across the roof. Tied on another rappel. Figured the rest would be easy-breezy.

CHAPTER THIRTY-FOUR

Payback

Ray's tranquil life in Piermont went on for so long that he sold himself on the preposterous notion that it would last forever. Then one cold rainy night he woke up and heard something on the roof. At first, he thought it was an animal, a racoon or something. But it sounded too heavy for that. He was just about to let out a holler, summon the law on the double, when it stopped, and he figured it must have just been his imagination, or a tree limb rubbing on the roof in the wind.

So, he dropped off again and next thing he knew—whoa!—there was a dude standing in the room, dripping rain.

How he'd found the safehouse; how he'd slipped past the Feds; scaled the wall; dropped down to the window from the roof; jimmied it open and swung through without a sound; Ray would never know.

One thing he did know, this guy was no mere second story man. He was a fucking Houdini. And Ray knew better than call for the FBI. A tall, thin man, he was all business, leaning under the low, sloping ceiling, waving a little .22-caliber Hit Man Special, with a silencer from one form to the other in the tangle on the bed.

"Ray?" the dude murmured, and right away he knew who he was dealing with.

It was payback time.

And Ray had imagined he was playing it so cool and cunning.

"Kill two birds with one stone," he had told himself, taking Agent Brown's advice. "Give out just enough anonymous shit to stir the bait, and the boss, the paranoid fuck, he'll tear the place down chasing his own tail before he finds the snitch."

Now, too late, he wished fervently that he had never picked up the telephone. And he made his final decision. In a lifetime of ignoble acts, this last would stand out like a pearl among fish eggs, a rose on a hill of dung.

"Easy down, Jim. I give you no trouble, bro, just don't hurt my wife."

"Your wife?" he croaked, twitching his head like the words were wasps buzzing around his ears.

"Yeah, my wife," Ray insisted, while she slept the deep, deep sleep of the just, her breath steady beside him. "The mother of your child or mine."

"Slide off that fucking bed!"

The dude was not listening. The boss had gotten to him. You could hear it in his tiny, screechy, off-tune voice.

"Stretch out on the floor, face down!"

So, very slowly, taking care to make no threatening

movement, Ray scooted on his thick and hairy haunches across the love-soiled sheets to face with only one fear, one regret, this infernal machine with the short-circuited eyes and the herky-jerky motions.

"Promise me," Ray begged, as he played dead for him on the floor. "Promise you won't hurt her."

"I promise," he breathed, and the dog star, Ray's star, sheared across the night sky and struck the dark horizon without a sound.

CHAPTER THIRTY-FIVE

An Unquiet Grave

He had a luminous digital watch to record the passage of the days. His rucksack was loaded with compact high protein bars and a five-gallon water container. He'd brought salt pills, prescription sleeping pills, and heavy tranquilizers to keep him quiet for hours on end. He had even remembered to carry along a watertight plastic bag to excrete and urinate in. He'd thought of everything, except his own demons.

In the tiny cubbyhole where he lay hidden under the roof, it was always dark, always close. In the daytime, it got too hot. At night, too cold. Even the smallest movement stirred up the fine dust that lay inches deep on the floor, plugging his nostrils, burning his eyes. Spiders and cockroaches crawled across his face. Fleas get into his clothes. He itched all over from lack of a bath. His breath reeked, and his teeth felt like they were growing webs. His limbs ached, and he'd developed bed sores from lying down so long in one cramped space.

To avoid detection, he could only empty his waste container at night, during a heavy rain, out of the ventilation duct under the eaves through which he had entered. Since this confluence of events occurred only twice, he spent most of his time in the attic sickened by the smell of his own wastes.

Meanwhile police helicopters clattered overhead, police hounds bayed after his scent, police voices sounded below as they searched the neighborhood.

Yet he could deal with everything, except his own demons.

In lucid moments, he understood that a family lived below him. A mother, a father, two boys and two girls, ranging in age from about fourteen to four. Their voices, the bustle of their comings and goings, floated up to him in the attic like characters in a 1940s radio program entitled "Family Life," complete with sound effects.

In his non-lucid moments, he believed that he was lying up in the attic of his parents' Folsom Prison guard's cottage, circa 1956, eavesdropping on the Range family.

In his very worst moments, he thought he was dead, that he had died one time when he was meant to die, at the age of seven when he fell off a boating dock and sank into the muddy Sacramento River.

A small, formless, voiceless ghost lost somewhere between heaven and hell, he was condemned to hover forever just above the heads of his nearest and dearest, listening to their conversations: "Your fault, Bill. Your fault, goddamn you to hell. Turned your back on that boy and he was gone. Just like that other time. Out at the toolshed . . ."

Sometimes he thought he heard another family in the house

below. Shelley and Toby in the future.

Toby is bigger now, about ten or eleven, going to school. Shelley commutes to the city to work. In the daytime, the house is empty for hours. Late in the afternoon, he hears Toby come in the front door. Raiding the fridge and cupboard for milk and cookies. Watching TV. Then Shelley pulls up in her car. Shelley in the kitchen, rustling up some supper. Toby, reciting his English lesson—the poems of Robert Service—in his room. After supper, he can hear her helping him with his Math, scolding him about taking a shower, putting him to bed, repeating the ritual *"Buenas noches, te amo, duermes bien . . ."*

At such times, he ached to be with them, ached from his own absence in their lives. Yet, with his eyes caked in dust and dried mucus, he was denied even the solace of tears.

This, he despaired, this is what death is.

And his state of mind grew more precarious.

He heard shrieks in the night. Heard a whole chorus of voices, Monika and a host of others he'd never heard before, crying, "Die! Die! Die!"

It was as if, in murdering Ray, he had somehow assumed all of Ray's guilt, and would have to endure forever the wailing of his victims. For hours, they railed at him, to the point where he would have done anything—thrust the bitter oily barrel of his weapon between his lips, suck on it like a baby—to shut them out.

Then, time and again, just as he was about to squeeze the trigger, they would fade away. And it occurred to him, as if in a revelation, that life is beautiful, if you can only get out of your shell, if you can only get rid yourself of the echoing voices.

"TO LIVE IS TO LIVE OUTSIDE YOURSELF," read the sign above the boss' infirmary bed.

How simple, he thought, how wise, how ancient, how true.

Why is it so hard to do?

The thing was, Al and his minion Steps had promised to create a diversion to enable Jim's escape. That had been the plan. She'd rented a car with a phony credit card and was supposed to be pretending to have trouble with it just down the street. For five minutes, Steps was supposed to sit out there gunning it, to disguise any sounds of struggle in Ray's safehouse.

Yet at the penultimate moment, standing at the foot of Ray's bed in the dark, dripping water, Jim had heard only wind and rain on the roof.

On the verge of aborting the mission, the assassin-to-be had mulled his options, and there came a moment when Ray's life hung by a thread. But in the end, Jim stepped on his neck and shot him in the back of the head anyway, not so much for the boss man or the clan, as for his own personal reasons.

Rappelling down the rain drainpipe, he could hear the FBI agents clomping up the stairs, banging on Ray's door, breaking it down.

For some reason, Molly remained silent.

He found neither Steps nor the car at their rendezvous, and wondered what had become of her, though he was still not overly concerned.

Driven by a suspicion that Steps and the boss might fail him, either by mistake or on purpose, he had taken the trouble to scout out a fallback hideout, a cubbyhole in a disused attic five blocks away, in case of just such an emergency. So, by the time the G-Men had collected their wits enough to organize a posse, he was ensconced in the unquiet grave where he found himself now.

CHAPTER THIRTY-SIX

The Kiss of Death

"The D.A. refuses to indict," Shelley said. "Calls it 'a face-off between two puffed-up bodyguards.'"

"Now wait a goddamn minute here," Ben seethed. "What about Tina the Ballerina? Did it ever occur to the silly bastard that this black ass sonofabitch, Jazeel, fits the description of *her* murderer too?"

"Ben, as a favor to me, can you just leave off on your racist—"

"Okay, let's call him a 'Negro gentleman,' then. How's that?"

"Not much better ... Anyway, yes. It did occur to the DA that Jazeel fit the description. And he had two of the witnesses view the body. But neither one of them was able to make a positive identification."

"Now don't tell me the Feds are fixin' to sweep the dust under the rug too." Ben stepped out from behind his desk now, and approached Shelley truculently, as if the whole thing were somehow her fault. "You ain't goin' tell me *that,* are you? Guy comes in there, whacks their star witness right under their fuckin' noses. They must be angrier'n hornets."

"What're they supposed to do? Molly couldn't describe the assailant. Knowing her, she probably slept through the whole thing."

Ben waved the air in a sign of disgust and futility. "What's the lawyer say? How's this goin' affect the government's case?"

"With no courtroom witness, he says, it's possible Al will get off. Juries don't like to accept the testimony of *live* murderers, leave alone dead ones."

"Aw, shit!" Ben fumed, smacking the wall with the back of his fist, setting all his framed boxing photos to rattling. "That slippery sonbitch is always two steps ahead of us. What pisses me off, we ain't even figgered out what *motivates* his ass yet."

"Relax, he doesn't know that himself."

"Now don't get cute on me, Shelley."

"Really, the more I learn about him, the more I'm convinced. You go up and ask him, 'Hey, Al, how come you do the way you do?' and I bet he couldn't tell you. It's like asking the lion, 'Why do you like raw meat?'"

Just then the phone on Ben's desk rang. He picked it up, frowned, and passed it to Shelley.

"A call for Ms. Shelley Friedman from a Mr. Jim Range. Will you accept the charges?"

"I will," Shelley answered, motioning for Ben to listen in.

"Hi," Jim said. His voice sounded muffled, as if he were talking from behind a scarf or something.

"Hi," she said. "Where are you?"

"I ... I'm out of town, not too far away, but I'd rather not say exactly where; at least not over the phone." Jim spoke more slowly than Shelley remembered, with a slight tremor that she didn't like at all.

"What happened in Streetlight? Why didn't you answer my call?"

"I got tied up."

"Would you like to set up a meeting?"

"That would be really nice."

For some reason they'd begun talking as if they were remote business acquaintances, rather than former lovers.

"All right. Is it okay if I bring my editor along?"

"I'm sorry, but that wouldn't be convenient. I'd rather meet you alone."

Across the desk, Ben shook his head firmly.

"I tell you what, Jim. I can't talk now. Is there some place I can reach you?"

"Not really. Could I call you tomorrow?"

"Of course. Same time?"

"That'd be great!" he exclaimed. And his tone, full of false enthusiasm, like that of some poor job applicant trying hard not to be put off, was enough to drive her to tears.

"Now Shelley, don't you even *think* about seein' that boy alone," Ben warned that night, as they rode the 6:07 out of Grand Central Terminal. "No tellin' how they got him brainwashed, what they put him through. Only way you goin' see him is in an empty room after he's been shook down, and two or three security guards lookin' on."

And by the time they reached Katonah, he had just about convinced her.

Wendy picked them up in the station wagon, with the back full of spaniels and squirming, squealing kids.

Toby was hollering, *"Mamá, Mamá, Mamá!"* at the top of his lungs, to be heard over Ben's kids—Eudora, William and Erskine, ages two, four and six—who were screaming, "Daddy, Daddy, Daddy!"

They piled in beside Wendy, a tall, gaunt woman in a flower-print, cotton dress with a Peter Pan collar, and she headed up Third Street past the old bottle factory and the graveyard while the kids continued to jump up and down in back and shout at the tops of their lungs.

Now it was, "Ice cream, ice cream, ice cream!"

So, she pulled over at the Tastee Freeze on Katonah Avenue while Ben got out to fill their request.

Then on their way up Quarry Road they got behind a dump truck and had to roll the windows up.

By the time they made it home to the Hirschberg place on Reservoir Hill everyone was sweaty, sticky, and covered in dust.

"Say, how come you brought the kids along today?" Ben asked, wiping his brow, as they were getting out of the car.

"Had to," Wendy responded, in her flat Kansas twang. "The nanny quit."

"Just like that?" Shelley asked, as Toby and the Hirschberg kids leapt out with the dog and made a beeline for the swings and jungle bars in the backyard.

"Yep."

"No notice?" Ben wondered. "No reason?"

"Nope. Just fed the kids their supper, walked out an hour early, and said she wouldn't be coming back. 'Well, at least let me drive you to the station,' I said, but she wouldn't hear of it. Started walking off down the road. Said her brother was picking her up at the corner. I owed her two day's pay, but she wouldn't take it."

"Well, goddamnit to hell!" Ben raged. They'd reached his long, low, ranch-style, front porch now, and he was fumbling with his keys in anger. "That is weird. Most bizarre fuckin' thing a nanny ever did."

"Won't do any good to curse." Wendy pushed past him, produced own set of keys with a flourish, and opened the door. "Just have to call the agency, start interviewing again."

"That's going to take time," Shelley said, as she and Wendy settled on the living room sofa, and Ben stepped up to the wet bar to make them all a drink. "I'm afraid Toby and I are just going to be an extra burden here."

"Not at all," Wendy replied. But she'd taken the time to clear her throat and swallow before replying.

Wendy had let it be known on several occasions, since Shelley's and Toby's sudden arrival in Katonah, that they were being suffered only at her husband's insistence. And she had proven impervious to all of Shelley's attempts to win her over.

"No, really, you guys," Shelley insisted, lighting a cigarette, accepting Ben's proffered bourbon-on-the-rocks with a forced smile. "I think it's about time Toby and I got our own place, anyhow."

"Well, suit yourself, hon," Ben said. He had slipped off his cowboy boots and rumpled suit jacket and was sitting before them on the rug now, leaning on an armchair, with his drink perched on a bony knee. "Long as you remember, you're always welcome here."

"Thank you, Ben, and I appreciate it," Shelley responded, gauging Wendy's veiled sidelong glance at her husband, "but I've made up my mind."

After another couple of drinks, and further speculation on the nanny's sudden departure, Shelley thanked the Hirschbergs and stepped out to collect Toby in the backyard.

"No, no, no!" he shrieked, as she dragged him from the jungle bars. "Wanna play, wanna play!"

"It's time for bed now, sweetheart," she cooed, stroking his sweaty little brow as he fretted in her arms. "The other kids are going in, too."

But he was inconsolable and squalled all the way to their little cottage out back.

"You know what you need, young man?" she said, when she got him in the door. "You need a nice hot bath."

"No, no, no!" he screamed, kicking out at her with his sneakers.

Struggling with him in the bathroom, she threw all his toy boats and rubber duckies into the tub at once, turned on the tap full speed, stripped off his tee shirt and bibbed overalls and dumped him unceremoniously in the water.

"Now, baby, isn't that better?" she asked, which only made him wail all the louder.

At last, in desperation, Shelley thought of Jim. Toby had loved Jim, and he'd missed him even more than he did Molly.

Though recently Toby's life had been full of new friends and new discoveries, and he hadn't mentioned his old amigo in some time, Shelley felt he might at least respond to his name.

"Toby, you know who I was talking to today?" She was washing his face now, and he had squeezed his eyes and mouth closed so that it made him seem decades older, like a tiny red-faced troll. "Do you know?"

Toby shook his head fiercely, scrunching his head down into his shoulders, as if to hide it there from her soapy, scrubbing hands.

"I talked to Jim. You remember Jim, don't you?"

"No, no, no, no!" he screeched.

He was not having any of it.

"You don't remember Jim? You don't remember how he used to carry you on his shoulders, and play Lego with you, and take you to the beach, and play the flute for you every night? You don't remember that?"

"Don' *like* Jim!" he cried, spewing soap furiously from his little mouth.

Later, much later, after she had combed him and powdered him like a baby and dressed him in his favorite flannel pajamas, she got him to calm down at last.

"*Mamá*," he sighed, as she carried him off toward his room. "You always be my mommy?"

"Why, of course I will, darling," she replied, laughing in astonishment. "But whatever makes you ask?"

In response, he merely smiled up at her, his dark eyes gleaming, with the wisest, most adult expression on his face.

"I don't know where you get these things, baby," she tutted, squeezing him to her breast, feeling the most terrific waves of pleasure when he put his little arms around her neck and squeezed her back. "I really don't."

Turning on the light in his room, making for his crib in the corner, she caught sight of Teresa curled up very still on the pillow beside Toby's teddy bear, Mimo.

It was not like Teresa to nap at this hour. She was usually mewing for her supper by now. And she rarely lay in the crib because Toby was a restless sleeper and had once rolled over on her in the night.

Drawing closer, Shelley noticed something ... *foreign* in Teresa's mouth. A folded piece of cheap, blue stationary, it looked like it might be a note.

Her heart gripped by a hideous premonition, Shelley halted for a moment in the middle of the room, unable to decide which way to move. Yet Toby, safe in his mother's arms, and already halfway to dreamland, appeared not to notice a thing.

Mastering her fear, Shelley tiptoed the remaining distance across the room, knelt with Toby in one arm and reached through the bars of his crib with the other.

Teresa felt stiff and cold. Even her fur, once so soft and lustrous, was brittle to the touch, like dead grass.

Reaching around with clumsy, tremulous fingers, grasping the paper between thumb and forefinger, tearing it at the seam as she removed it from between Teresa's sharp little clamped teeth, she flattened it out on the pillow and read, in crude block letters:

SEE HOW EASY IT WOULD BE?

She crumpled the note in her hand, flung it down on the pillow beside Teresa, grasped Mimo by an arm, and tried to rise. But the room was spinning, and the light had grown dim, and she was afraid she might drop Toby, so she let Mimo fall to the floor and eased back down on her behind.

Still clasping her child tightly to her breast, she leaned forward as far as she could, to clear her head.

Having rested a moment, and regained her equilibrium, she recovered Mimo, without whom Toby would never sleep, and sniffed him compulsively all over, even tasted his fur to make sure it wasn't poisoned. Then she got up and staggered out into the hall with them.

"How's about sleeping with *Mamá* tonight?" she murmured tenderly when her son's eyes fluttered open for a second. He smiled up at her again, hugged Mimo to his chest, and went out like a light.

Tucking Toby and Mimo in bed side by side, kissing them both goodnight as required and whispering the incantatory, "*Buenas noches, te amo, duermes bien,*" Shelley decided that she dare not leave the room.

Instead, she took the phone off her night table and dialed Ben in the big house.

"Ben, I want you to bring over one of your shotguns right now."

"What you want it for?"

"Just bring it over, okay?"

"Well, I'll be go-to-hell!" he snapped.

"Is it loaded?" was the first thing she asked when he carried it into the room.

"Yeah," he said, crankily, fiddling with the safety catch, "but you sure you know how to handle one of these things?"

"You damn right I do"! she retorted, picking up the phone again to dial Ibiza. "My husband taught me."

"What the goddamn hell you think you goin' *do* with it?"

"I'm going to sit right here by Toby for the rest of the night. Go look in his room."

Then she dialed Tobias in Ibiza.

When he came on the line, his *"Hola"* sounded quivery and ancient and a world away, as if he were answering from beyond the grave.

"Tobias," she said in an undertone, "something terrible has happened. Your son is safe for the moment, but he's in danger. I want you on a plane for New York tomorrow. You may have to bring someone along with you to help. Maybe one of the twins could meet you. I want you to take Toby back to Europe. I want you to keep him somewhere safe, somewhere he can't be traced, until this whole thing blows over. Will you do that for me?"

"Mais bien sur, ma chère ... por su puesto," he replied, mixing his languages as he always did when caught by surprise. *"Aber, ich kann nicht..."*

"There's no buts about it, Tobias, I'll explain when you phone me with your flight number," she said in English, and hung up.

"Tell me something, now," Ben said, when he stepped in from Toby's room, pale and wispy as a ghost in his slippers and old-fashioned nightshirt. "You think the nanny's involved in this some way?"

"Who else?"

"Damn."

"I wouldn't be too hard on her though. No telling what Al put her through."

"Yeah, no tellin'," Ben agreed. And then he did something that until this very moment Shelley would have thought completely out of character, something that endeared him to her forever.

Raising his eyes toward the ceiling in a dramatized yet highly convincing display of humility, bewilderment, and helplessness, he spread his arms and silently wailed, like some cagey, old, country Jew, appealing to a remote and preoccupied deity for enlightenment.

"Ben, will you do me a favor?" Shelley inquired, when he was done. "Will you bury Teresa for me?"

"'Course I will, hon, I'll even say Kaddish, you want me to."

"Thank you very much, dear, but that won't be necessary," she laughed, dabbing her eyes with the edge of Toby's sheet. "You might say a prayer for Manny though. And one for Tina the Ballerina too. And while you're at it, say one for Jim and me, will you? I've got a feeling we're going to need it."

Two days later, she arranged to meet Jim in the most public place she could think of—the terrace bar overlooking the main floor of Grand Central Terminal, just outside the gates of the Conrail Police Station.

Wearing a brown tweed suit and a tan trench coat, she arrived early, ordered a double martini, lit up her thirty-fifth cigarette of the day, and sat looking out over the milling horde of commuters, hoping to spot Jim before he spotted her.

She had waited perhaps ten minutes, only vaguely aware of the great flickering representation of the cosmos on the station dome high above her head, when a bald, cadaverous, homeless man with haunted eyes and filthy, ragged clothes came stooping and shuffling across the bar toward her.

Fishing in her purse to hand him a quarter, she realized that it was Jim.

"Oh my God, what have they done to you?"

"How . . . how're you doin', Shelley?" he wheezed.

He had ignored her outburst and looked down upon her now with an almost beatific fondness, his lips trembling with the effort to smile.

Trying hard to keep the pity and revulsion from her voice, she reached out a hand to steady him into his chair.

"I . . . I'm fine."

"And Toby?"

"He's all right. He's visiting with relatives in Europe."

Shelley tossed this off, but she still burned with the memory of their leave-taking last night at JFK: Toby, meeting his tall, whitehaired father and his gangly, towheaded, half-brother, Janusch, sweetly, timidly, as if for the first time, and then shrieking in terror when his mother left him, as if she were abandoning him forever to these tweedy, well-mannered strangers with their odd foreign accents.

"Toby's in Europe?"

Jim blinked and shook his head. And he looked so dejected at the news that she reached across the table again to touch his hand.

"Yes, but don't worry, he's doing fine," she lied, falling into the tone that one uses with old people or invalids. "It's you I'm worried about. You look like you ought to see a doctor."

"I ... I've had to sleep under a bridge for the last f-few nights," he panted, coughing into the crook of his stained coat sleeve.

It was such a transparent appeal for her compassion that it seemed to take even Jim by surprise, and he avoided her eyes.

"So, what would you like to drink?" Shelley asked, trying to sound brisk and cheerful when the waitress came around. "I'm having a Scotch, but I think maybe you ought to have a Guinness Stout. It's supposed to be good for you."

"Well, that's what Molly used to say, anyway."

"Oh, Molly." Shelley waved a hand in derision. "She doesn't even know what's good for herself."

"Is ... is she okay?" he asked, as the waitress departed with their order.

"Of course, she is. 'God,' as my husband used to say, 'has got this thing for fools.' Now tell me, what happened in Streetlight?"

"Well, the boss man, he had me to the point where I was like completely spaced out," Jim began, the words tumbling out, his eyes flitting back and forth, as if in a sudden fever. "Had me like some kind of zombie. Didn't know whether I was coming or going, didn't ..."

"I was beginning to think you'd be locked in there forever," Shelley interrupted, pressing his hand, sensing it was time to slow things down.

"Me too," he said, grabbing up the frothing mug of beer as soon as the waitress sets it down and taking a long, long pull.

"But finally, he just let me go."

"What for?"

"To do a job."

"What kind of job?"

Shelley remembered now to slip a finger down to her purse and switch on her wire.

"I'll tell you later," he responded, wincing, as if pained by the thought. "Anyway, he sent me out to do a job. So, I did the job and then I had to play Hide and Seek for a week. I was in this little cubbyhole in an attic, lost in a kind of dream-world, still like . . . in his orbit.

"Then one night toward the end I guess his spell wore off because everything just came clear to me. I could see my whole life, all the wrong turns I'd made, all the clever traps I'd laid for myself, all the traps I'd watched other people lay for me, like a road map laid out behind me. And I tried with all my heart to understand the feeling I'd had, when I was in Al's power, this feeling of numbness, of existing without a will of my own, of . . ."

"Let me tell you something, Jim," Shelley interjected, alarmed at the degree of pain and self-loathing in his tone. "Wiser heads than ours have tried to figure out what draws people to guys like Al Rakozi, and no one's come up with an answer yet."

"Maybe it's some kind of hypnosis," he said, his eyes cast up, unseeing, toward the gleaming galaxies on the ceiling.

"Yes, perhaps, but it's more than that. It's the charisma of a hyper-narcissist, a cult leader, and it's as old as time."

"At first, I tried to blame it on my upbringing, right? My old man was always coming down on me—'Sissy, sissy, you swing that bat like a girl!' Like he was afraid I might be permanently affected by what happened to me one time when he left me alone with a pervert to go off and play poker with the boys. But that's bullshit, you know? Look at Monika. She was raised in a Swedish *parsonage*, for Christ's sake, and how'd she end up? So, I racked my brains, trying to figure it out. But in the end, there was only one thing I knew for sure. I was in prison in that attic. And it wasn't Al or my old man or anyone else who put me there. It was me. I'd been in prison in Streetlight, on shipboard, in the Army, in Folsom, in prison my whole fucking life, one way or another, no matter how I scampered around the world trying to avoid it. And you know what? I swore to myself, if I ever got out of there, I'd never be in prison again."

Across the table, Jim was resting on his elbows and gazing at her searchingly once more, as if she might provide some answer to his dilemma. His eyes, she remarked, were not a clear green, as they had seemed to her before, but a muddy riverine green, with childhood turbulence and adult foundering revealed in every swirl and eddy.

"I tell you, before we start talking about solutions . . ." she said, and then held up two fingers to the waitress for another round. "Why don't you just lay everything out for me? Tell me about the job that Al put you up to."

"It started with an anonymous caller," he replied, obliging her instantly. But then he halted, sat back in his chair, and screwed up his eyes to recall the rest, as if it had occurred years ago, instead of mere days.

"Well, no one ever more richly deserved it," Shelley said, after Jim—amazingly detached again—had described Ray's end. "Even though it's wreaked all kinds of havoc on our federal case."

Yet under all her bravado, she felt shocked and disgusted, as much with herself as with Jim.

'Jesus, I'm like the kiss of death,' she thought.

"Don't think I've lost sight of my guilt," he said. "Don't think I have any illusions on that score."

"I don't think that, Jim."

She shook her head and patted his hand again.

"The worst part of it is," he muttered, so low she could barely hear him, "I still can't imagine life without you and Toby."

"Please, please don't say those things," she said, but she was being disingenuous, for she knew that he *would* have to live his life, whatever remained of it, without her and Toby. For she could never let a man like Jim, as he'd revealed himself to be, into her heart again, into the presence of her child. She went cold at the very thought.

"You know what I've been thinking?" he said, as if he'd read her thoughts. "I been thinking I haven't got a fucking prayer. There's only one thing I can do."

"What?"

Shelley held her breath.

"Rid the world of Al Rakozi."

"Look, I tell you what," she replied, expelling air in sudden relief. "I've got a better idea. We'll get you a lawyer. He'll go to the federal prosecutor, and they'll have a little talk. It'll be a lot less messy that way."

"I can't go to prison . . . I can't."

"Who said anything about prison? They've just lost their star witness. You tell them what you just told me, that Al ordered you to kill Ray, that he *hypnotized* you into doing it, and they'll cut you a deal."

CHAPTER THIRTY-SEVEN

A Plaything of the Fates

"Pack your bags, Jim, they're sendin' a car over at noon," Ben said, beaming a smile at him. "And I want you to remember, from the moment you get in, you're under federal protection and subject to all the terms we worked out with the prosecutor. So, don't give 'em any bullshit. You hear? And Shelley, I want you to ride shotgun with him. Keep that wire runnin'. I like them authentic de-tails."

"They find the informer at the NYPD?" Jim wanted to know.

"Naw, they polygraphed the entire fuckin' force, they say, even the janitor, and they all come up clean."

"Oh yeah? Then how did Al get the address of that safehouse?"

"They ain't got that figgered out yet."

"Well, I'm not leaving this apartment," Jim said, grateful to find another excuse to delay the inevitable, "till they come up with an answer."

"Say, lemme tell you somethin', bubba. You cain't hide forever. Gotta come out of your hole sometime. And look at it this way. Shelley and me, we're in this thing, too. You ever thought about that? He's got no love for us either."

"Sure, but there's a difference. He *wants* me more than he wants you. I'm a traitor to the cause."

"The hell you say," Ben said, starting for the door.

"Which is why I'm not going into a place that's riddled with Streetlight moles!" Jim yelled after him.

"Think of it this way, Jim," Shelley consoled, when Ben had gone. "They just can't afford another public relations disaster like the last one."

"So what?"

"So, they're going to use all the resources of the federal government to make sure Al never gets near you again."

Jim took a deep breath. It appeared that he could resist Shelley even less than he had resisted the boss.

For two weeks now, while their lawyers negotiated with the federal prosecutor, and the prosecutor scrambled to find the informer in his office, Jim and Shelley and their security guards had been holed up in this tenth-story, Chelsea apartment, courtesy of the *New York Star.*

Long and narrow, with high ceilings, a green slate fireplace, and two tall windows looking out on to leafy West Twenty-First Street, the place belonged to a *Star* foreign correspondent—on assignment in China for the embalming of Chairman Mao—and was furnished in what Shelley termed "Manhattan Minimal" style, with bare, white walls. The bare floors were polyurethaned wood. There were also three or four pieces of expensive, unadorned furniture by fashionable contemporary designers.

Shelley had the bedroom nearest the bathroom. Jim had the one nearest the kitchen. Their security guards—squat, dark, thatch-haired young men from Peru and Ecuador wearing garish blue and yellow uniforms—came and went singly, changing shifts every eight hours, and making themselves at home in the library, where they sat glued to Spanish language TV.

Every morning promptly at eight a guard rapped at Jim's door, and he rolled out of his loft bed, climbed down the ladder, and dragged himself off to the bathroom.

By the time he finished shaving, Shelley was out in the kitchen/living room, dressed in sneakers, jeans, and an old college sweatshirt, rustling up some breakfast. Eggs and whole wheat toast and hash browns, blueberry pancakes and maple syrup, orange juice and café-au-lait, a handful of Solgar Natural Vitamins . . .

"Trying to put some meat back on your bones," she said one morning, as he sat at the counter waiting for her to join him.

She cracked a smile when she said it, flinging her thick, wavy black hair out of her face with a hand, and he thought he might die of pleasure.

Yet, at the same time, his heart went out to her, for the smile was painfully thin, and there was nothing she could do to hide the distraught look about her eyes, the look of someone who'd just lost everything she valued in life.

After breakfast, they always spent the next eight or so hours—with a short break for lunch—on the living room sofa with Shelley's tape recorder and notes spread out on the lacquered black coffee table in front of them.

"This is a great story, this is really newsworthy stuff," she kept saying, quizzing him relentlessly on Al Rakozi and Streetlight.

And though it was clear to Jim that her enthusiasm was forced, that she had superimposed it over a mother's profound and immutable sorrow at the loss of her only son, he answered her honestly, no matter how unsavory the disclosure.

Why he did this, he couldn't say. He felt no particular need to confess, no sense of remorse or responsibility because most of the acts that he had committed seemed to him *involuntary,* or at worst reactive and defensive in nature, and to a certain extent he thought of himself as a mere plaything of the fates.

Shelley herself seemed gratified by his frankness, at least on a professional level. Yet, sometimes she appeared shocked nonetheless, and she ran over the steamier parts of the tapes—especially those that dealt with the Aardvarks' bedtime antics, and Al's odd sex life—two or three times, as if to assure herself that she'd heard right.

At such moments, to distract her from any serious assessment of his own behavior, Jim made enormous efforts to be cute and charming, to entertain her the way he had on West Eleventh Street.

Once, after an impromptu flute concert of Briccialdi's "Carnival in Venice" that she applauded with a show of ardor, he was unable to resist the temptation—anticipating failure with a kind of fatalistic thrill—to lay his instrument aside and walk his trembling index and middle finger up her leg ... A little, drunken man following a crooked path home from the pub. But she flicked him away like an errant bug, long before he reached his unrealistic goal, and continued with her questioning.

". . . Now tell me again, Jim, how Al made you go after Ray. You say here, 'He made me feel like I owed it to the clan.' What exactly do you mean by that?"

With nothing else to hold onto, Jim clung to the present. He offered her endless details, endless insights into himself and Al and Streetlight. Whether they were accurate or not, he could have cared less. When he ran out of things to say, he began to elaborate, to exaggerate, to make things up.

The truth of the matter was, he just never wanted to leave this apartment. Never wanted this interrogation to end. Never wanted to stop looking at Shelley, smelling her, hearing her voice. He'd do anything, he told himself, *anything* to stay. Slander not only Streetlight but *himself.* Mortgage his future for the present. Give up life itself . . . for just one more moment, an instant, with that beautiful, bountiful lady with the dark, suffering eyes.

And the funny thing was, the longer they stayed together, worked together, dined together, played house together in that Chelsea apartment, the longer he heard her going tappety-tap on her typewriter late into the night in the room next door, the longer they slept just a wall apart, the more Jim convinced himself that despite everything, maybe—just maybe—all hope was not lost.

'Now the tables have turned,' he said to himself. 'Now, because of Toby, she needs me as much as I need her. She just doesn't know it yet.'

"I want you to tell me the truth," he said to her once over

nightcaps at the kitchen counter, with the guard's TV blaring down the hall. "Do I still have a chance with you or what?"

"Oh, for Christ's sake, Jim, you know the answer to that," she scoffed. "Why are we going over this again?"

"Then what about just friends? Can we be friends?"

"Friends? What does that mean? When this is over, Jim, I'll try to get you a little grubstake from the paper. And then you're going out to the Coast, where you were headed in the first place. Get yourself a job. Maybe go to graduate school? I don't know, audition for the San Francisco Symphony. You sound good enough to me. You might surprise yourself. You might even be happy."

"If you won't be my lover or my friend," he said, beaming his most irresistible grin at her, "then how about mothering me a bit?"

"What do you think I've been *doing,* Jim? I mean, when are you going to grow up? That's the kind of thinking that got you into this shit in the first place . . ."

Even her scolding felt like petals upon his ears. He'd listen to her forever, he told himself, asking for nothing more.

But he was talking trash, and he knew it.

Her logic was irrefutable.

Under it all, he thought, she was afraid of him, afraid of what he he'd done, what he'd let be done, what he might do in the future.

He couldn't blame her.

He was afraid of that too.

So, he tried to put the best face on things. Tried to plan a future without her and Toby. When that failed, when he thought of leaving them behind, heading out to Coast as she'd suggested, contacting his old friends and family, trying to get a job, it seemed to him a fate far crueler than death, and he promised himself to just take life one day at a time, to build his strength back up and try to survive.

Then, this morning Ben rang the intercom buzzer downstairs. And even before he answered it, Jim knew the inevitable had come.

Jim and Shelley were waiting just inside the vestibule with the security guard when their car—a shiny, black, Plymouth Fury, with a two-way radio aerial in back—pulled up at the curb.

To expedite their departure, and to ensure their anonymity, they'd been instructed to calmly walk over together and get into the car as if it were a private taxi and their guard a doorman.

Yet now, pushing through the door, pausing at the top of the stoop to look around, Jim spotted a couple of battered, blue and white, NYPD squad cars cruising halfway up the block, and smelled a rat.

Grabbing Shelley by the hand, whispering, *"Cuidado, hombre!"* to the guard, he hustled her down the steps and across the sidewalk.

The guard threw open the back door to the Fury, and Jim shoved Shelley into the back seat beside a stout, perspiring young lawyer from the federal prosecutor's office.

About to jump in beside her, he heard a grunt behind him, and what sounded like a falling body. A pair of beefy, blue-sleeved arms clamped around his middle, and suddenly he was being yanked backwards.

With the breath squeezed out of him, he let go of the door.

Next thing he knew, he was lying flat on his face on the concrete with a knee in the small of his back, and someone was clapping a pair of handcuffs around his wrists.

Craning his neck around, he saw the security guard in a like position by his side, and a pair of muscular Irish cops smiling down at them.

"You're under arrest," declared the largest of the two. "You have the right to remain silent..."

"I'm sorry, officers," Shelley said politely, emerging from the Plymouth Fury as three more blue and white squad cars careened up with red lights glaring and screeched to a halt in the middle of the street. "But that man is under federal protection."

"Says who?"

"Says me," announced the lawyer, coming up behind her, flashing his U.S. Attorney's I.D.

"This man is wanted for murder in New York, and I got a warrant for his arrest," the cop said, dragging Jim off toward one of the squad cars while his partner covered the security guard. "You got a problem with that, talk to Inspector Ron Nelson at One Police Plaza."

CHAPTER THIRTY-EIGHT

Ball and Chain

"Send her right in," Shelley said, when the newsroom receptionist buzzed to say a Mrs. Pagano wanted to see her.

Dressed all in black, wearing a maternity outfit that she had no need of yet, Molly looked like a plump, apple-cheeked, young widow in mourning, and made her way across the teeming newsroom with a dignity far beyond her years and station. In a dreamy sort of way, Shelley thought, she almost seems to be enjoying her tragedy.

"I've come to you for advice," she announced, when she reached Shelley's cubicle.

"Of course, Molly."

Shelley motioned for the girl to sit beside her at her desk.

"I know who killed Ray," she said, enunciating every word slowly and dramatically, "and I should like to know what I'm to do about it."

"I thought you told the FBI that you had no recollection of

the murder."

"It's just come back." Molly sighed and shut her eyes. "It's like a dream. I see Jim coming in through the window with a gun in his hand, Ray standing up to meet him."

"What makes you think it's *not* a dream?"

"Too real," Molly replied, shaking her head, with her hands folded demurely in her lap.

"So why come to me with this information? Why not the police? Why not some other newspaper?"

"Because you owe me," she retorted, turning to fix Shelley with eyes as cloudy, gray, and shallow as the Irish Sea, "for what happened to me at your apartment."

"And you share no responsibility for that?"

"I was just a student, a part-time nanny, wasn't I? And you were my employer."

"I still don't see . . ."

"Tell me then, Shelley, who else am I to turn to? My auntie's thrown me out, and the FBI's lost all interest in me since Ray's death. There's the New York police, of course. But Ray warned me about them. I must admit though, I have thought about it. Ever since a visit I had the other day—from an Inspector Nelson? Such a dream, he was. I swear, I'm tempted to just ring him up and spill it all out."

"Alright, you want my advice, if I were in your shoes, I think I'd probably just hold my peace," Shelley said, anxious to keep her quiet at least until after Jim's arraignment in the Monika Thorssen case. "I doubt the police would believe you now, and even if they did, I don't think your second thoughts about Ray's murder would stand up in court."

"Yes, but you see, I believe it's my duty to pursue the matter," the girl went on, daubing at her cheek with a hanky. "After all, this is my husband, the father of my child we're talking about."

"I wish I could help you, Molly, I really do. If it's money though . . ."

"I must say, I could do with a bit."

"I'm sorry, I haven't got any," Shelley said, truthfully. "And my editor won't give me anymore because he says I've already spent too much."

But Molly wasn't buying it.

"I warned you, Shelley, I did," she said firmly, when she rose to go, "so don't be surprised now at anything that happens."

Jim's arraignment was supposed to be held in Courtroom 670B, in the Criminal Courts Building at Centre Street and Leonard. But when Shelley arrived, an hour after her interview with Molly, a trial was going on involving another defendant.

"Changed to another venue," the court officer explained, when Shelley asked what happened to the Jim Range arraignment.

"What venue is that?"

"Bellevue Hospital, Detention Wing."

"Why there?"

"Well, let's see here," he said, reading from a computer printout. "'Defendant injured in precinct holding cell.'"

"Oh, my God, what next?" Shelley cried out, more in vexation than sympathy, for ever since she married Tobias, she had subscribed to his notion that people make their own luck and are in some sense responsible when it goes consistently bad.

Reaching Bellevue Hospital fifteen minutes after Jim's arraignment was due to begin, Shelley bullied her way past the security desk in the Detention Wing with her press tags and raced up the stairs to the fourth floor.

There were six beds in the room, each inhabited by a patient in cheap blue pajamas with BELLEVUE HOSPITAL DETENTION WARD stenciled across the chest, and a crowd of visitors, so it took her a moment to sort out who was who.

The patient at the far end of the room, with a bunch of professional-looking people in dark business suits gathered around his bed, was Jim, of course.

The tall, dignified, old, black lady standing at the foot of his bed was the judge.

The stout, red-faced gentleman beside her was the Assistant U.S. Attorney.

The frail, balding, young fellow standing to Jim's right was the defense attorney.

The stubby, curly-haired Hispanic with the bandido mustache to his left was the prosecutor.

And the tall, dark, handsome man in the natty, tweed jacket and designer jeans leaning against the radiator was Inspector Ron Nelson of the NYPD, whose ex-officio connections to the Streetlight Foundation were a matter of public record.

"Prosecutor," the judge was saying, "would you like to talk this over with the defense counsel now? I don't see why you can't come to an agreement here."

"I'm sorry," the prosecutor answered, exchanging glances with Inspector Nelson across the room, "but I really don't understand, Your Honor."

"Mr. Range is a valuable witness in a federal RICO statutes case," the U.S. Attorney explained, "and I can assure the court that if he's released to my custody today, he will remain under government protection and supervision for some time."

"Does this set with you a little better, Prosecutor?"

"Absolutely not, Your Honor," he argued, exchanging glances again with Inspector Nelson who—Shelley noted with some alarm—had just been signaled that he had a telephone call and was slipping out the door. "The federal government is notorious for withholding the most vicious criminals from local justice, in return for their help in landing so-called 'bigger fish' who are rarely convicted. I ask that Mr. Range be returned to police custody until the New York City District Attorney's office has time to examine this sudden 'miracle evidence' in detail and verify its specifics."

"To be frank, Prosecutor," the judge opined, after reflecting a moment, "Mr. Range has not fared very well in local police custody thus far, and the defense, not without good reason, has voiced some strong concerns for his safety. Moreover, this is a rather thin murder case that you've brought before me today. Mr. Range was on the premises at or about the time of Ms. Thorssen's murder, he knew the victim, and therefore he must be guilty. The defense, on the other hand, has produced convincing material evidence, including a murder weapon, fingerprints, FBI ballistics tests, and—most compellingly—a signed confession linking a Mr. Raymond Pagano to the crime. It is my judgement, therefore, that there are insufficient grounds to indict Mr. Range at this time . . ."

"Does . . . does that mean I can go now?" Jim asked from his bed, as the members of the court filed from the room.

"You bet it does," the U.S. Attorney replied, patting him on the shoulder. "Just as soon as we can order an ambulance."

"I tell you what," Shelley put in, "if Jim feels up to it, I really think we ought to get him out of here right now. No telling what they've got up their sleeves next."

"Okay by me," Jim agreed. "It's not much more than a scratch, anyway."

"How'd it happen?" she asked, as he eased out of bed and into his county-issue bathrobe and slippers.

"This Puerto Rican kid named Key I used to know in Streetlight? He was in the holding cell when they locked me up. I wasn't there five minutes before he came at me with a sharpened bedspring. I jumped back when he swung, so he just kind of nicked me across the ribs, and my cellmates pinned him down. Luckily, they did. The guard was nowhere in sight. Another couple of tries and he might've had me."

"How many stitches?"

"Seventy-six."

They were in the elevator now with Jim's lawyer, the U.S. Attorney, a couple of uniformed policemen, and several black and Hispanic visitors, all of them listening intently.

"I wouldn't call that a scratch, but it may be your lucky number," Shelley said, and everyone laughed.

With the U.S. Attorney running interference, Shelley got Jim released from the hospital and past the security desk in record time. But he balked when they approached the black, government-issue Plymouth Fury in the parking lot.

"Uh-uh, no way," he said, shaking his head. "Last time I was offered a ride in one of these things, I ended up in jail. I mean, I appreciate your help, sir, but until you find the informer, I think I'd prefer to fend for myself."

"I'm afraid, Mr. Range, that you have little choice in the matter," the U. S. Attorney answered, removing a collapsible umbrella from his briefcase, and holding it over Jim's head to protect him from the rain which had just begun to fall. "You've been released to federal custody as a material witness."

Jim shook his head again, stubbornly, and Shelley motioned that she wanted to talk to him alone. Taking the umbrella, they stepped off to the side while the attorney got in the car to wait.

"Listen, Shelley, I don't see the point anymore, you know? I'm starting to think I might as well just split."

"Right, I can just see you," she sniffed, as the rain comes down harder and harder. "Out on the road again, a fugitive from justice, dragging your own prison around with you like a ball and chain . . ."

"I don't see any other way; you get any ideas, let me know," he replied, then turned from her when he became aware of a commotion under the brick portico at the Detention Ward entrance. Police were milling around, and a tall, dark-haired man whom Shelley recognized as Inspector Nelson was gesturing to a small, plump young woman who stood behind him in the crowd.

With a sinking heart, Shelley saw Molly come forward, scan the rainswept parking lot, and point at Jim.

Jim must have spotted her at the same time because he shrugged, rolled his eyes at Shelley as if to say, "I told you so," and took off running, full out, his slippers flying off his feet, his bathrobe flapping out behind him.

"Stop that man!" Nelson shouted. "Stop him! He's wanted for murder in another case!"

Hurtling past the astonished security guard at the Bellevue front gate, splashing barefoot through the overflowing gutter and out onto First Avenue, Jim flagged down one of the dozens of yellow cabs passing by and disappeared in traffic before Inspector Nelson and his retinue of men in blue got even halfway across the parking lot.

That night Shelley stayed up late, long past the changing of her guards at twelve, sipping vodka gimlets, trying to read a paperback bestseller that she'd picked up at the corner drugstore. But she didn't get far because she kept worrying about Jim, waiting for him to appear at her window any second.

Then about three in the morning she heard the security guard slip out, hours before his graveyard shift was due to end, and all her alarm bells rang.

Running to relock the front door, yelling, *"José, donde vas?"* she switched the burglar alarm back on, spun about and raced through the apartment, latching windows, searching rooms and closets.

Just as she was getting her breath back, just as she was about to phone the security company and ask them what the hell was going on, she recalled that she'd forgotten to look in the shower . . .

"Peek-a-Boo! We see you!" Al shrieked, when she pulled

back the curtain, camping it up with his big Mohawk bodyguard, Tall Boy. "Peek-a-Boo, we see you!"

CHAPTER THIRTY-NINE

The Unholy Saint

Seeking refuge that night under the George Washington Bridge, Jim stumbled upon a makeshift village of cardboard, plastic sheeting, stacked rubber tires, plywood, scrap lumber, and abandoned automobiles.

In the reflected light of city streetlamps, he could see that people were sleeping there, on the ground, in the cars and shacks, all wound up in twos and threes for warmth.

Stepping gingerly over limp human bodies, he came to a tin-roofed, scrap-lumber hut on the edge of the encampment which, for some reason, was empty when he'd sought to make use of it a few days ago, on his way back from Piermont.

Inside, out of the wind and rain, amidst bottles, tin cans and God knows what other trash, he covered himself with plastic bags and soggy newspapers and tried to sleep, as scenes from the last hectic hours flash before his eyes:

The interior of a yellow cab was festooned with beads, bits of strung glass and bright dangling cloth. Its Haitian driver eyed Jim's BELLEVUE HOSPITAL DETENTION WARD bathrobe suspiciously in his rearview mirror.

Eyeing him back, Jim swung the door open at a stoplight, leapt out barefoot—"*Stop zat man! Stop heem! He no pay mah fare!*"—raced into the East Thirty-Third Street IRT station, wriggled through the teeth of the turnstile before the unastonished eyes of the token teller, and lost himself in the crowd.

Emerging from the subway at One Hundred and Eighty-First Street and Saint Nicholas Avenue in the rain, Jim lifted a pair of jeans and some sneakers from a sidewalk sale rack on Broadway, outran the irate Hispanic proprietor, and changed in someone's backyard. He climbed the spiral concrete stairway to the pedestrian walkway of the George Washington Bridge and paused to admire its graceful mile-long arch to the Jersey Palisades.

At mid-span he got caught in a blinding gale, one that swayed the bridge, hummed in its girders, and drowned the sound of traffic entirely.

Stepping onto the humid, dripping, Jersey side after the storm, he stood there facing traffic with a thumb raised till he was nearly blind from the oncoming headlights and deaf from the sound of accelerating traffic. The whole time, a police dog in one of the tollbooths kept barking at him suspiciously, as if to warn off any perspective rides. Then the rain again, a cold persistent drizzle that soaked through his clothes and chilled him to the bone.

At midnight by the tollbooth clock, he turned on heel, marched past the growling police dog and back across the dark river in the rain, making for the great, luminous island beyond the clouds.

Hunger buzzed in his ears. Tiny popping lights went off behind his eyes. Gas pellets skittered painfully down the long runnels of his intestines. The slash across his ribs burned like fire. Yet brain, skin, body, and bowels tingled with supreme anticipation—a sensation that he'd never been, nor ever would be, more alive. Spreading his arms, raising his palms, he shouted his defiance at the invisible sky . . .

"Yaaaaagh!"

An hour or two in the tin-roofed shack and Jim was awakened by the cold and damp. Shivering in the semi-darkness, trying to sort out what was real from what was only in his head, he heard a heavy footfall.

Someone appeared in the doorway, blocking the light from the street. A huge man, black as night, stooped and entered, dragging twenty-six years of bad dreams along with him. Breathing heavily, raggedly, he stepped across the dirt floor and bent over, smelling of blood, of rancid egg, of all the ills of mankind.

"White boy," he murmured, running a huge trembling hand up Jim's thigh. "I see yo head, peepin' out dere. White boy, you white in de night."

"AAAAAAAAAAAGH!" Jim screamed—Little Jim screamed, at the top of his three-year-old lungs—and the man jumped up, banging his head on the tin roof.

"Now, why you holler like dat?" the black man demanded, in an aggrieved tone, rubbing his head, backing toward the doorway. "What you doin' here, man?"

"I . . . I had to find shelter," Jim replied, and slipped from under the paper and plastic that covered him, ran his fingers along the trashy floor, searching for the pistol and extra clip of ammo that he had buried there on his return from Piermont.

"Dis be *my* home you sleepin' in, cracker."

"I'm sorry. I . . . I didn't know anyone lived here. I had nowhere else to go. Now, would you please let me by."

"Maybe . . . maybe I will . . . if you pay."

"Listen, I told you I'm sorry," Jim said and found what he was looking for. Digging it out, tearing it from its plastic cover, he flung the silencer aside, pocketed the extra clip, and rose to assume a defensive posture. "I didn't mean to cause you any trouble. But I don't have any money."

"How's about you pay another way?"

"Huh?"

"You nice to me, white boy, I be nice to you."

"I got a gun here, man. Lemme go or I'll fucking blow you away."

"You ain't got no gun, fool. You too po' for dat."

The guy stepped forward.

It was only a peashooter, a little .22-caliber automatic designed for close-up work and easy concealment, and when Jim fired it didn't sound much louder than an air gun, even without the silencer. But it lit up the shack and made a neat hole in the tin roof just over the man's head.

"Don't shoot!" he cried and fell to his knees in the doorway. "Please, don't shoot."

"Outta my way, man, outta my fuckin' way!"

His heart drumming it out in a savage, childish rhythm, Jim kicked him in the groin, swung the pistol, knocked him to the ground with a blow to the back of the neck, and ran right over him.

Sprinting through the doorway, he weaved in and out of the shacks and upturned automobiles at top speed, hurdling piles of refuse and reclining bodies, splashing through fetid water.

"Stop dat white motherfucker! Stop him!

Jim stepped on people.

He tripped and fell onto piles of people.

Someone got hold of his leg.

Kicking, flailing, rolling in the stinking mud, he broke away, popping stitches across his ribs, and made for the light, for the surface, for reality, for life and love, for One Hundred and Eighty-First Street, where he could see bouncing red, blue, green, and yellow neon blurred by rain.

He ran all the way to the BMT subway line on Cabrini Boulevard. Leaping the turnstile, he raced down the stairs three at a time and caught an A Train just as it was about to leave the station.

The five passengers in the car gazed up at him in horror.

Panting for breath, Jim glanced at his reflection in the window. From head to toe he was covered in green slime. His hair was matted with it. His ears were plugged with it. It ran from his nostrils. It was in his eyes, down his neck, in his shoes. Out of the muck on his chest blood oozed, ran down his leg, dripped on the floor.

"What are you looking at?" he screamed at the passengers, and started to laugh, to wave his arms around and mug in the mirror of the window. He couldn't help himself. It seemed the funniest thing in the world. "What're you looking at?"

Forty minutes later, heading up West Twenty-First Street from the Eighth Avenue subway station, he spotted a Streetlight van parked on the opposite side of the street, under a big, dripping, chestnut tree, and thanked the fates for turning him back on the Jersey side.

Another six minutes and he was climbing up Shelley's fire escape, over her railing, and into the light spilling from her living room window.

He leaned over a soggy, flower planter, peered cautiously through the cross-barred, burglar-proof window and viewed Shelley splayed out on the sofa in a sopping wet night-gown, with her hands tied behind her back.

Mouthing words that Jim couldn't catch, she rolled her head weakly from side to side, while Al danced about her with a cigar in his mouth, grinning like a satyr, pointing to a brimming pitcher of water in his hand. Then he leaned down, squeezed her nose shut with his fingers, and poured water down her throat until she choked and spat and vomited.

Out in the center of the room, leaning against an armchair, Al's big Mohawk bodyguard, Tall Boy, looked on, solemn as a cigar-store Indian, with a .357 Magnum stuck in his belt.

Vainly scanning the apartment for some way of getting inside, Jim went over his options.

He could whip out his peashooter and fire at Tall Boy; but at this distance, through double-glazed glass, it probably wouldn't even hurt.

He could run downstairs and call the police; but by the time they arrived, Shelley might well be drowned. He could scream bloody murder and hope the neighbors, or someone down in the street, would call the cops; but this being New York he didn't like his chances.

Or, using the slight advantage his position gave him, he could strike a deal.

While Al, full of false good cheer, pointed to his pitcher of water and tried to convince Shelley that she really ought to give him what he was looking for, Jim spent another moment assessing his prospects in life. Concluding that they were bleak, if not nil, and taking a certain paradoxical comfort in that notion, he fondly recalled his one night with Shelley, his days with Toby, and daydreamed a happy ending.

Then he took a deep breath, reached out, and gave the window a tap.

"What was that, boss?"

"How the fuck do I know? Probably just a pigeon or something. Why don't you go check it out?"

"What if someone's out there?"

"Huh?"

"What if he's got a gun?"

"Get over there and check it out, fuckface, before I shoot you myself."

And Jim lamented his decision: He hadn't noticed another weapon in the room, hadn't counted on Al having one at all. Yet, he might just as well have lamented human mortality, or the course of his own life so far, for events had been set into motion, and no one could tell where they might lead.

Tall Boy stepped over to the window, unlatched the burglar-proof grating, swung it open toward the inside, and pulled up the window.

The long fat black barrel of his .357 Magnum poked through, sweeping to and fro across the dead chrysanthemums in the flower planter, causing their leaves to rattle and fling off beads of rain.

The Mohawk craned his smooth, copper-domed head out.

And Jim, with the feeling that all his life, all his experience, had been nothing more than a rehearsal for this one brief act, jammed the muzzle of the .22 in his ear.

"Careful, man, this thing's got a hairpin trigger," he whispered, and Tall Boy dumped his weapon on the fire escape in a panic.

"What the fuck is that?" Al called from inside.

"Let her go, Al! I'm the one you want!"

"You're wrong there, Brownie, I want you both!" he hollered back, almost gleefully, it seemed, and fired off some huge, heavy bore weapon, a .45 automatic, perhaps, shattering the window over their heads, showering them with glass.

"Hold it, hold it!" Tall Boy pleaded. "Have a fuckin' heart, boss."

Al let a minute go by in silence.

"Go on, get out of here, bitch," he said at last.

"Let me know when you're out, Shelley!"

"Who asked for your two cents, asshole?"

"I'm out, Jim!" Shelley shouted a moment later, from the

doorway at the back of the apartment.

"So, what're you waiting for now?" Al demanded, indignantly. "Put that fucking gun away and let's talk this over."

Considering his options again, Jim pulled the trigger. The Mohawk jerked and fell on his face in the flowers, trailing a thin line of smoke from his ear.

But already Jim had whipped his little weapon around and was firing into the room to keep Al's head down while with his left hand he stretched out for that large, essential .357 Magnum which lay just beyond his reach on the fire escape.

Al fired back twice and missed, the rounds glancing off the iron window frame, whining over the building across the street.

And finally, Jim reached the weapon.

Then Al fired again and got lucky.

Jim felt something slap against his left forearm, looked down and saw a gaping hole a few inches from his elbow, pumping dark arterial blood.

He dropped the Magnum, lost his balance, and fell forward, rolling for the stairs on the other side of the fire escape.

But Al fired again—BOOM—very loud from up real close and after that Jim found himself in a state of disorientation:

He could hear, he could smell, he could see everything in minute detail and his brain was working like mad but he couldn't feel anything.

He looked at the iron railing above him, at the pair of roosting pigeons who calmly alighted there again after the shooting stopped and knew that he was still on the fire escape, that he'd been hit in the side and flipped over onto his back.

He glanced at the building across the street, saw lights going on, and neighbors peering out in sleeping clothes, goggle-eyed, as if impervious to harm, as if it were all a TV show.

Looking down, he saw a big, tattered hole in his nightshirt, just below the armpit, with pink and red froth breathing in and out, in and out.

Across the metal floor of the fire escape, past spots of rust and black mold and splattered blood, he saw the Mohawk lying face down in a bed of dead mums, and Al behind him in the window, in a cloud of gun smoke, grinning.

And he heard him call, almost gently, it seemed, "Let it go, man, let it go."

Jim stared down at his own right hand. Saw it unclench. Watched the little peashooter fall. Heard it bounce once, twice, three times on the metal steps.

And suddenly the sounds of the city—street traffic, horns, the rumble of the subway, late night stereos and TV sets—came on strong in the background, like someone just had turned up the volume.

The world, it appeared, would go on as before, whatever happened to Jim.

And he watched helplessly as Al leaned through the window over Tall Boy, snatched up the Magnum, and tossed it back into the room.

Watched him grab the big, limp Mohawk by the ankle and drag him inside with one hand, banging his pistol butt against the wall with the effort.

Saw him climb out through the window over the flower planter and onto the fire escape.

Heard him yell at the gawking neighbors across the street,

"Police action! Police Action! Get away from those fucking windows!"

Yet, when Al squatted on Jim's chest and jammed the .45 between his eyes, it didn't even hurt.

"You should've known, man," Al lamented, shaking his head. And it was amazing how little rancor, how much sincerity there was in his tone. "You should've fucking known."

"Sh-should've known what?"

"See, what you lived through in the past, Brownie, you can't unlive. You blame others for that, right? But it's you, you, and you're whole fucking life. You got diddled in that toolshed, man, and after that you never had a chance. Just playing it out, again and again, with your soul in torment. Streetlight offered you the only peace you ever knew. And what'd you do? You blew it.

"But hey, that's not to say we're perfect," Al hastened to say, employing the royal "we." "Think of our quest as flawed, but essentially noble. Think of us as holy sinners, unholy saints, ordained to suffer a sublime passion that raises us above the rest of ordinary mortals and yet, at the same time, condemns us to the gutter of history. So, what we're asking you now, Brownie, in these last moments of your agony, is for love and pity and forgiveness, in return for the love and pity and forgiveness that we feel for you. Remember, life is merely a transitory state. And it won't be long now before all of us, all of Streetlight—and Shelley too, when we find her—follow you down. Will you do that for us, man, will you?"

Looking up that long gunmetal gray barrel to the calm, dark, Magyar eyes beyond—eyes unknowable, an enigma even unto themselves—Jim read his answer and knew it to be brief.

"No, never."

"I'm truly sorry to hear that," Al said, smiling, and pulled the trigger.

The gun went "click" and misfired.

"Damn," he said, only mildly irritated. Smacking the butt with his palm, forcing the loose clip back into place, he prepared to fire again.

In the meantime, Shelley, or some friendly wraith in her guise, had miraculously reappeared behind Al.

Could it be?

Shelley had not tried to save her own ass, as any rational being might, but had lurked somewhere nearby and was now creeping up to the window—fiery-eyed, fearless as some avenging goddess—with something heavy and shiny and metal in her hand.

It looked like a .357 Magnum.

It looked like the gun Al threw inside.

Raising it up in both hands, she aimed it at Al just as he turned toward the sound of her footstep and uttered a small, almost feminine cry of dismay.

BAM!

She fired and smacked him between the eyes. He dropped like a stone, bounced on the metal floor of the fire escape, and lay there with his eyes staring up at nothing.

Yet even after Shelley had dragged Al's body off Jim, wrapped a tourniquet around his arm, cradled his head in her lap, ran her fingers through his hair, crooned his name, wept real tears in his face, looked him in the eye, swore she'd phoned 911 and called his attention to the wailing sirens to prove it, Jim still could not convince himself with absolute certainty that she was what she appeared to be.

"Don't you give up on me now!" she cried, when her image began to fade, and slapped him, shook him up. "You hear? You stick around, Jim, and I'll stick with you."

"You promise?"

"I swear!"

But it was a purely hypothetical bargain because her image was slipping away again, and this time it wouldn't be coming back.

Still, it helped to ease his way.

For such small pleasures as these, he thought, we live and we die.

THE END